MARKED BY FATE

ORIGINS

Marked by Fate Origins

Beginnings. Secrets. Deleted Scenes.

Kristin D. Van Risseghem | Rhonda Sermon
Melissa A. Craven | Kelly St. Clare
Amalie Jahn | Melle Amade | Debra Kristi
Ingrid Seymour | Alisha Klapheke
Lena Mae Hill | Sarah K. L. Wilson
D. L. Armillei | Jamie Thornton
Hilary Thompson | Erin Hayes

Beginnings. Secrets. Deleted Scenes.

Transport yourself to other worlds with 15 Marked by Fate teen warriors …

… encounter shadows, queens, witches, and wizards who battle against immortals, angels, vampires, demons, genetically engineered soldiers, robots and gods. Let yourself be swept away by adventures in magical fantasy worlds, mind-blowing dystopian lands, space stations, galaxies, and alternate timelines.

The short stories and deleted scenes in Marked by Fate: Origins are exclusive to this collection and they go away--some of them forever-- when the Marked by Fate full box set releases in October 2017.

Gain a glimpse of where the action begins, including a deeper look into some of your favorite characters! Get the Marked by Fate: Origins collection today to join these teen warriors in their adventures.

CONTENTS

Purchase Marked by Fate

Defined by Their Choices

A collection of 25 Fantasy and Science Fiction YA coming of age novels from New York Times, USA Today, International, Amazon bestselling and Award-Winning authors!!

This action-packed boxset is filled with teen warriors who encounter queens, witches, wizards, werewolves, shifters, angels, and gods. Follow genetically engineered soldiers, cyborgs, and robots discover magical hidden fantasy worlds, encounter mind-blowing dystopian lands, space stations, and galaxies they could never have dreamed existed while traveling through time into uncharted territories. Marked by Fate to complete these deadly and dangerous quests filled with nonstop action and adventure!

NINJAS & NEPHILIMS

An Enlighten Series Short Story

Kristin D. Van Risseghem

Ninjas & Nephilims © 2017 Kristin D. Van Risseghem

CHAPTER ONE

"Son, what's bothering you?"

"Nothing, Dad."

"Don't give me that. I feel your discomfort from here." He slowly rose from the boulder and rolled his shoulders, as if they were sore. But I knew the truth. He didn't show fatigue. Ever. It was his way to 'play' human. "I know something's up with you. Now what is it? If you don't tell me, I'll grab it out of your mind. You know I don't like doing that."

"I know. It's just that ..." My eyes stared out toward the calming blue water. "I don't want to be 'special'."

"Where's this coming from?"

"No place." I turned my head; I couldn't look at him. If I did, he'd see my pain. "A group of co-workers were going to play football in the park and—"

"You know you can't." He shook his head.

"I know. I just wish I *could*."

"I understand." He placed his warm hand on my shoulder. Another loving movement. "Remember when I first brought you here? I think it was a bit warmer than it is now. You recall what I told you?"

How could I forget something as monumental as what he had said that day? Before he had confirmed my suspicions, I figured out we were different, but couldn't put my finger on exactly what *it* was that made me unlike all the other kids in the neighborhood.

Dad took me here to this exact spot along the Mississippi River when I was in grade school. He thought it was 'time'. Time for a man-to-man talk. I was eight, then. I wasn't a man yet.

What right did he have to lecture me?

He wasn't around because he had some sort of a sales job. Or that's what my parents agreed to tell me. So, it was Mom and me living in southern California until we moved to Minnesota with a bunch of *his* rules. There were many days when I longed for him to live with us. To be with us. But there were times, too, that I didn't want a constant reminder that I was different.

And yet, I idolized him. There was something mysterious about him. After all, it wasn't like he mistreated me, or Mom. I could see the love in his eyes for her, and me. I felt his love, too. He never missed a birthday, a major human holiday, or a special event at school. We did take a few vacations over the years, but he mainly worked.

Was I being selfish? Probably, but I was a kid. I didn't understand it, or why, or what he really was.

I didn't grasp what I would become until I was older, either.

They told me their story many times. How Mom had been waitress at a diner in Santa Clara when they met. One summer day he—Gabriel— had stopped in for a late lunch. It was a slow day, so they had plenty of time to talk. He returned the next day and the next, eventually convincing her to have dinner with him and did whatever other young couples did back in the 1930's.

She *knew* she was in love with him. She would have done anything he asked. Dad told her what he was, and why he couldn't marry her. All because of the *rules*. He said she was with child and that the child would be special.

I'd live longer than normal people. I'd have abilities that no ordinary boy should have.

Gabriel loved Mom so much he asked God to grant her a longer life, too. That way she could raise and protect me, since he couldn't be a normal dad. God had sympathy, but didn't grant his prayer. So, Gabriel gave some his life force to her.

If you hadn't followed some of the key words, I'd spell it out for you.

There's no such thing as a chance encounter. Not with Gabriel, or his 'co-workers'.

Prayers were wishes that humans asked to God. But what Gabriel requested wasn't a wish.

Life force? Longer lives?

So yeah, I remembered what he had told me.

"I'm an angel, Shay."

I remembered that sentence; still do.

The lilt of his tongue with the slight accent that made him sound ancient. What does an eight-year-old say? I had said: "I knew it! Well, not that exactly. Never in a million years would I have guessed that. I thought maybe you were really wealthy and that we were going to be rich and famous ..." Or along those lines. I really don't recall the exact wording. After all, it was a long time ago.

It was not what I expected him to say. Well, okay, it was.

If he was an angel, what did that make me?

Slowly the pieces fell into place, but it took me years to really comprehend it.

His 'sales job' was to recruit others like me to the good side of the coming war.

All I wanted was to be like everyone else.

I wasn't born an angel. I'd be taller, stronger, and faster than other kids my age. And it'd be wrong to use my strengths to weaken others. No one liked a showoff. I would get wings and have heightened human senses. I would grow up and look normal, but live a very long life.

That day on the river front, Dad continued to talk about the difficult choices he made and sometimes he was forced to sacrifice for the greater good. Then he told me that when he'd met Mom, it hadn't been by chance. He'd been watching her for a while, and he'd seen the good in her. He knew she would make the sacrifice needed for me one day.

Mom had told me that when I was a baby, people volunteered to look after me. She worked at the diner while putting herself through nursing school; it helped on a single-parent income since no one would accept money for babysitting me. I never fussed, never cried, never threw tantrums. By the time I grew to be a toddler, people raved how cute I was. They made comments about my striking blonde hair and startling aqua eyes.

By high school, I had a body every guy dreamed of and every girl wanted me on their arm. I never worked out, besides running, but had arms and legs of steal and abs that put body builders to shame. I wasn't sure if the others like me had the same attributions or not because I never met another.

When I turned eighteen, I received the Heaven's Mark: two silver iridescent wings with the golden Triquetra symbol in the center. I ran my fingers over the mark, remembering what Dad said about my special gift that all people like me received, "Now you're marked to be His warrior." Then he presented me with a silver sword, blessed by God, and told me to treat it with the utmost respect for it's a reward for being His servant. Silver wings sprouted from my shoulder blades. And just like my wings can appear and disappear, so does the sword; each unique to the individual and plays to his or her strengths.

All the years I'd gone to school, students and teachers alike swooned over me. Being part angel definitely had something to do with it.

After college and getting my business degree, it was easy for me to get a sales job. Following in Dad's footstep, so to speak. I only applied to one place, Merritt's Cars. I probably could've had a higher paying salary or *any* job in the world but I wanted to be an honest guy who sold a product to the average, working family.

And I loved cars.

That's how I managed to get my black '57 Chevy Bel Air.

A lot of things came naturally to me. Sure, I had to work hard, but my looks got me further. I had lived on my own during the nineteen-fifties until the seventies. Mom moved back to California after I graduated high school. She couldn't continue in the cold climate. We had moved around a lot to various cities in Minnesota, every decade or so. Mom loved the last house in California we'd been living in and maybe that was why Mom moved back there. She missed the warm weather. It was also just time to move on.

And so I stood, on the banks of the Mississippi River in Minnesota. Next to my dad—*the* Archangel Gabriel—who was about to give me some sort of speech.

I wasn't born an angel.

I was born a Nephilim.

Chapter Two

"Shay, I know this is going to be a lot for you to take in. It's your mother."

"What about Mom?"

"She plans to move back to Minnesota."

"But she loves it in California."

"I know. She loves you more. You've been here in the Twin Cities by yourself for a while and you'll be here for a bit longer. Michael thinks you'll be needed here soon. Your mother found a house that she absolutely adores. It's in Buffalo, a small town just north of Minneapolis. You both enjoyed living near water so I sort of already purchased the property for you both."

"*Her?*"

"Yes. It's almost time. There's been rumblings on earth, in Fairyland, and even in Hell. You remember the prophecy?"

"How can I forget it?"

"Tell it to me then, since I'm getting old and forgetful."

"You're not forgetful." I shook my head, but proceed to recite the words instilled into me since I could first speak:

Glory!
Babe born.
First and last.
Heaven and unto Earth.
Receives the highest in jubilation.
Enlightens will unite, they shall band.
Triumph be if darkness is driven back.
Help found who love, the world will stand.

"So, where is the house?" I asked.

"On a lovely body of water called Lake Mary," he replied. "It's surrounded by dense forest on the north, and rolling hills as far as the eye can see to the south. You'll love it."

"I'm sure we will."

"That's the spirit, my son. Duty comes first. You'll be so busy with the new house, keeping your mother company, and missions that you won't have time for anything else."

Yeah, duty always came first.

I've had little to no friends over the years, but maybe that was part of my doing. I pushed them away, didn't really try to become close since I knew I'd outlive them. *Duty always comes first.* I sighed.

"Alright. I'll start moving my things over the next couple of weeks. When will Mom get here? I should at least clean and fix the house before she comes."

"We'll work on the house together. Just like a father and son would. And maybe you'll find some people your own age."

"Let's just get what needs to be done."

Over the next few weeks, Dad and I repainted the exterior and interior of the house to brightly colors that reminded me of Spanish style living. Dad took up shingling while I addressed the plumbing and electrical needs. By the time Mom arrived everything was in order.

I wasn't there the weekend Mom moved in, which I felt bad about. But Dad hired movers to unload the furniture and her belongings. A mission was needed in the next town over and that's what took me away from greeting her. And of course, Dad was correct; as always. We loved the house, the land, and the lake.

June 24, 1997, 3:26 P.M.
St. Joseph, Minnesota

The tiny wail of a newborn baby vibrated into the earth's core. I heard it deep within my soul. Never had I felt anything like that. Of course, I had to go and inspect things for myself.

"Who are you?" Before me stood a tall, blonde teenager. "What are you doing here?" I asked him.

"You can see me?"

"Yes. You're an angel." His eyes widened slightly at my statement. "I'll take that as a yes."

"But you're not." It wasn't a question.

"No, I'm not." I shook my head. "My dad's an angel."

"Ah." He nodded.

That didn't explain anything. If he was an angel, he'd know about Nephilims, right?

"So, why are you here?" I asked again.

"I asked you first."

I crossed my arms, not wanting to say anything further.

"Yes you did."

Boy, was he infuriating; dodging questions.

"Who's *your* dad?" He matched my stance.

"Gabriel."

"All right, then."

When he didn't elaborate further, I said, "Something called me to this spot."

"Same here. Yesterday afternoon I felt a rumble. My friend, Sidelle, said that the earth would tell me when...I needed to be here."

"We must be on the same mission."

"So it seems." He relaxed his shoulders. I did the same. "Look. Since we're on the same side, we might as well make the most of the situation. There's a baby girl," he pointed to a yellow house a few yards away, "who lives there. She was born yesterday. She almost didn't make it, but...never mind. I think she could be the one we're looking to protect."

"How do you know that for sure?" I asked.

"I don't, but she's the only girl who was born yesterday about the time the earth told us. And ..." He fidgeted.

"And what? What did you do?"

"I might have brought her back from dying."

"You intervened!" I shouted.

"Yes, but Michael knows what I did."

I didn't want to be associated with this rule breaker. He was going to distract me from missions. I could feel it. This was not good.

"She was born with a natural white glow around her, but when she died and came back, her aura turned purple."

"What does that mean?"

"I'm not sure, but we need to stay vigilant. I've spotted a few demon knights hanging around the city. Nothing to worry about though. I've dispatched them already."

"It sounds like you don't need me." This would be an easy mission. An angel was already here watching and patrolling. I could go back home, take care of Mom, and ... All right, I didn't have much going on in my life.

"If you want we could take turns watching the area, until she's grown a bit more," the angel said.

"Fine," I conceded. "I'm living in the next town over. I suppose that a baby will be with her parents most of the time and we won't see much action."

"You're probably right."

I turned to leave to get back into my car, then stopped. Looking over my shoulder I watched as the angel faded from my view. He must have already known what I was going to ask.

"My name is Kieran," he whispered on the wind.

"Name's Shay," I responded.

Chapter Three

The weeks turned into months and I understood why Kieran had brought the little girl back to life. Her parents named her Zoe. She was a bundle of joy for them; their first child. Zoe did have a unique presence about her. She drew in everyone around her with a charming smile, an infectious giggle, and the largest brown eyes that told the world she was special.

Months turned into years and Kieran and I established a schedule to watch over Zoe and her parents. Then Kieran took it a step further. He befriended her. Told her that he was her imaginary friend and that only she could see him. I watched them play together as he became her best friend and there wasn't anything I could do about it. How would I explain an actual guy in her life who looked like a teenager without raising suspicion or being creepy? Kieran could make himself invisible and change his appearance. I couldn't compete with that. So I stayed in the shadows.

And then it happened. A chance encounter with demon knights.

Zoe was about three years old. Old enough to walk and talk. I watched as she and Kieran played in the front yard while Kevin and Jackie, Zoe's parents, packed their vehicle with their vacation belongings. It was time to prepare their cabin for summer. This was the first of many weekends traveling up north.

"Did you grab the cooler, Kevin?" Jackie shouted from the front door.

"Yes, it's in the car. You just need to get in so we can hit the road."

"I know, I just feel like I'm forgetting things."

"You do this every year and if we do forget something, we'll buy it when we get to the cabin or we'll bring it the next time." Kevin dangled the keys from his index finger.

"You're right. Go grab Zoe and let's go."

"Zoe! It's time to go. Come on, get into the car."

I watched as Zoe's short legs carried her from the yard, and then launched into the car seat. Kieran, who remained invisible, floated to her side and sat on top of the cooler. The door slid shut.

They backed down of the driveway, out of the cul-de-sac and turned onto Sandbar Lane; taking the Jabril family and Kieran away. At the very last minute, Zoe turned and stared directly at me. I slouched down into my car seat, but those brown eyes pierced right into mine. Her little hand slapped against the window.

Without a doubt, I knew she saw me. A small smile stretched across her lips.

I was hooked.

Of course, I had to follow them to the cabin. There really wasn't any other option for me. I must protect her. Some*thing* told me to look after her.

While keeping an eye on their red minivan, my hand turned the key to start the engine. I shifted into gear and checked the rearview mirror. A dark shadow crossed the lawn. I opened the car door and ran to where the figure stood.

Nothing. Whatever it was had disappeared.

I sprinted back to the car and stomped on the gas; needing to catch up with Zoe.

It didn't take me long to find them, St. Joseph's a small town with only a few streets. I spotted them turning onto the street near the The Coffee Grind, but stayed a couple car lengths back.

When suddenly, a black pickup truck missed the stop sign and slammed into the driver's side of the Jabril's minivan.

Tires squealed. Metal crunched. Air hissed.

People ran out from The Coffee Grind, shouting and screaming.

By-standers stood there on the sidewalk, mouths gaped open.

I drove my car as close as I could get it to the accident. Searching for Kieran in the mangled vehicles. His body laid across Zoe's; protecting her from the impact.

Her screams chilled me to the bones. I felt her heartache, and anger.

But Kevin and Jackie...their bodies. Kevin was slumped sideways over the center console while Jackie's hung halfway out of the passenger side opened door.

I slid open the side door to check on Zoe. She remained securely fastened in the car seat.

"She's okay, Shay," Kieran mouthed. "I protected her, but her parents...They need help. Now!"

"Fine, just make sure Zoe's okay. I'll check on her folks."

Broken window glass crunched beneath my boots as I dashed to the passenger side to evaluate the mom's injuries. Blood ran down her face from a deep gash in her hairline; she didn't move. I pressed my ear to her chest. No sounds. Gently, I released her seatbelt and slid her to the ground.

Making my way carefully in front of the minivan, I checked for a pulse on Kevin's neck.

Nothing.

"No, this can't be happening," I mumbled to myself. "I won't let it. Zoe needs her parents to help raise her; to protect her."

"There might be a way," Kieran said from the back seat. "But it's not exactly legal and the Orders won't like it. And we need to find someone else to help us. You and I aren't powerful enough to pull this off on our own." He disappeared.

"Kieran!" Zoe shouted from her carseat. "Don't go! Don't leave me!"

Above Zoe's cries, sirens wailed from off in the distance, getting closer as every second ticked by.

"Shh. It's okay," Kieran said as he reappeared. "Your parents will be okay."

"I don't think they will be," Zoe whimpered.

"Why do you say that?" I asked as I came around to stand next to her.

"Because their spirits aren't in their bodies anymore."

Kieran and I gaped at each other.

"But they are in a better place," Zoe continued. "The people in the truck though, they aren't." She pointed to her left and over my shoulder. "They're bad people. And they killed my parents." Fat tears dropped from her sad eyes.

A dark cloud slithered across the sky and settled into Zoe. Something changed in her at that moment. She balled her hands into tight fists. Energy crackled in the van around us. Then it was gone. The moment passed.

Police cars, ambulances, and fire trucks encircled around the accident. Officers ushered the spectators out of the way, took statements from witnesses as medics addressed the injured.

I wouldn't say to myself her parents were dead. I wouldn't accept it.

Kevin and Jackie were lifted out of the wreckage and into the ambulances.

A medic tapped me on the shoulder. "Excuse me, are you injured?" he asked.

"No, I wasn't in the accident. I came upon them and stopped to see if I could help."

"Ah, okay. If you could step aside so I can check the girl please."

"Sure. Her name's Zoe." I moved to let the medic get closer.

"Hi, Zoe. I'm Finn. Can you tell me if anything hurts?"

"I'm okay," Zoe said. "But my parents died, right?"

"Um. That I'm not sure of. I just need to make sure you're okay and then I'll see about your parents." He pressed his hands on the sides of Zoe's face. Faint blue light emitted from his palms. Then Zoe's eyes closed and her body slumped over into Kieran's lap.

"What the hel—" I tried shoving Finn out of the way.

"No, let him work," Kieran said. "I asked him to be here. He'll help us." He stroked her brown hair.

"Help us with what?"

"It's better if you don't know all the details right now, Shay."

"I don't like this." I shook my head.

"Neither do I, but Zoe needs her parents and this is the only thing I can think of."

Finn mumbled something and the blue glow grew brighter. I looked around, but no one paid attention to us. It was like they moved in slow motion and I viewed them through a dirty, glass bottle.

"No one can see us, Shay," Kieran said. "We're in the Void. We're safe here."

"She's fine, guys," Finn said.

"All right, let's get her out of here and back home," Kieran said.

"Wait a minute, she can't go home without her parents," I said.

"We know, that's where I come in," Finn said. "Let's just get her back in familiar surroundings and we'll go from there."

"Take my hand." Kieran extended his arm to me after he lifted Zoe. "It's faster we travel this way." He grabbed my wrist when I hadn't moved and then we disappeared.

I found myself standing in Zoe's bedroom.

"Are we doing this or not?" Finn asked when he appeared next to me.

"Yes," Kieran said as his arm that cradled Zoe glowed a soft white. "Shay, are you in or not. You said you wanted to do anything for her."

I looked at her sleeping form and breathed in. "Yeah."

Kieran placed Zoe's body on her bed, never breaking contact with her. "It's done."

"What did you just do?" I asked.

"I erased her memory of the accident and replaced it with memories of her actually going to the cabin, unpacking, fixing it up and getting ready for summer."

"Then what do we need Finn for?"

"I'm here because I'm a Winter Fairy and as such, I'm going to swap Zoe's parents for changlings. Zoe was right earlier. They are dead and no one can bring them back to life. So, the next best thing is this. Now, before you go all noble on me, I should warn you both that it doesn't always work for adults. Normally changlings are done when humans are infants. I can't guarantee how long this glamour will last. It could be a few years or it could be their lifetime. Depends on what happens during their lives and in hers." He nodded to Zoe. "After I do this, we're even, Kieran."

"Not quite, Finn. We'll need help setting up the wards. Then I give you my word as an Angel, that I won't say anything to *her*."

"Fine." Finn turned and stood in the middle of the room, blue light shooting from his skin that wasn't covered from his clothes.

The small dresser mirror frosted and the windows changed to solid, white ice. My skin chilled from the coldness. Tiny snowflakes swirled around us and as each moment passed, the flakes grew larger. The snow clumped together, gradually forming into shapes—humans. I could make out a man and a woman's body. Blue swirling light bounced off the walls, making prisms flash against the shiny objects in the room. Every now and then a faint green streak mixed in with the blue.

Finn's face jerked up toward the ceiling, the temperature dropped forming a sheet of ice on top of the beige carpet. Long icicles hung from the lavender curtains, sleigh head board, and the desk lamp.

Two solid figures stood before us, resembling Zoe's parents. I watched mesmerized as their skin warmed and turned from snow white to flesh. Brown color filled the man's eyes. His hair cropped short was a dark brown. He grew to stand just under six feet.

The woman's eye morphed into blue orbs. Tan hair draped down her back. She stood average height next her husband.

They drew in a breath at the same time.

Life sparked in their faces.

And then they turned to face each other.

"I am—" the man said.

Finn looked at us.

"Kevin," Kieran said.

"Kevin," the man who now resembled Zoe's father repeated.

"I am—" the woman said.

"Jackie," I said.

She nodded.

"Let's get this over with so I can go home," Finn said. "Come on, follow me outside."

"What about Zoe." I turned to look at her peaceful, sleeping face.

"She'll be fine for a couple of minutes," Kieran said. "She won't wake until Finn allows it. And besides, she doesn't need to see this either. It's better if she doesn't know about her parents."

"We should tell her when she's older," I said.

"No. She won't forgive either of us—"

"I disagree. She has every right to know—"

"Would you two stop." Finn turned and glared. "Just don't tell her unless she brings it up. She'll never know unless the glamour doesn't hold and there isn't any reason to bring her more pain. So shut it already and let's set up the wards."

He led the five of us to the outside of the house. I never used what little Angel Light I had to create a ward. There weren't times when I needed to. Granted, I could do small protections that I could call upon when fighting. But those only appeared around myself. This would be interesting.

"Okay everyone, stand about twenty paces from each other," Kieran said. "Jackie, you stand to the west of the house. Finn, go behind the house and take Kevin with you. Show him where to stand, just east of you." Finn took his changlings and positioned them accordingly to where Kieran said. "Shay, you stand over there to my right."

"I don't know what to do," I said when I took my designated place on the lawn.

"Just follow my lead," Kieran said.

Kieran's arms lifted upward. White Angel Light emitted from his hands. He slowly brought them down in an arch and extended his palms toward me and Jackie, like he wanted to shake our hands. He nodded to me and then to her. We followed his actions. I could only assume that Finn and Kevin were doing the same.

Silver glow lit my palms and on my left it merged with Kieran's white Light. To my right, I watched as blue tendrils of Kevin's light made its way to me. I glanced to where I knew Jackie stood and watched as the same blue-colored ribbons wound its way to meet Kieran's. We were all connecting. As soon the circle completed, the light mixed the three colors and then crept over the house. It stretched above the roof and settled onto the grass, making a sphere around the entire property.

The light pulsed, and then shrank inward, like a sponge absorbing water.

Thunder crackled in the sky.

I looked up, but not a cloud could be seen.

We dropped our hands and stood there.

A moment passed, then Jackie and Kevin walked inside the front door.

Finn came around, nodded to Kieran and disappeared.

Kieran never spoke to me again. He never sought me out. We never spoke of that day. There wasn't anything to say. We went back to our schedule of watching; protecting.

That encounter with Zoe, the accident, what we did was seared into my mind. I'd have nightmares for a long time.

It was good that Kieran erased her memory. I think. We watched Zoe grow up to be a happy child. That darkness I glimpsed never came back.

Only time would tell.

I knew then that Zoe ensnared me into her life. I'd never be able to leave her side again. Of course, I knew that we couldn't be together even when she got older. Orders couldn't mix. I was a Nephilim and she was a—I wasn't sure what she exactly was. All I knew for sure was that Zoe would be well protected.

And I was going to make sure that she would never know pain again.

WANT TO FIND OUT MORE?

Purchase the Marked by Fate boxset and get Swords and Stilettos plus 24 other full-length novels

FUN. ROMANTIC. EPIC!!

Zoe Jabril needs to devise a kick-ass plan to save the world ASAP. Otherwise, Armageddon starts the day she turns eighteen—and if that happens, everything is going to hell. Literally.

She could be any other 17-year-old attending parties and checking out cute guys—except she discovers her best friend is a Guardian Angel and the boy she crushes on is a Nephilim, both sent to protect her from the demons who want her dead.

Now Zoe has to deal with growing feelings toward the Nephilim, who spreads a strange electrical current through her body every time he touches her. And she's under constant attack from Demons, trying to stop her from fulfilling the Prophecy: a girl will be born who will unite Angels, Nephilim, Fairies and Werewolves to battle evil. Then she has to control newly found talents if she's to prevent the devil from escaping Hell.

CONNECT WITH KRISTIN

I hope you've enjoyed Ninjas & Nephilims

To find out what happens next,
check out the rest of my series available now.

Swords & Stilettos (Book One)
Daggers & Dresses (Book Two)

Follow me online
Instagram: @kristinDVanrisseghem | Twitter: @KVanRisseghem
| Facebook: @kristinvanrisseghem.Author |
| Pinterest: @kristinDVanrisseghem |

ABOUT THE AUTHOR

USA Today bestseller and award-winning young adult author, Kristin D. Van Risseghem grew up in a small town along the Mississippi River with her parents and older sister. Currently, she lives in Minnesota with her husband and a Calico cat. Kristin also loves attending book clubs, going shopping, and hanging out with friends. She has come to realize that she absolutely has an addiction to purses and shoes. They are her weakness and probably she has way too many of both.

An avid reader of YA and Women's Literature stories, she still finds time to read a ton of books in-between writing.

Kristin's books are published by Kasian Publishing LLC

Jonah's Curse

A Midnight Chronicles Short Story

Rhonda Sermon

Jonah's Curse © 2017 Rhonda Sermon

This is a work of fiction. Names, places, characters and incidents are either the product of the author's imagination or are used fictitiously, and any resemblance to any actual persons, living or dead, organizations, events or locales is entirely coincidental.

Chapter One

There's a ridiculously high probability that each day will end with my death. Let me explain.

An excruciating, burning pain pierced Jonah's eyes as he struggled to open them. It was as if someone had superglued his eyelids closed while he was in his chemical-induced coma. He raised his hands to cover his face as a sliver of light sliced through the darkness.

Little by little, agonizing second after agonizing second, light continued to poke more holes though the darkness until suddenly the darkness admitted defeat and vanished, sending a wave of light crashing over Jonah. The pale blue walls and wooden floorboards of his bedroom at Rose Cottage, where he lived with Rose and Austin, came into view.

He gasped, blinked a few times, and rubbed his fists into his eyes. Something moved on his left near his pillow. A child's hand holding a glass of black liquid appeared so close the cold rim banged his nose. The leather cuff around the child's wrist with Jonah's family crest told him the hand belonged to Austin. He shared no family blood with the young boy, but he and Rose had been Jonah's family for as long as he could remember.

His mind instantly went to the two of his family members that had died before the migraines made him incoherent and unable to function.

"What day is it?" Dread filled him as he waited for the answer. How many more people had died while he was unconscious?

"Excellent. You're awake." Ice clinked as Austin rattled the glass in front of Jonah. "Hold this with two hands and sip it slowly. Don't spill it on the bed." This wasn't the first time Austin had been there when Jonah regained consciousness. He was an old hand at managing Jonah's recovery from his migraines.

Jonah took the glass and leveraged himself into a sitting position on the bed. His arms felt like little pieces of string, his hands like dangling bricks. Every muscle ached with exhaustion and his head pounded. The aftereffects of dealing with the unrelenting pain from the migraines were similar to the fatigue after an epic bout of the flu. "What day is it, Austin?"

"Rose said I wasn't to tell you anything until you drank that tonic." Austin settled back on the white leather wingback chair, both legs draped over one of the arm rests and his chin on his hands. Jonah's eyes were drawn to the leather cuff on his wrist. The purple, red and black family crest comprised crossed swords behind a phoenix, which seemed increasingly poignant each time Jonah emerged from the flames of his illness unscathed. He had been close to death when Rose arrived with his medicinal narcotics, his body burning as if engulfed by flames. The pain and heat were more intense than ever before. As the narcotics pushed him into the dark, soundless world of unconsciousness, he had feared death would finally claim victory in this protracted battle.

His debilitating migraines had become increasingly frequent. Rose had needed to travel back in time to Cleopatra's palace for the medicine Jonah required to stay alive more and more often these last few months. Every trip took Rose exactly two hours in Jonah's time, no matter how long she spent in the past. It was one of the rules of the ancient magic that allowed them to travel through time. "Tell me what day it is. It's important."

Austin pointed at the glass in Jonah's hand. "Drink your vitalizing tonic and I'll tell you. Better you than me. I hate that stuff." The impish grin on Austin's young face as he ran his hand through his shaggy brown hair instantly made Jonah feel brighter. Austin's smile was infectious and he absolutely knew it. He already used it regularly to charm people and get his own way.

Jonah sipped the liquid in the glass and grimaced. "You and me both, buddy. Now, tell me what day it is and what the time is."

Reaching into the pocket of his shorts, Austin pulled out a familiar pocket watch. Jonah had given it to him for his tenth birthday just a month ago, and the boy was glad for any excuse to look at it. It had belonged to Jonah's father, a man he had never met, before it had been Jonah's—at least that was what his mother told him when she gave him the watch on his tenth birthday. And though Austin was not Jonah's son, Jonah loved him as if he were, and it had felt right to pass the watch to him. Neither of them had met their fathers, a fact that brought them even closer. "It's just gone noon on Tuesday. My favorite day of the week, because it means we get to have tacos for dinner. You were unconscious for three days. I think that's a new record." Austin grinned. He leaned toward the bed and held up his hand. "That deserves a high five." His smile didn't reach his eyes, which were filled with apprehension.

The last day Jonah remembered was Thursday. His stomach lurched. If Mortez had continued to make good on her threat, she would have killed five more people. Waves of nausea rolled through Jonah. What had he done? He needed to speak to Rose.

Austin interrupted his thoughts. "Don't leave me hanging!" He waved the hand he was waiting to Jonah to high five.

Jonah placed the half-full glass of vitalizing tonic on the white bedside table. He raised his arm and delivered a weak high five. "I was always coming back to you and Rose, buddy. I'll always come back."

"It doesn't make it any less scary," Austin said very quietly. He dove off the chair onto the bed and hugged Jonah fiercely. "Thanks for coming back."

The force pushed Jonah back against the pillows. When Austin started to pull away, Jonah held him a little bit tighter. "I'm not ready to let go just yet." Austin chuckled as he squirmed and wriggled his way out of Jonah's grasp.

"By the way, that was a truly pathetic high five." Austin reached behind Jonah and adjusted the three pillows so to better support Jonah. He screwed up his nose and shuddered. "Those pillows reek. They're all damp and sticky. I reckon you've sweated out your body weight and then some." He handed Jonah the vitalizing tonic from the bedside table.

Jonah sniffed gingerly at his t-shirt. "Eek. I think the only thing that smells worse in this room than them is me." He pressed two fingers to the base of his temples. A dull ache had settled inside his head. "Shouldn't you be in class?"

"Not gonna argue with you. You're very smelly." Austin padded over the floor toward the leadlight bay window that stretched along the wall of the bedroom.

He was tall for his age, and already built like an athlete, but still had to stand on his tiptoes to fling open the heavily-embossed silver and white curtains. The house had a spectacular view of the pristine white beach and turquoise and sapphire blue ocean. The sun poured into the room, catching the flecks of gold in Austin's shaggy brown hair from the hours he spent at the beach. "Naitanui took me surfing this morning."

The sparkle in Austin's eyes made Jonah smile. Austin loved the water and the sea. "Nice. How was it?"

"Awesome. Would have been better if you were there though. Naitanui said I should sit with you while Rose was on her mission, so I've got a free pass from classes all day." Austin beamed at Jonah. "It's a sweet deal."

There was no one in the world who had a smile that lit up a room like Austin. Jonah vividly remembered the first time Austin smiled at him. His heart had melted, and he knew instantly he would do anything to protect this young boy. Anything.

"Rose should be back pretty soon." Austin tugged at the window handle until it moved and then pushed the leadlight window open.

The smell of salt mingled with the scents of rose and lavender wafted into the stuffy bedroom. Jonah closed his eyes and breathed deeply. The gentle sea breeze invigorated his drained senses and the rhythmic crash of the waves calmed his raw emotions.

Austin opened all three of the windows. "All the fresh air in the world isn't going to mask your smelliness. You want a shower?"

Jonah gave him a thumbs up. He gulped the remaining vitalizing tonic down and threw the damp sheets back. When he sat up and placed his feet on the smooth floorboards, the room tilted. He grabbed for the edge of the bedside table to steady himself.

Austin sprinted over from the window and grabbed his shoulders. "Let me help. If you fall and hit your head on my watch, Rose will be very unhappy." He put both arms around Jonah's waist. "Lean on me all you need. Ready?"

Jonah nodded and braced himself to stand. Austin's arms tightened around his middle. When they stood, Austin's head was pretty much level with Jonah's waist. Being six foot five, there weren't too many people Jonah had to look up to.

"You're getting pretty strong there, buddy," Jonah said as they staggered across the room toward the bathroom. He kept one arm over Austin's shoulders, and the other pressed against the wall for support.

"You and Rose always say we have to be strong for the people we love. So I want to be strong for you." Austin pushed the bathroom door open wide with his foot.

Jonah's heart skipped a beat. "And I want to be strong for you too, Austin. Always remember that."

"You're the strongest person I know. That's why you always come back when you're sick." Austin slowly released his hold on Jonah and stepped backward, feeling his way along the wall to turn the taps on in the shower. His eyes never left Jonah, his body poised to grab him if he swayed again. He checked the water temperature with his hand a few times and adjusted the hot tap. "Perfect." Austin stood between Jonah and the shower, contemplating his next move.

"I've got it from here." Jonah took his hand off the wall. "See, steady as a rock." It took every ounce of his concentration and determination to stand without swaying.

"I'll wait in the other room." Austin backed out of the bathroom and closed the door.

Jonah immediately collapsed against the wall.

The bathroom door opened again and Austin returned. "Some rock you turned out to be. I'm going to leave this open in case you need a towel or soap or maybe collapse and break a bone or hit your head." There was a pause. "And don't forget to wash your hair. OK. Well ..."

Jonah's gut twisted at the concern and uncertainty in Austin's voice. He hated that Austin had to see him like this. "I'm good, Austin." His head was foggy and his body ached but he forced a smile. "You don't have to babysit me."

"I'll sit out here anyway. It's that or class."

Jonah peeled his damp shorts and t-shirt off, then carefully stepped into the shower. The tiled floor was cold under his feet. The warm water washed over him, soothing his tired, aching muscles. He wondered what mission Naitanui had sent Rose on. Naitinui was the leader of The Midnight Society, the army of time travelers which Jonah and Rose were part of. They were both Timesurfers. This was the only life either of them knew. Both their parents and any other family they had were long gone. The Midnight Society was their family now.

At ten years old, Austin was too young to go on missions, but because he and Rose were at the top of The Maligo Order's most wanted list he'd done more time traveling than most Timesurfers five times his age. The complex magical wards set up here at Rose Cottage kept them safe from The Midnight Society's sworn enemy, but when he was very young Rose refused to trust anyone but herself and Jonah to protect him. The three of them went into hiding and never spent more than a month in any one time or place. The moment Mortez discovered Rose had sworn to protect Austin, he became her prime target. An innocent victim in Mortez's ongoing crusade to destroy Rose and her family. There was so much bad blood between the two of them. Their feud was well known throughout the Timesurfer world. Only Jonah, Rose, Naitanui and Mortez knew how it started and it was a secret that Jonah would take to his grave.

"Rose has arrived back at The Break," Austin called from the next room. "She'll be here in ten minutes. I'll have a shot at making the bed. Rose left a pile of clean sheets on one of the arm chairs. I assume that's code for 'make the bed.'"

The Break was the headquarters for The Midnight Society, where all the Timesurfers set off on and returned from their missions. Austin's tuneless whistle from the other room as he tidied up made Jonah smile as he washed his curly, chocolate-colored hair.

Austin's head popped around the bathroom door. "Oh, and Rose said to tell you Mortez has gotten seven so far."

Seven. His worst suspicion was confirmed. Jonah felt like someone had rammed a dagger into his heart and was now twisting it. That changed everything. The heartbreaking decision he had fought so hard against making suddenly become inevitable.

"Seven what?" Austin asked. "Are you OK? Your face has gone very white."

Jonah mustered a weak smile. "I think the hair washing took it out of me. That or the vitalizing tonic is disagreeing with me."

Austin nodded knowingly. "It's so gross, but it works. I'll go and wait for Rose."

Jonah held his breath as Austin's footsteps became more and more faint. The shock that seven people had died because of him landed like an enormous weight on his chest. He gasped and pressed his back against the cold tiles as he struggled to breathe under the sadness which now pinned him against the wall. His legs wavered and he slid slowly to the floor of the shower. His pulse raced. All the signs were there. The migraines untreated were unbearable, the narcotics to keep them under control were becoming more and more ineffective and weakened his heart every time he used them. Now on top of that, innocent people were dying. As a soldier, he had seen and done unthinkable things, but never during that time had he been confronted with a decision as monumental as he now faced.

He stretched to turn the hot and cold water taps off and crawled out of the shower onto the bathmat. With two deep breaths, he braced and levered himself off the floor. As he dried himself off haltingly with the sky-blue towels he and Rose had picked out together, the deep, aching fatigue began to leave his body. The vitalizing tonic was finally kicking in. He wiped the steam from the mirror. His face and body hadn't changed since he turned eighteen, which was more than a century ago now. Today his cheeks were flushed and there were large, dark circles under his grey eyes which now had a familiar brightness to them. The glow wasn't from the vitalizing tonic, but from the narcotics that kept him alive from week to week. Other than that, he looked like the same immortal, time-traveling warrior he always did.

Mortez, the leader of The Maligo Order, was the only person with the magic to lift the migraines Jonah had been cursed with since childhood. All he had to do was defect from The Midnight Society, but Jonah had so far refused to leave everyone he loved and abandon all his beliefs and values.

It had always infuriated Mortez that Jonah continued to choose The Midnight Society and a life with Rose over joining The Maligo Order. After she successfully overthrew the previous leader of The Maligo Order and assumed control of it last week, Mortez became more determined than ever to have Jonah and his unique magical gifts working for her instead of against her.

Aside from Rose, he was the fiercest warrior The Midnight Society had ever trained. He was also a conduit, and they were rare. There had only been two of them in the last five hundred years. A conduit could channel the magical powers of any other Timesurfer by touching them. These things coupled with the fact she would be denying Rose of her one true love made Mortez determined to have Jonah defect to her command without further delay. So much so that she had begun executing people who shared family blood with him. She killed one at noon every day he chose not to concede and join her. To have their blood on his hands made it difficult for him to breathe.

"How's our patient doing today?" Rose's voice floated in from the other room.

Austin squealed with glee. "Rose!"

Jonah pulled on the black jeans and purple t-shirt that sat neatly on the stool near the door of the bathroom. Rose must have put them there sometime over the last few days for him. He threaded a black leather belt through the belt loops as he sauntered into the bedroom, his heart aching as he prepared mentally to face his most arduous decision ever.

Rose and Austin were having a tickle fight on the freshly made bed. Austin giggled uncontrollably as he thrashed around trying to maneuver his way out of Rose's grip. He was the most ticklish person Jonah had ever known. So many conflicting emotions washed though him. Delight at seeing Rose and Austin like this together one last time and then a heavy sorrow that he would not be part of these precious, loving moments after today. It was the sorrow that lingered.

"I give up! I give up," Austin panted between giggles.

Rose released him and knelt on the bed. The adoration on her face as she gazed at Austin made Jonah's heart swell with love and pride. There was no one better able to protect Austin. Her flushed cheeks were a sharp contrast to her porcelain complexion. She pushed her long, wavy black hair away from her face and smiled tenderly at Jonah. "You look much better than the last time I saw you."

Even filled with melancholy, he smiled back automatically. His heart squeezed out a few extra beats and his breath caught in his throat. Rose was the most beautiful woman he had ever laid eyes on, and she made his life complete in every way. The familiar butterflies flittered in his stomach. They had appeared the very first day he met Rose and had never gone away. "Thank you for traveling to Cleopatra and getting my medicine."

Rose held up her hand and smiled. "I do it because I love you."

Regardless of her smile, her grey eyes lacked their normal sparkle. Her eyes told Jonah she was desperately worried. He had spent the last few days suffering debilitating pain, as if someone were taking an ax to the back of his skull. But it was nothing compared to the dread that now consumed him. They both knew what was coming. That it was no surprise didn't make it any less gut-wrenching.

Austin pointed to Rose's calf-high combat boots. "No boots on the bed. House rules."

Rose gasped in mock horror and stood in one graceful movement. At six feet, she was tall for a woman. Her athletic and curvaceous body drew many admiring glances, but it was her presence that made people stare. The slight tilt of her chin and the self-assurance that came with being the most accomplished warrior The Midnight Society had. She brushed imaginary lint from her fitted black trousers and straightened the lace sleeves of her white cotton shirt.

They moved toward one another at the exactly the same moment. Jonah wrapped his arms tightly around Rose, his chin resting on top of her head that was pressed hard against his chest. She had a very distinct way of hugging him. Rose didn't wrap her arms around him in a circle; instead, she wrapped her arms around him, bent her elbows and crossed her arms upwards on his back so her hands pressed against his shoulder blades. The only two people he knew who did that were Rose and Austin.

Jonah closed his eyes and breathed in the scent of roses, lavender and Rose's distinct floral perfume. To him this was the fragrance of family, home, and unbreakable love. Knowing he was about to leave this for a different life, he held Rose extra tight. He staggered as Austin tunneled his way between them.

His happy face beamed up first at Jonah and then Rose. "Seeing I'm on a class free day, can we all go for a walk down the beach and build the biggest sandcastle ever?"

Jonah choked back tears and fought to regain his composure.

"Nice try." Rose ruffled Austin's hair. "Naitanui is waiting outside to take you to the weapons room for some training. I want to talk to Jonah for a bit."

Austin groaned. "But I've taken down every kid under fifteen. Where's the challenge?"

"Austin." There was a sternness to Rose's voice which made it clear the training was non-negotiable.

Austin sighed. "Fine. But can we go to the beach after that?"

Rose and Jonah exchanged glances. They had agreed to say nothing to Austin when the time came for Jonah to leave. Their plan was to tell Austin Jonah was on a special mission only he could be entrusted with and to keep Rose and Austin safe, he was forbidden from making contact with them. As Austin grew more aware of The Midnight Society and the responsibilities that came with this life, Rose would explain things more fully. While they both clung desperately to the possibility Jonah would find some way to return before the time came for Austin to know the truth, the reality was that it became virtually impossible the moment Jonah walked out the door. A decision like this could not be undone.

Jonah knelt on the floor so his eyes were at Austin's level and grasped Austin's shoulders. Feeling sick to his stomach, he forced a smile onto his face. "We'll see, buddy. Now give me the biggest hug you can muster and get on your way. Warriors can never train too much."

Austin wrapped his arms around Jonah's shoulders and squeezed. "Is this tight enough?"

"That's perfect." Jonah's heart pounded in his chest, panicked at the thought of leaving Austin.

Austin rested his head on Jonah's shoulder, and his chest tightened with sadness. He glanced at Rose and saw her eyes were glistening with tears. This would be his last chance to hold Austin for a very long time, maybe forever. A little piece of his heart broke away. It would never be complete again without Austin and Rose.

When Austin moved to pull away, Jonah held on tight. "Two more minutes."

Austin chuckled and began to squirm. "Nope. I've got places to be." He planted a kiss on Jonah's cheek and hugged Rose before sprinting out of the room without a backward glance.

Jonah sank onto the floor and rested his head on his hands, desperate to call to Austin to come back so he could see his smile once more. Hold his small body close one last time. But he couldn't. How did he say goodbye to someone he had been a father to for all these years? An enormous mass of grief lodged itself in his chest and made it nearly impossible for him to breathe. Silent tears rolled down his cheeks.

"There's no other way, Jonah." Rose cradled his head against her warm body. "You were unconscious for three days after you had the medicine and delirious, not to mention in agony, for the two days prior to that. You aren't likely to survive many more. We can't put this decision off any longer."

Jonah gently extracted himself from Rose's embrace. He thought it was impossible to love her more, but somehow, with every new day, he did. "My head knows that. But my heart is consumed with a pain that is far worse than anything I've ever experienced with the migraines or medicine. This is fresh torture I never imagined possible. With prodigious love comes phenomenal pain."

Rose stroked his shoulder tenderly. "If there was any other way ... This is the *only* choice we have."

The inevitability of leaving The Midnight Society made Jonah's stomach turn. Bile rose up his throat. For over a century, he had protected history from the magical manipulation of The Maligo Order. He was a soldier who fought to protect peoples' rights to make mistakes and learn from them. He ensured history unfolded as it should. There was no grey in his world. Only black and white. His commitment to his duty had never wavered. "Working with Mortez goes against everything I believe in."

Rose tucked one of Jonah's wayward curls behind his ear. Her fingers trailed along his jaw and across his lower lip. "What's to say the purpose of our magic and being able to time travel isn't to alter history and avert tragedies with the benefit of hindsight? Who really knows whether Mortez or Naitanui are on the correct path? Or even if there is a correct path? The only certainty is that people will continue to die, irrespective of whether history is free from manipulation or not. Don't let innocent people die because of you, Jonah. Don't be a martyr. Your death will not help end this battle that has been going on for hundreds of years."

Jonah jerked away from Rose's touch.

She flinched like he had slapped her. "You have been my family and lover for more than a century," she said. "I will never give my heart to another. Nothing you say or do will ever diminish my love for you. Leaving is the most tremendously selfless and brave choice. You're the only person I know with the strength to do this." The anguish in her voice and raw emotion on her face was unmistakable. She began to pace back and forward along the bed.

A tsunami of conflicting emotions raced through his body. Fear, grief, anger. He stood and moved to the window where he could just distinguish the outlines of Austin and Naitanui making their way along the beach to the weapons room at The Break. Never had he felt so weak and helpless. "Magic or no magic, no one has the right to play God. That's what Mortez is doing. It's wrong. People should be free to make their own mistakes and shape their own futures, irrespective of what that is. I've always fought for people to have freedom and choice."

"You can't fight for anyone if you're dead!" Rose yelled. She strode over and stood in front of Jonah, her body rigid and fists clenched by her side. "I can't live in a world without you, Jonah. I don't want to live in a world without you. Mortez has proven her healing powers will keep your migraines away. Go to her. Please, Jonah."

She wrapped her arms around his waist, pressing her body against his. "If you stay here, there's no doubt you'll be dead in weeks. Either from the drugs or the migraines. They're both killing you. This is your chance to live."

Jonah broke away from her embrace. "If I defect to Mortez, the people who have loved me and cared for me since I was young become my enemies. I'll be alive and fighting a war against the two people I respect most in the world." Jonah clenched his fists. "I think I'd rather be dead."

Rose gasped, her eyes wide with disbelief.

Jonah moved to turn away and Rose spun him around to face her with the strength and speed that only an exceptional warrior could display. Her eyes now burned with a fierceness he had never seen before. "You'll be dying with the blood of innocents on your hands, Jonah. Seven innocent people have died simply because they share some small amount of blood with you. If you won't do it for me or yourself, then do it for them."

He dropped to his knees and shrieked. His body was so filled with torment he felt like it might explode. Colossal sobs racked his body, so fierce that his ribs threatened to shatter with each one. He closed his eyes, focusing on breathing in through his nose and out through his mouth. He fought with all his strength against the emotional turmoil which threatened his sanity until a momentary calm settled over him. This was the moment. He stood and stepped away from Rose, his eyes meeting hers for the briefest of seconds. "I would do anything for you and Austin."

He turned on his heel and marched from the bedroom along the passageway, ignoring the photos that lined the walls. The three of them smiling in front the Sydney Harbor bridge in their last summer holiday, him with Austin behind their sandcastle just before the tide washed it away, and the three of them dressed to go trick-or-treating last Halloween. He headed out the front door of the cottage, unable to risk a backward glance. With every step he took, another brick went up in the wall he was building around his heart. He never wanted to feel the agony of this type of loss again.

Mortez wanted a soldier and that's what he would be. He would fight for her until this war was over or until he took his last breath. His conscience would be clouded and his soul tormented forevermore. He would be Mortez's most valued and trusted soldier, but his heart would remain eternally with Rose and Austin. Every day his heart would be agonizingly empty, and every night he fell asleep with that pain would be a reminder of the enduring love he had for Rose and the lengths he would go to for her.

Mortez was continually attempting to capture Rose's stepmother and sisters. He would do everything in his power to sabotage those attempts and ensure Rose's family remained safe. It was because he knew he could never stop being in love with Rose that he would risk a slow, torturous death every day, which would be his fate if his actions were ever discovered. It was the only way he could live with his choice to betray those who had shown him love and support all these years and to sacrifice the values he had fought so hard to protect.

WANT TO FIND OUT MORE?

Purchase the Marked by Fate boxset and get The Midnight Society plus 24 other full-length novels

Incredible powers. Hidden worlds filled with magic and time travel. A deadly and brutal challenge.

Cate was always different. Five years of witness protection has made her an outcast. When the world and everyone except her seem to freeze at the bus stop one day, she feels more alone than ever.

As she tries to understand what's happening, a group of teens appear out of thin air, lift the bus over their heads, and disarm a bomb placed underneath it. They seem surprised she can see them as they disappear once again.

After the mystery teens show up at her school the next day, Cate is drawn into a world of time travel and magic she never thought possible. It turns out she has powers of her own, but only she can decide whether she uses them for the forces of good or world-altering evil…

CONNECT WITH RHONDA

First of all let me say thank you so much for taking a chance on me as an author. This short story is a prequel to my debut novel *The Midnight Society*. I am thrilled to have my first book in this series out. You can find the Midnight Society on Amazon

To be notified first about the release details of The Midnight Chronicles Book 2: *The Midnight Elites* you can sign up for my newsletter at Rhondasermon.com/newsletter. You'll also have access to exclusive giveaways, content and other cool stuff.

I can't wait to share more of my stories with you!

Rhonda

Follow me online
Instagram: @rhondasermonyaauthor| Twitter: @RhondaSermon
| Facebook: @RhondaSermonAuthor |

ABOUT THE AUTHOR

Rhonda Sermon lives in Perth, Western Australia with her husband and two children. Her debut novel, *The Midnight Society*, was a finalist in the Young Adult category and overall runner-up in The Strongest Start 2012 Contest hosted by TheNextBigWriter.com. On the good days, she adores writing, on the challenging days, it's still awesome. Her two ragdoll cats can often be found helpfully walking over her keyboard, chasing her mouse or generally complaining loudly about the lack of priority their needs are being given.

EMERGE THE CATALYST

An Emerge Short Story

Melissa A. Craven

Emerge: The Catalyst © 2017 Melissa A. Craven

For more information contact: Hello@Melissaacraven.com or visit the author's website at www.melissaacraven.com

Midnight Hour Studio

CATALYST

[kat-l-ist]

Noun

Something or someone that causes activity between two or more persons or forces without itself being affected.

A person or thing that precipitates an event or change.

THE IMMORTALS

Immortals have existed since the beginning of the beginning, long before we yielded the world to our mortal children, who have forgotten us. In the modern world, we thrive, hidden from our enemies who would see us extinct. I am the oldest living Immortal, known as the Scholar—a myth to some and purely fiction to others. I have watched from afar as the governing body of the Immortal world has grown corrupt and lazy.

We stand on a precipice, waiting for the catalyst event that will propel us into the next age. An uncertain age our prophecies cannot predict.

—From The Journals of The Scholar

CHAPTER ONE

"Livia, your father will retaliate if he hears you asking these questions." Porcia glanced nervously across the gardens that resembled an antebellum rendition of Versailles.

"He's not here," Livia said patiently.

"And you know he doesn't need to be here to discover what you're up to."

Her mother was one of the most intelligent women Livia had ever known, but she was never one to stand up to Livia's father, not in all the centuries of their long marriage. Porcia was always more of a pampered prisoner than a respected wife.

"Mother, I am over two hundred years old. I can handle my father." Livia stood under a canopy of huge oak trees draped in Spanish moss as she watched her mother paint her toenails a vicious red. In her faded black fatigues, Livia felt downright dowdy next to her stunning mother.

She loved Porcia more than any daughter could, but she always seemed so fragile. She was the only real family Livia had ever known, but Livia had taken on the protective role in their relationship, bearing the brunt of her father's ire to spare her mother the punishment. Marcus never dared to hurt either of them physically. But he was a controlling man, and Livia had learned a long time ago that the only way to earn his respect was to play by his rules. She'd done that for most of her life, working to help him achieve his agenda. But Marcus had never even noticed when his daughter stopped trying to win his approval.

"The questions you are asking." Porcia shook her head. "You have no idea the can of worms you are opening." Her mother enjoyed the fine things Marcus provided, and on most days, she didn't seem to mind her walled prison. But her eyes occassionally still shone with ageless wisdom and a spark of defiance. Livia often wondered if Marcus ever noticed that about his wife or if he thought she was just a simple woman who liked pretty things. Porcia was once a notorious woman of the Roman Empire, and even centuries later, she was not one to be underestimated.

"There must be a reason these memories are coming to me so clearly now. It's like ... recalling another life you never knew you had. Or recovering after a long battle with amnesia only to remember the insignificant details—enough to haunt you but not enough to fill in the missing pieces."

"I always knew this day would come, my daughter. You are *my* daughter. I've loved you and raised you inside this gilded cage until you grew strong enough to face him on your own."

"Nothing about my past will change the fact that you are my family. But I need to know what these memories mean, Mother." Livia sat beside her in the shade of the ancient oaks at the farthest reaches of the garden. Marcus rarely allowed Porcia to leave the grounds of their Atlanta home, and this was as far as she could go without escort. Beyond the brick wall laid the hustle and bustle of the modern world. Marcus claimed he kept his wife sequestered for her own safety, that too many people would try to use her against him. But Livia always suspected that if given her freedom to come and go as she pleased, Porcia might not choose to return.

"Tell me what you remember."

"Four women, all fussing over me when I was just a child. A blond woman with eyes like mine held my hand. She was with three younger women who looked a lot like her. I think they were her daughters ... or maybe her sisters. They seem so happy in the fleeting memories I have of them."

"And why do you think this is important?" Porcia screwed the cap back onto her bottle of nail polish.

"I used to think it was just a dream that I could dismiss. But it only grows stronger. The memories are mine, and I need to understand them. I feel connected with those women somehow, like once upon a time they were my family."

"They were." Porcia said with a bitter sigh.

"Who are they? Are they dead?"

"I don't know. I don't have the answers you deserve. But if you are determined to dig into your past, I can lead you to someone who can help."

"Who?"

"Her name is Lily. She is mortal."

"Mortal? What would a mortal woman know of my past?"

"You will have to ask her."

Chapter Two

"Sir! Sir, you need to return to your seat!" The flight attendant chased the ancient Immortal down the narrow aisle of the plane as it began to move.

Livia felt his presence the moment she boarded the plane and took her seat in first class. He was probably the most ancient Immortal she'd ever encountered, and the thought of being trapped on a fifteen-hour flight with such a man made her nervous. She'd even thought about waiting to catch another plane, but after taking the red eye from Atlanta to L.A., she didn't want to delay her trip to New Zealand any longer.

"Sir, we are about to take off," the flight attendant huffed in irritation when she caught him at the juncture between coach and first class. "Please return to your seat."

"Humor an old man, dear lady? I've never flown first class, and I see so many empty seats."

"I'll take you back to your seat. Now, sir."

"I'd really love to sit with my granddaughter if it wouldn't be too much trouble," he said, gesturing toward Livia. "Look, she even has my nose, bless her. Although, it looks much better on her than it does me."

Livia cracked a smile at the old man. If manipulation was an artform, he had a talent for it. He'd seen many thousands of years, but he looked to be about fifty. His dark hair, threaded with silver, stuck out in disarray.

Dressed in flip-flops, faded jeans and a tshirt that said, "Driver picks the music, shotgun shuts his cakehole," he didn't look like anyone's grandfather.

"Just … sit, please," the flight attendant begged. "Wherever you want."

"Excellent. Could I also trouble you for a brandy and a few snacks? I do enjoy the roasted cashews." His oblivious smile probably won him just about anything he wanted.

"After take off, sir." She gave him an exasperated smile.

"Mind if I join you?" he asked once they were alone.

"Please," Livia said. He was up to something, and she'd rather have him close by so she could keep an eye on him.

"My presence can be unsettling," he groaned as he took the seat beside her. "I figured the long flight to Auckland would be more comfortable for you if I came to introduce myself—that and the comfortable reclining seats."

"Not to mention the superior snacks?" Livia teased.

"A man could starve back there with those sad little packages of peanuts."

"How often do you do this?"

"What?"

"Talk your way into first class."

"Oh, only every time I fly. I'm Alexander, by the way." He offered his hand. "And you are Livia, daughter of Marcus Servius and Porcia Catonis of Ancient Rome. Lovely to meet you."

"How did you—" Livia's eyes widened in surprise as she realized who this man really was. "You're the Scholar."

"Indeed I am."

Some believed the Scholar was a myth, a man so ancient even the Immortals had forgotten him. It was said that he was responsible for the writing of history, for he had seen it all.

"Unfortunately, once we reach our destination, you won't remember meeting me. It is the nature of my gift—the thing that protects me from my enemies … men like your father."

"My father?"

"Marcus is an ancient himself. But of course, you know that. We go back to the time before mortals existed, centuries before the Great War. I didn't like him much then, and he's only gotten worse with time. Not to speak ill of him, I'm sure he's managed to be a good father."

"He has his moments," Livia said.

"He's always blamed my family for that mess of a war a million years ago. And we've always blamed him for the rise of the *idiocy* that pushed us all into the war to begin with. All water under the bridge as far as I'm concerned, but Marcus never could let it go."

Livia didn't know what to say to that but was rescued by the flight attendant arriving with the drink cart.

"Brandy for you, sir." She set the tiny bottle in front of Alex along with an assortment of snacks.

"Keep 'em coming."

"The drinks or the snacks?" Livia asked.

"The snacks, of course." Alex gave the flight attendant his best smile.

"And for you, miss?"

"Water is fine, thank you."

"The question isn't about Marcus, though," Alex continued without missing a beat. "He is predictable in his sameness. The question is about you, dear girl."

"Me?"

"I know exactly what Marcus is planning. And he knows I know what he's up to. But I don't know where you fit into it all. The fact that you're here, on this flight, heading to New Zealand to seek out Lily Carmichael suggests you are on the right path. But it remains unclear where your loyalties will lie once the proverbial crap hits the fan."

Livia choked on her water, wondering how the man knew so much about her. *He is the Scholar. He knows everything.*

"It is simply the age-old question of nature verses nurture, Livia." Alexander gave her a penetrating stare. "Will you become the woman your father has created, or will your roots be strong enough to set you on the right path? It is up to you, but you must make a decision soon."

"A decision about what?"

"You and I both know what Marcus wants. He will stop at nothing until he finds the boy my wife predicted would change the course of our world. Will you be the one to help him do it?"

"A prediction?" Livia's mouth went dry. She knew exactly what he meant, and she wanted no part of this game of cat and mouse.

"Everyone in our world knows about the child of prophecy," Alex said gently.

"The Power is corrupted and will remain so until a new generation is born with the strength of their ancestors, led by one with an unsullied, natural connection with the Power. His heart will guide him, giving him the restraint to wield his Power wisely. He will gather his equals, and together, they will stand against those who persist in the corruption of the natural order. He will be strong and fierce in his beliefs and steadfast in his love. Born the second child of the seventh daughter of his line, he alone will possess the skills and the knowledge to heal what has been broken. He alone will have the courage to judge unbiased and mete out the ultimate punishment. Until the time of his birth, may we prepare the way and hope for the future of all the races of men."

"Your wife is the ancient prophet?"

"She is."

"Then you know prophecy can only be understood by those who have access to the one who gave it." She turned to meet his gaze.

"I do. And so does your father. I haven't seen my wife in a very long time." Alex stood to stretch his legs. "But I will see her again. And soon. Make a decision, Livia." He turned and headed toward the facilities.

Livia reclined her seat, feeling pensive about the task ahead of her. She felt almost foolish in her mad dash across the world.

It's silly, but I have to know what this woman knows of my past.

Livia shook off the uneasy feeling she'd had since she boarded the plane. It was nothing more than the presence of the old Immortal making his way back to his seat in coach. For one as old as he, it would have been nice if he'd taken a moment to come set her at ease for the long flight.

CHAPTER THREE

Livia paced across the porch of the little beach cottage. She'd flown halfway around the world on the spur of the moment to come here, and now, she lacked the courage to knock on the door.

My father would die of shame if he could see me now, afraid of a mortal.

But Livia was determined to find the answers. She was desperate for some clue that would give her direction. If this woman somehow knew of her past, she needed find out. Without another moment's hesitation, Livia raised her fist and knocked on the acid green door.

"Livia, I've been expecting you," Lily Carmichael said as she opened the door.

For the first time in all of her two hundred years, Livia was at a complete loss for words. This insignificant mortal woman couldn't possibly have known she was coming.

Maybe this isn't a wild goose chase after all. She gave Lily a nod and stepped into the warmth of her shabby-chic home along the Rona Bay. It felt like a real home, friendly and inviting—nothing at all like the home Livia grew up in.

"Did my mother call you?" Livia asked. That was the only plausible explanation.

"No. We both know Marcus would punish her if she did. I've been expecting you to show up for a while now. Come in, we have much to discuss." Lily guided her to the back of the old house to a small study filled with books on archeology and anthropology. "I imagine you're quite confused," Lily said as she went about making tea at the small bar in the corner of the office. "Have a seat."

"I don't understand." Livia sank into the old leather armchair opposite the ancient oak desk. "How did you know I would be here?" Livia let her normal harsh and demanding tone return to her voice. Livia had lived a hard life and was no stranger to dangerous situations with other Immortals. If this were some kind of trap, she would come out on top. Of that, she was certain.

"Relax. I imagine your mother told you where to find me, yes?" Lily placed a steaming hot cup of Earl Grey in front of her as she took her seat behind the desk. "

"How could you know my mother?" Porcia was so rarely allowed to venture outside of the mansion she shared with Livia's father, there was simply no way Lily was old enough to have ever met her.

"I've never met the woman who raised you. But I've known other members of your biological family. They were good people."

"Biological family?" Livia shook her head, taking an absent sip of her tea. "That's not possible." Natural born Immortals were rare. She was adopted just like most of her kind was. *Then why do I remember another life? Another family? Isn't that why I'm here?* The memories were vague, and Livia was never truly certain if they were memories or dreams of a life she only wished she had. But the memories were getting stronger, and she could no longer overlook them.

"I never knew your biological parents," Lily said. "But you are a natural born, Livia. You have an aunt who was there the day you were taken from your family. You were barely four years old, and it was more than two hundred years ago. Of course, you wouldn't remember."

"How is it that a mortal woman knows of the Immortal world?" Livia raised her brow in suspicion.

"I knew an Immortal woman many years ago. She helped me through a tough time, and in the process, I discovered her secret. Since then, her family has remained close to me and mine. She was your aunt."

"If what you say is true, then where is she?"

"I haven't seen nor heard from her in twenty years," Lily said as she stood and crossed to the mirror on the wall. She moved it aside to reveal a safe in the wall. A moment later, she produced a velvet lined jewelry box. "This belonged to your aunt, Sophia—although I believe she was once known as the poet, Sappho. I was told you would seek me out some day, and she always wanted you to have this."

The woman was lying—and doing a good job of it because most of what she said seemed to hold a grain of truth, which begged the question, how much could she trust Lily Carmichael if she was only getting half-truths? Livia opened the box to find an heirloom necklace. The teardrop pendant was made of pewter with stones as black as night. She'd seen it before—or one like it. The woman she saw in her memories wore such a necklace.

"Why did my mother send me to you?" Livia snapped the box closed, her heart thudding in her chest.

"I believe your mother, Porcia, was once close with your natural grandmother. I imagine your grandmother knew you would need answers someday, so she told your mother where I could be found," Lily said, as if she were talking about a matter as simple as the weather.

"What does it all mean? The memories of the woman who wore this necklace?"

"It's not a complicated thing, dear. They are your family. Your blood. They lost you in an incredible tragedy. They mourned for you—and probably still do—wherever they are now."

"What am I supposed to do with that?"

"Well … you can be thankful you had a loving family who missed you when you were taken from them. You can let it stay in the past and move forward with the family you've always known. Or you can find them and get definitive answers to the question of your past. Find out once and for all what happened the night Marcus Servius took you from your home. And why."

"You think he took me from my natural family for some nefarious reason?"

"You work for your father, don't you?" Lily asked.

"Yes."

"Then ask yourself if maybe you were the first of many?"

If there was one thing Marcus liked, it was to recruit the best and brightest young Immortals to his cause. He wasn't above using force to collect someone he wanted. Was Lily right? Was Livia his first? And if she was, did she owe him anything?

Chapter Four

Livia shut the acid green door behind her, taking an absent step across the porch. If anything, this trip had only confused her even more.

Or confirmed my deepest fears.

Anger swelled inside her. She came here for answers and was leaving with even more questions. Hate for her father ignited her anger. If he'd taken her from a loving family, what kind of life had he robbed her of? Who would she be if she'd never known Marcus Servius?

As Livia walked down the narrow street to her rental car, she stopped and turned to see a car quickly retreating. The girl inside was Immortal—young and powerful, just on the cusp of her Awakening. She would likely be one of the strongest of her generation, exactly the kind of Immortal it was Livia's job to collect. Her father would want this girl.

On any other day, Livia would have gone after her, but there was something about her, something she'd seen in the brief moment their eyes met. The girl was trouble and Livia had enough drama in her life.

Will you become the woman your father has created, or will your roots be strong enough to set you on the right path? It is up to you, but you must make a decision soon. The errant thought felt just like her forgotten memories—a ghost of a past experience.

"Perhaps another time," she muttered as she slipped into the driver's seat and headed back to the airport.

WANT TO FIND OUT MORE?

Purchase the Marked by Fate boxset and get Emerge: The Awakening plus 24 other full-length novels

Allie Carmichael has always believed life is simple. You're born. You live. You die. She has no cause to believe those rules don't apply to her.

All her life, Allie has suffered in silence as those around her shrink from her touch, too intimidated to take the time to get to know her. It's left her feeling like an outcast for fifteen years.

When an unexpected move to Kelleys Island brings Aidan McBrien crashing into her life, Allie is thrown by his reaction. He isn't affected by her touch. He doesn't stutter or make a quick exit. He smiles and welcomes her into his circle of friends.

For the first time ever, Allie knows what true friendship means. Finally, she has a real shot at normal--until "normal" crashes and burns when she wakes in agony on her sixteenth birthday. Aidan calls it her Awakening, a rite of passages he and their friends have all faced. Allie struggles in ignorance through the experience, uncertain of what is real and what isn't. When she emerges, she is different. She has always been different, but even among her extraordinary friends, she and Aidan are special.

As Allie struggles to maintain her tenuous grasp on the power that threatens to overwhelm her, she worries she will lose herself in this strange new world of ancient Immortal beings. A dangerous world where she will have to fight tooth and nail to defend the power and freedom that is her birthright.

Connect with Melissa

I hope you've enjoyed Emerge: The Catalyst
To find out what happens next, check out the rest of my series available now
Emerge: The Awakening | Emerge: The Edge | Emerge: The Judgment |
Emerge: The Scholar | Emerge: The Captive |

Visit me at Melissaacraven.com for to hear my latest news and to get your free copy of Emerge: The Scholar

Follow me online
Instagram: @Melissaacraven | Twitter: @Melissaacraven
| Facebook: @MelissaacravenAuthor | Pinterest: @Melissaacraven |

About the Author

Melissa A. Craven was born near Atlanta, Georgia, but moved to Cleveland, Ohio at the age of seventeen. She still thinks of Cleveland as home, so it was only natural for Emerge to take place there.

Today, she's back in Atlanta—for some reason she can't seem to stay away from the ungodly heat that makes her long for things like "lake effect snow" and wind that will knock you flat.

Melissa decided a long time ago that the "life checklist" everyone else was clutching so tightly in their fists just wasn't for her. She does everything backward because she's weird like that. (With a proven history of doing things the hard way.)

She is an avid student of art and design, and received a Bachelors of Fine Arts from the University of West Georgia in 2009. She works as a part time interior designer for an Atlanta based Design House – but only when she's not in the writing cave.

In her spare time, if she has any, she enjoys playing dorky board games and shopping for derelict furniture she refinishes to exercise the interior design part of her brain.

THE APPLE REBELLION

The Tainted Accords: Prequel

Kelly St. Clare

The Apple Rebellion © 2017 Kelly St. Clare

CHAPTER ONE

I slow my steps as the thatched orphanage comes into view. My veil flutters in time to my shallow breaths. Coming here seemed a good idea at the time, but now I'm here, all my prior ambitions seem foolish.

What was I thinking? The villagers don't even like me. They're *terrified* of me. I'm a fifteen-year-old girl who the Solati people won't get within ten paces of. Possibly, the fact I'm the Tatuma, next in line to rule this world has something to do with their fear ... And maybe because the only villager friend I'd ever had ended up with a blade drawn across her throat.

Most of the time, I *prefer* their avoidance. When people get close, they tend to hurt or ridicule me. Distance is safe. Distance is secure. My mother taught me *that* by imprisoning me in this black veil from the cradle. The coarse, heavy fabric represents a very real cage to me. I hate it, but wouldn't be caught dead without it—simply because others die when I dare to think otherwise.

...It is how the villager girl ended up with her throat slit. And it is how I came to be locked in the tower of my childhood for another year.

I can't bear to be locked in the tower again. Never again.

It's ironic; When my mother—the Tatum and ruler of Osolis—let me out for the first time all those years ago, I'd never felt such excitement. To be amongst the beautiful people my brother told me of each week;

their elaborate hairdos and brightly colored robes. Even when I'd been allowed out to watch Olandon train with old Aquin, I was snuck through the palace and never got to glimpse them.

How I'd longed for friends… When you spend ten years in a tower, you have a long time to wonder what you'll say when you come face to face with another person—what they'll think of you, and how you'll appear.

I wasn't left wondering for long.

'Shunned' would be the word I'd use. The royal court saw something in me so ugly, they turned against me as one—or so I'd thought for several years after my release. In time, I came to see they were merely mimicking my mother's attitude toward me. My mother hated me, so the court hated me. Their choice was as lacking in substance as that. The court members didn't seem so beautiful after this realization, and I no longer want to be friends with any of them. If I ever thought to forgive one or two who might defy my mother, that yearning slowly extinguished to cold ashes over the years.

I am free of the tower, but sometimes I wonder if I will ever be free of my loneliness.

I look up at the orphanage, gliding to a halt, feeling the telltale slide of my gray robes settling around my ankles and wrists.

I know what the villagers see: a slight girl who wears a black veil that covers her entire head to the collarbone and base of her neck. They likely speculate as to why my mother covers me—am I ugly, am I beautiful, is there something wrong with me?

It's nothing I haven't wondered myself.

I gave up caring somewhere along the way; This is my life. Though … that mustn't be completely true, or I wouldn't be here, in front of the orphanage.

Maybe, deep down, part of me holds hope for more.

The orphanage is made of thatch, like most of the village houses. This building is bigger than most due to necessity. Osolis is a treacherous place. A single spark can surge to a white-hot flame in seconds, so dry and hot is our world. Many parents die, and many will continue to die. That is the way of life here. Which is why there are so many orphans.

I hear hushed whispers behind me, and swallow back fear as my chest tightens. *Panic.* I've been staring at the orphanage for too long. The villagers have noticed. They're looking at me and talking to each other. It's too late to change my mind.

Closing my eyes briefly, I swing open the door.

Noise. Children laughing and squealing. Playing. No hushed silence and shared looks—this is why I love children.

I take a deep breath and enjoy the sounds around me.

"Tatuma Olina," a weathered voice calls out. "You honor us."

I turn to the sound, barely making out the outline of a strong-backed woman. Her shoulders are tense. She curtsies low and I wince as her knees crack.

"I am the matron of this orphanage. I hope I can be of service to you."

I have to commend her bravery. I don't think a villager has uttered a word to me in years. Not since … that day—though, I haven't walked into their place of work, either. Perhaps the matron feels forced into conversation.

"Well met, matron," I say. "As it happens, I would like to be of service to you."

The matron inhales sharply, and I do my best to make my words unhurried and confident.

"I would like to work here. Without pay," I say coolly. Too cold? I want her to agree. I inject more warmth into my voice. "I want to help with the children."

Silence.

"The work here is not fit for one of your standing, Tatuma," the matron says slowly. She has made sure to phrase the comment submissively, but doesn't quite make it.

I smile under my veil. This is a woman who is used to telling others what to do. "I know what the work entails; I will change diapers, wash and feed the children, play with them and put them down for naps."

"...The reality is ... different. It is plain, thankless work, Tatuma Olina."

"Surely you do not find it thankless, matron."

The woman pauses. "No. I do not—"

But I am a villager, I finish her sentence silently. "Matron, I understand my position in the palace. I understand your hesitations in accepting my help. Let me reassure you I have cared for my young twin brothers for the last three years. I am well aware of the challenges of the job and well aware of the rewards, too."

A slight tilt; The matron is deliberating.

Really, she can't say no, but I won't force my presence here. If she will not accept me, I will not stay. Yet I cannot remember when I last wanted something so desperately.

I want to be needed ... I want to show someone there is a person under this veil.

"Solis knows I could use the help," the matron says, wetting her lips. "My concern is ... well—"

"You can be assured I come here with my mother's blessing," I interject smoothly. "She is aware of my visit here and of my intention to help."

The matron sags ever so slightly.

Such is the fear my mother inspires.

I feel it, too. *More* so because I have seen her true face. The Tatum's real character is something even the fiercest warrior should quail with fear before.

Recently, however, I discovered a weakness to my mother's hate of me, and I'd exploited this weakness to get her permission to work here.

The court and my mother think nothing of the villagers. The villagers are beneath their notice—merely here to do work. To the court, the poor are uncivilized and hardly better than our enemies on Glacium. A court member *interacting* with villagers would be unthinkable, an embarrassment. The member would be ridiculed.

This is the weakness I exploited.

There is nothing my mother loves more than humiliating me. She gets twisted pleasure when the court laughs at me behind my back and sometimes right in front of me. She enjoys my lack of standing in the court, and I knew by being in the orphanage, and by doing this work, the court would gossip about me for months. My mother knew it, too. She'd agreed to my coming here with more ease than to my request to go to the underground baths to wash myself each day.

The matron takes a few shuffling steps.

I lift my head, outwardly calm, inwardly a mess—always a mess. I watch as her cheeks lift and know she is smiling. At me. A smile for *me*.

I want to cry.

The matron speaks. "Tatuma Olina. You are most welcome to help us here. Whenever you wish."

Chapter Two

I slam my fist into my brother's stomach. He wheezes and I hold back a grin. It disappears as he picks me up and throws me to the ground, using his weight to pin me.

Veni.

My old trainer, Aquin, hits me with his stick. "Poor form."

We are deep in the kaur forest which separates this rotation from the next. Aquin has a special training shed here, far enough from the palace and village that I am safe from discovery. When my mother began letting me out of the tower to attend Olandon's training—and only after my brother begged her for months—Aquin quickly decided I should benefit from the training sessions, too. If my mother ever found out, he'd be killed, and I would go back into the tower. Or worse.

It was a grave secret the three of us kept.

I hear Olandon's soft laughter at Aquin's reproof. Unfortunately, so does Aquin.

Crack!

"Quiet, boy," Aquin snaps. "She cannot see and she kept you fighting for ten minutes."

Olandon rolls to his feet gracefully. He stretches out a hand to help me up.

Crack!

"She can get up herself," Aquin says, with hard eyes.

My brother knows better than to cradle his injured hand to his body, but I bet he wants to. I'm wise enough not to laugh aloud.

Aquin, doesn't think my veil should be an excuse for weakness, though it blinds me almost completely. I haven't gotten around to agreeing or disagreeing with him. I just want to keep fighting. Fighting is power, I've found. If I keep training, I have the power to fight back against my mother's men when they beat me. And when I don't fight back, which I never do, it's because I've *decided* not to.

"Lina," Aquin says gruffly. "Over to archery."

I hold back my groan.

Aquin's 'no excuse' rule extends to me blindly shooting arrows into the constant darkness. Once every few weeks I hit the target through sheer luck.

"You have worked at the orphanage this entire week," Olandon commented, releasing his arrow. I hear the thud as it hits the target.

"I have," I answer neutrally.

He releases another arrow. *Thud.* "You do not seem any dirtier."

I roll my eyes.

I love my younger brother. He's one of my only friends in the world. We've always been there for each other. He is the person I crawl to after beatings. He keeps me sane. But my mother *loves* him and it has made us see the world differently. Olandon was never locked in a tower, nor veiled. Olandon is accepted by the Solati court. He likes them and has many friends there. In some ways, because of our different experiences, Olandon thinks as the court does—especially regarding the villagers. It is a source of constant friction between us.

"They are dirty because they live in the dirt, Landon," I say. "If we lived in the dirt, no doubt we would be dirty, too."

I draw a bow and aim in the general direction of the far wall. I can hear the tap of Aquin's cane behind me, and Olandon is well clear. I let go, wincing as the arrow ricochets off something to the left.

"The children do cry a lot, though," I add to appease him.

Aquin whacks his stick between my knees to widen my stance. "They cry because they are hungry as all children do."

I release another bow. "The palace has so much food. It does not seem right there is not enough for the orphanage."

The old man stops by my side and rests a hand upon my shoulder. "No," he says after a pause, "it does not."

He moves away to bark directions at Olandon, and I dare to drop my bow for a second.

...I've found whenever Aquin acts strangely, and a hand on the shoulder from him is *definitely* strange, the old man is trying to tell me something.

What was Aquin telling me?

That *I* should do something about the hungry children?

CHAPTER THREE

"The children adore you," the matron says.

She has relaxed a great deal in my presence in the last week. I'm glad. She wouldn't have relaxed if my mother were here and it's nice to know I'm not like the Tatum. It gives me hope that one day, if I survive long enough, things on Osolis can change.

"Thank you," I say softly. Her compliment fills me with a warmth I'll treasure. I like to collect memories like this to replay when night falls.

"I knew you were kind, of course," she continues. "My sister has spoken of you."

My eyebrows arch under the veil. People say I'm kind?

"Oh," I say, a question in my voice. It is rude to ask questions on Osolis, but if ever I wished to ask one, it would be now.

"My sister is a cook in the palace kitchens. Afranca is her name."

"I know of her." I smile. "You both have the same bearing about you." Posture tells me a lot about a person. I rely on it heavily during conversation. In Solati culture, it is considered an embarrassment to show strong emotion, which made it difficult for me in my early years. I'd learned to listen and observe, instead—these were my only signals to discern true meaning behind words spoken in my presence.

"I'm sure we do." The matron smiles, cooing at an infant while rocking another to sleep in her arms. "Just like our mother had, and just like my niece will."

I lift the young girl from where I'm changing her and place the toddler on the ground. I wrap the messy diapers up for cleaning. As I do so, Aquin's strange behavior of two days before niggles at my mind.

...The matron's sister works in the kitchen. If memory serves me correctly, she works as the head cook.

"Matron Atrudi," I call back to her from the doorway. "The children do not eat as often as they should."

She shakes her head sadly. "I'm afraid most only get a slice of bread and a few mouthfuls of meat each day."

I look over at the thin children playing at my feet.

The matron continues, "Alas, the younger ones do not understand why they cannot have more, poor wee things."

And why could they not have more? I find myself questioning.

My mother. That's the answer. My mother and her attitude toward her 'inferior' subjects.

A plan forms in my mind, but stills on the tip of my tongue. If I utter the plan aloud and my mother finds out, it will mean more than a beating or exile for me—it will cost the lives of any whom I involve.

Panic claws up my throat.

My first instinct is to put my head down and continue on as I always do, in the shadows. Yet carrying the secret of my training with Aquin makes me stronger and gives me hope in my darkest moments. This would be another secret to hold, and might make me stronger again.

But I'd also have to trust the matron and her sister not to turn against me. Maybe others, too ...

I'd need to place my safety in their hands ... And they would need to put their safety in mine—which, considering my mantle as Tatuma, actually held much more risk.

I bite my lip, thinking of the crushing loneliness in the tower, and how it hadn't seemed to lighten all that much since being let out. At least if mother locked me in there again, I'd have the thoughts of this tiny rebellion to keep me company.

If the matron and her sister can trust me, knowing who my mother is, and what may happen to them, then I need to take the leap and trust them in return.

But can I do that? Trust another?

Is it worth it?

I listen to the squealing children around me and firm my resolve.

"Matron Atrudi, I may have a solution for you."

Chapter Four

"You wish for two cartons of apples to be delivered to the kitchen each week especially for you," Satum Jerin repeated slowly.

Jerin is the Satum of resources, and the only Satum out of the three I like. He's always kind—though careful not to show me too much favor in Mother's presence. I don't begrudge him for it. He's just protecting himself.

As the Satum of resources, Jerin has access to all of the food in storage.

"That is correct, Satum Jerin." I hesitate. "The thing is, I would sincerely appreciate if you were not to ever tell my mother of the extra apples. I—" Is there a good explanation for requiring two cartons of apples each week? Probably not.

He scratches his chin before controlling the gesture. "I see, Tatuma Olina. You wish for the apples to be delivered to Cook Afranca in secret each week, and for me not to mention it to anyone else because the apples are to treat a malady you suffer from." He trails off.

I grin under the veil. "Yes. A malady requiring apples. I do hope they may prove effective in helping my illness, but it will take a long time for me to be sure—maybe years. It is a rather delicate subject and I'd appreciate your ..."

"Delicacy," he finishes, humor in his voice.

I dip my head, and my chest relaxes. It took me a whole week to summon enough courage to broach the subject with him. I even had a plan. One which flew out of the opening as soon as we began to talk.

First, the matron and cook decided to help me. Now Satum Jerin wants to help, too. Just like that. I lift my head and study his outline. Why is he helping me? He doesn't know who the apples are for.

I put away the confusing thought for when I'm alone. "Satum Jerin, I feel compelled to warn you that if my mother ever hears of this—"

"We must consider how you will get the apples to the orphanage itself, Tatuma Olina," he says, ignoring my confession.

He does know! A laugh is startled out of me. "It seems my plans are completely transparent, Satum."

"Only your heart, Tatuma."

Heat fills my cheeks. I would write off the comment as empty flattery if Jerin was the kind to flatter. I hurry on. "I had thought to ask the blacksmith. He comes to the palace weekly to make deliveries with his dromeda and cart."

"A sound plan," Satum Jerin said thoughtfully. "I will speak to him for you on your behalf, if you should wish."

I can't help my relieved sigh. "I would appreciate that."

I've spoken to more people in the last few weeks than I've spoken to in my life. I'm proud of that fact, but instinctively wish to avoid any future interactions at the same time.

Jerin begins to talk, but I feel my brows drawing together at my last thought.

...Maybe I *shouldn't* avoid talking to people any longer. Maybe it should be me who speaks to the blacksmith ...

I open my mouth to tell the Satum I've changed my mind.

Jerin bows low. "I will let you know what the blacksmith says tomorrow. He is a good man, and I am certain he will be eager to help."

My brave declaration stutters in my throat. I swallow the words back.

Maybe it will be easier this way.

Jerin knows the blacksmith. The blacksmith will be more comfortable talking with a Satum.

I don't want to ruin this with my awkwardness.

It will be easier this way.

My heart sinks, inexplicably. "Satum Jerin," I say. "Thank you. Truly."

Chapter Five

I stand in my third-floor room, gazing out the window as I have so often done over the years. I like to watch as the smoke layer lifts for the day. I don't see much, but my view goes from pitch-black to dim, so it still feels like the start of a new day to me.

Today, I watch for a different reason.

The villagers run on different time than the court Solati, so when the blacksmith's dromeda clops across the cracked ground to make deliveries, the sound is impossible to miss.

The noise is loud.

Is it louder than usual? My hands are slick with sweat, and he hasn't even reached the apples yet.

I hear the call of the guards who wave him through the gate. He's coming. This is actually happening. Fear clutches at me, and my heart splutters sporadically as I think of what I've done. They'll all die. The matron, the cook, Satum Jerin, and the blacksmith. My mother's eyes see everything. What was I thinking? She taught me the lesson of obedience in the harshest way and long ago. Have I forgotten that lesson so quickly?

Is this foolish and selfish?

I lean against the opening for support. Darkness beats at my thoughts and I stagger under their weight as the booming 'clops' of the horse seem to echo across the space toward me.

Solis, why am I so worthless? My breaths are coming quickly. Too quick. I roll the fabric of my robes together and focus on slowing them, my body shaking in the aftermath of my loss of control.

...It takes me a while to realize I can't hear the clops anymore.

I can't see a thing from up here, but going down to the kitchen would be to risk revealing our carefully knit plan.

The waiting game is dreadful. But I do it.

I wait.

Hours pass ... firelight begins to stream into my barren room, and I am able to see a few of the objects within its confines. The water basin against the wall to my left. The trunk at the foot of my bed. The outline of the wardrobe on the other side.

A sound meets my ears. *Clop.*

I leap to my feet and rush to the opening, straining my ears for all they're worth.

Clop.

The blacksmith is leaving. Does he have the apples? I dare not set foot outside my room, but I listen to the receding sound of the dromeda's hooves, and I hope.

I continue hoping until the palace is busy with the sound of stupid court members. Only then do I exchange my grey robes for a dull brown set and slip from my room. I use the servants' stairwell. This isn't unusual for me. It won't be considered suspicious.

The kitchen is in a breakfast flurry when I arrive. The kitchen hands don't stop in their work when they see me. I like to think it's because they're comfortable in my presence, but it's more likely they've adopted the snobbish attitude of the court.

Cook Afranca, the matron's sister, stands the middle of the chaos, throwing orders left, right, and center, and wielding a heavy-looking pan.

I'm too nervous to grin about it, and I don't dare speak to her with so many ears close by.

I slip through the kitchen and perch atop a kaur-wood barrel in the cellar. People slip in and out, taking my presence in and ignoring me. I don't speak to them.

The number of people coming into the cellar slowly dwindles. I listen as the uproar on the other side calms, and as the smell of food dissipates.

The cellar door creaks open at last. A strong-backed frame is illuminated there, and it occurs to me it must be completely dark in this room with the door closed. How odd I must seem to others.

"Tatuma Olina." Afranca greets me.

"Cook Afranca. I apologize if I've been in the way this morning."

The cook laughs from her belly. I smile at the chortling rumble.

"You can be sure if you were in the way, I'd be telling you."

I blink at her response. I'm not all that sure she wouldn't, either. A glimmer of respect spreads through me.

"The blacksmith paid a visit," I say.

"He did. He brought deliveries, and took a delivery in return."

I hop off the barrel, excitement coiled in every muscle. It worked!

"I'm glad," I say quietly, though the tension underneath is unmistakable. "I am so very glad."

The cook leans over and squeezes my hand. The gesture shocks me so much I freeze on the spot.

"I'm glad too, lassie. You've done a good thing. A great thing. And we thank you."

My tongue untwists as she drops her hand. The place she touched burns even after she's done so. A simple touch, yet it is wreaking havoc inside of me because it is a mother's touch.

I tremble slightly as I push the thoughts away. Doing so is more difficult than it should be. "You are all doing the hard work," I say. "I just watch."

The cook holds the cellar door open and I slip past her into the kitchen.

"That's where you're wrong, lass. You made it possible. Don't you be forgetting that. Now! You've had the morning meal, I hope."

I shake my head. "No, I—"

"Sister," a voice says urgently from across the room.

Aquin would whack me with that accursed stick of his if he knew I'd missed someone approaching. But then Olandon walks as softly as I do.

"Brother," I say calmly, my heart not following the tone of my voice at all.

He crosses to my side without looking at Afranca. "It's Mother. She's sent her Elite to collect you from your room."

Horror floods through me.

She knows. Solis, she knows.

"Her words, brother," I say. It comes out harsher than intended.

I can tell Afranca hasn't missed the implications of Olandon's announcement.

Most people in the palace know about my mother's treatment of me. It's hard to hide when you are absent for three months with a broken leg. Or hunched in half with a cracked rib. Bile rises into my mouth as fear fills me. More fear than I've ever felt because this time it might not just be a beating. This time others might die.

Olandon clutches my hand out of sight of the cook. He's shaking. He always does. Ever since my uncle made him watch one of my beatings. "She said, 'I haven't seen my beloved daughter in a while. I must take care she is not becoming a savage like the villagers. Bring her to me.'," he repeats.

Is it her true reason for summoning me? Or does my mother know about the apples? I force my shoulders to relax for Olandon's sake.

There's only one way to find out though I so badly wish I could run the other way and escape her.

"Very well," I say evenly. "I will not keep her waiting." I give Afranca a smile she cannot see. "Cook Afranca, thank you." There's more I want to say to her; "Be ready to run" is at the top of the list—though the cook understands as well as I there is nowhere on Osolis to escape the Tatum's retribution.

"Tatum Olina, you are always welcome."

I pick up the fear in her voice. The cook has a daughter. I wonder if my mother will kill her as well.

I link arms with my brother. "Landon, please go to my rooms and wait for me there. I will not be long."

He leans his head to me and whispers. "I am to bring the usual."

He's talking about bandages, compresses, and tea for the pain.

I disregard the idea of lying to him and telling him it's okay. He knows as well as I what will happen next. "...Yes, brother. I think that would be best."

CHAPTER SIX

A large fist connects with the soft part under my ribs. I tense my stomach, but it only does so much against the blow. The air is forced from my lungs and I fall to all fours on the ground before my mother.

Blood drips from the edge of my veil onto the carpet below.

"I hear you've been having fun in the village." My mother's voice drips with disdain.

For years, I thought I might be able to make her love me. A part of me still hopes one day she'll see Olandon and I are the same.

I've yet to ascertain if she knows of the apples. My mother likes to play with her food, but I would've thought the beating would be worse if she'd found out about my little rebellion. I don't dare to hope though. I have no control in this room—the Torture Room, as I dubbed it years ago.

"I work as a villager might," I wheeze. It is best to play on her enjoyment of my humiliation again.

She sneers. "I don't know how someone could love one like you; your ugliness seeps from under that veil—as thick as it is. I don't quite know how you manage it. If it were any other skill, I would almost deign to congratulate you."

I focus on the floor.

...First, I'd punch my uncle in the throat. Then I'd break my mother's face with the heel of my foot. I'd need to pillage a weapon from the Elite to have any chance. That would be the tricky part...

"You may be going to the village now, daughter. But do not think to get too close to the peasants there. You know what happens when you do..."

The words hang, and my insides quail. *Throat slit, blood spraying.* Yes, I know what happens. I will never show my face to another again.

"I do it because you are my child," my mother says. The sad tone is at odds with the mocking tilt of her head. "I know no one will ever love you. I am protecting you."

She's out of her mind, and I'm the only one who sees it.

The blood still drips from my nose, but I barely feel it. Just as the flurry of blows her men landed on me hardly registered moments before.

The pain will come later. Right now, I'm numb with fear for the people who have put their trust in me.

I'm careful not to lift my head. These sessions only end when she thinks I'm beaten.

"That is all," the Tatum says.

A distant thrill reaches me through the fog.

It takes a few seconds to realize we've gotten away with it. *I've* gotten away with it. My mother doesn't know what I am doing under her very nose. Her eyes haven't reached to the palace kitchens, or to the village orphanage. Not yet.

Though she has hurt me over and over again, inside and out, there are places she cannot find me.

There are places I am safe.

For now, the orphans have enough to eat, and when later comes, and my body aches and I want to give up, I'll console myself with the same resolve burning through me right now.

My mother cannot take everything away from me.
Now I have two secrets to keep me strong.
I have my fighting.
And I have my apple rebellion.

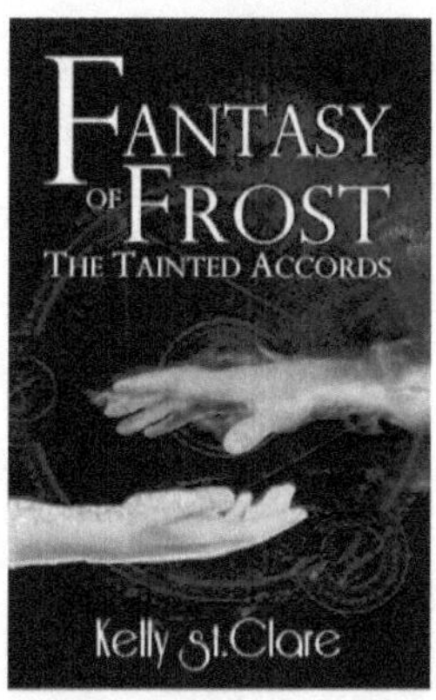

WANT TO FIND OUT MORE?

Purchase the Marked by Fate boxset and get
Fantasy of Frost plus 24 other full-length novels

I know many things. What I am capable of, what I will change, what I will become. But there is one thing I will never know…

The veil I've worn from birth carries with it a terrible loneliness; a suppression I cannot imagine ever being free of.

Some things never change…

My mother will always hate me. Her court will always shun me.

…Until they do.

When the peace delegation arrives from the savage world of Glacium, my life is shoved wildly out of control by the handsome Prince Kedrick who, for unfathomable reasons, shows me kindness.

And the harshest lessons are learned.

Sometimes it takes the world bringing you to your knees to find that spark you thought forever lost.

Sometimes it takes death to show you how to live.

CONNECT WITH KELLY

I hope you've enjoyed The Apple Rebellion

To find out what happens next, check out the rest of my series available now
Fantasy of Frost | Fantasy of Flight | Fantasy of Fire |Fantasy of Freedom

Visit me at kellystclare.com to hear my latest news and to get your free copy
of His Fantasy & Tainted Accords Coloring Pages

Follow me online
Instagram: @kellystclare | Twitter: @kellystclare
| Facebook: @kellystclareAuthor | Youtube: @kellystclare |

ABOUT THE AUTHOR

When Kelly St Clare is not reading or writing, she is lost in her latest reverie. Books have always been magical and mysterious to her. One day she decided to start unravelling this mystery and began writing.

The Tainted Accords was her debut series, and her second series, The After Trilogy, is now available.

A New Zealander in origin and in heart, Kelly currently resides in Australia with her soon-to-be husband, a great group of friends, and some huntsman spiders who love to come inside when it rains. Their love is not returned.

TIME TRAVEL

History and Legal Procedures

A Manual for Travel Candidates

Amalie Jahn

Time Travel:

History and Legal Procedures

A Manual for Travel

CANDIDATES

Sixth Edition

Compiled and Edited by Winston F. Mulvane

Published by the United States Department of
Traveling Services

Table of Contents

History of Time Travel
Initial Discoveries

For many years following the discovery of gamma/magnetic fields, scientist worldwide sought to be the first to use them to create circulating light beams in an attempt to warp or loop time. Toward the end of the century, researchers at the prestigious Bernstein Institute in Seattle, Washington successfully twisted space in such a way that the universe's first artificial gravitational force was produced using the electromagnetic radiation of a unidirectional ring laser. After trapping light inside a photonic crystal, the light began to circulate. The energy of the circulating light caused the space inside the circle to twist, producing the gravitational force.

Subsequent years saw similar reconstructions of numerous gravitational forces produced by other laboratories around the world. While many strove to be the first to prove the existence of time manipulation, the distinct honor went to Dr. Myra Kingston of the Time Control Technology Research Facility (TCTRF) in Johannesburg, South Africa. At the turn of the century, she stunned the world with her online videos showing polarized neutrons (neutrons spinning a single direction) visibly changing direction in the center of the circulating light, thus indicating that space was indeed being twisted inside of the crystal. Within months, this same team under the direction of Dr. Kingston proved there was also evidence of time bending inside the circle of light.

Using this information, scientists at the Quantum Time Travel Institute, located in Tempe, Arizona, prepared two identical samples of the radioactive substance beryllium-14 which had identical half-lives of 4.84 seconds. The first sample was introduced into the rudimentary time machine spinning in the same direction as the light, the second in the opposite direction. They discovered the first sample decayed further than the second, supporting all known theories of time travel.

NOTES:

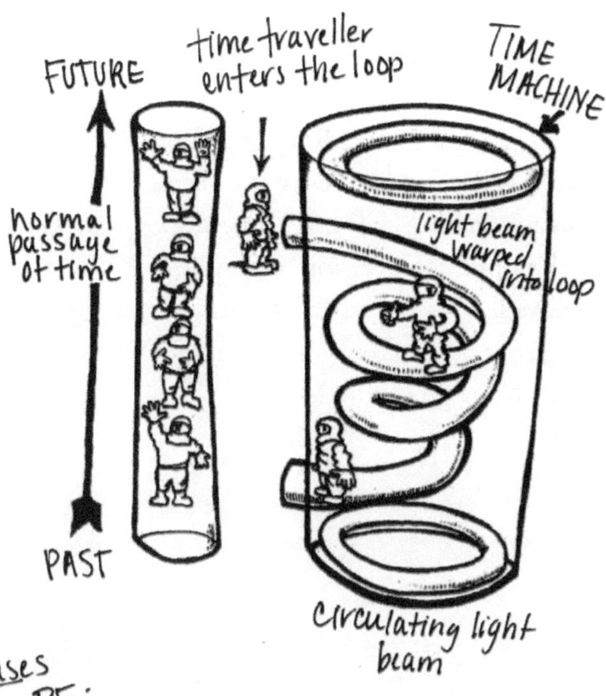

Possible causes
of Branson's PF:

Silica
hard metal dusts ➡ research this more
bacteria
animal proteins ?
nitrofurantoin
meds ⎰ amiodarone
⎱ methotrexate

* remind mom about
borrowing the car
tomorrow

In the years following evidentiary proof of the existence of time travel, scientists argued as to what would become of people should they be sent back in time via circulating light beams. At that point, the parallel-universe theory had not been directly supported by experiment, but scientists moved forward, encouraged by both the Uncertainty Principle and quantum mechanics. Both worked on the theory that one could not make a definite prediction about anything that would happen next. Therefore, the parallel-universe theory worked well. What would happen next could not be predicted because, in fact, everything happened next. They surmised that for every decision we make, another version of us makes the opposite decision and splits off into a parallel universe. Thus, when traveling into the consciousness of the past, each time traveler would simply be creating an alternate universe in which to return, never resuming the original timeline.

NOTES:

Methotrexate treats :
Psoriasis
~~PRP~~
~~Sarcoidosis~~
~~Lupus~~
Eczema ?
↑
Was Branson treated with this when he developed that rash on his shins during soccer?
FIND OUT!!!

DON'T FORGET:
Meeting w/ Dr. Rudlough
2pm tomorrow

Initial Non-Human Trials

Within two years after initial testing indicated time travel would be possible using the gravitational pull of circulating light, three separate agencies created large scale time machine prototypes within weeks of each other. Initial testing took place at each of the labs simultaneously, but the Bernstein Institute holds the distinction of being the first to successfully send an inanimate object back in time. They attempted to send a crystalline timing mechanism approximately five seconds into the past and return it to the resulting alternate version of the present timeline. They were encouraged when the crystal's display jumped from five to ten seconds instantaneously, indicating an extended passage of time which was otherwise undetectable to the scientists. This mechanism would become the prototype for all future time-testing devices and would be sent back with all subsequent subjects.

The first living entity, a single-cell plankton, was also successfully sent back in time by scientists at the Bernstein Institute. After scores of increasingly complex plant species (lichens, mosses, ferns, hydrangeas) survived being sent back in time repeatedly and for trips up to one hour in duration, the world watched live online as the first animal species, a single-cell paramecium, was sent sixty seconds into the past. After it returned to the present seemingly unharmed, dozens of other species quickly followed in laboratories around the world, working through the animal kingdom from simple mollusks to rodents and eventually primates.

NOTES:

Hard Metal Dust Exposure = ASBESTOS?

<u>Branson</u> <u>possible</u> <u>exposure</u> —
  ✶ insulation materials - pipes, furnace, attic
  ✶ Shingles
  ✶ Siding and roofing tiles
  Soundproofing
  Plaster / joint compound
  paints
  adhesives

Research this more!

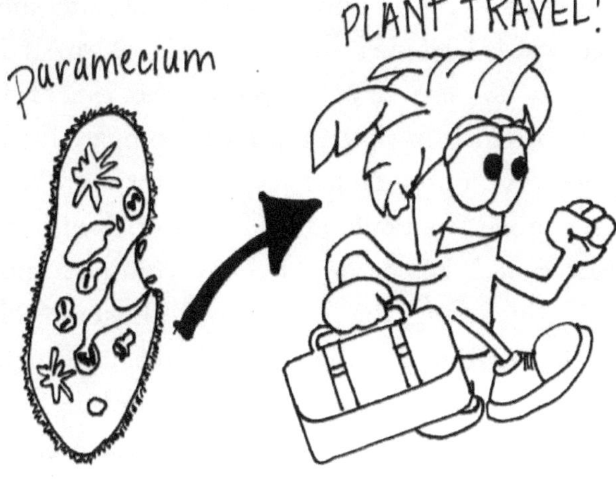

Human Pioneers

The first human to travel back in time was Dr. Bridgette Tate, a quantum physicist at TCTRF. Millions around the globe watched as she stepped into the machine and emerged only seconds later, describing how she'd been sent back five minutes into the past to relive the same series of events she had experienced only moments before. During these early trials, several key scientists were instrumental in uncovering the drawbacks and dangers associated with traveling back in time as well as developing a means of documenting changes between original and new timelines.

Scientific Studies and Conclusions

Because the creation of additional parallel timelines was inherent in the course of each time travel event, individual travelers during early human trials were the only ones with absolute knowledge of the specific changes caused by their trips at their return. It became imperative for researchers to also have access to the established trajectory of each subject's original timeline in order to compare it to the altered post-travel timeline. A solution eluded scientists for months until it was discovered that a simple manipulation of each citizen's standard issue tracking implant could be recalibrated to continue monitoring the original timeline, bypassing the time travel altogether. Retaining information about the original timeline through the implant allowed researchers to quantitatively and qualitatively compare the two resulting timelines beyond the narrow scope of the travelers themselves.

One of the most noted early travelers was Dr. Muhammed Khanna. His research pressed the boundaries of how far back it was possible for a person to travel in time. Over the course of his testing, he traveled as little as an hour into his past and as far back as thirty-six years, determining there was no limit as to how far back one could travel into one's own timeline.

Dr. Emmett Wilberton's research focused on how long it was possible to stay in the past before returning to the present timeline. His longest trip into the past lasted just short of four years, but he reported that his life was nearly unrecognizable at his return, cautioning others against such lengthy trips.

Dr. Ronda Smallson chose to relive her honeymoon dozens of times to test how small changes affected her new timelines. Initially, she tried to replicate the exact same chain of events which was documented via microscopic digital surveillance. Over the course of subsequent trips, however, she began to make slight variations of her speech and activities. At first, it appeared the changes caused no significant shift in her timeline. Her trips ended in the same way and researchers agreed that successful mainstream time travel looked promising. But Dr. Smallson continued on, reliving her honeymoon a total of sixty-four times in all. By the final trip, so much had inadvertently changed along the way that she and her husband returned home on separate flights, by choice. When she arrived back to present day after the sixty-fourth trip, she found that she was without her wedding band and she'd been divorced for twelve years.

NOTES:

Time travel monitoring !?!?! 

? to ask:
who gets monitored
for what purpose
is everyone checked

AM I SAFE?

men > women ✓
wealthy > low/mid income ✓
nontrustworthy score > trustworthy score ✓

Doctor on tv who got arrested:
man / wealthy / trustworthy?

Ramifications of Unmitigated Travel

Although the scientific community advised against it, as the technology behind time travel became easier to replicate and cheaper to create, more and more average citizens were able to gain access to the equipment that would allow them to travel back into their own lives. With growing numbers of voyagers came larger and larger problems.

One of the earliest and best-documented problems with time travel involved what has come to be known as the "snowball effect." In essence, when early travelers returned to their lives at previous points in history, some researchers assumed that since the past had already happened they would be able to simply relive the same paths step-by-step without consequence. They quickly found this was nearly impossible and that changes (as well as the resulting outcomes) were inevitable. Initially, timelines seemed unaffected by very small discrepancies in day-to-day activities. However, after travelers began returning to the past repeatedly and for longer periods of time, it appeared that those infinitesimally small changes began to accumulate into what would become more noticeable changes.

In an attempt to mitigate this effect, scientists encouraged travelers to limit the duration of their trips and not to travel especially far into their past. Unfortunately, as more people traveled back to relive wonderful moments in their lives, those infinitesimally small changes began to affect not only the traveler's life but also the lives of innocent bystanders. Inadvertently, travelers were changing the futures of the people around them without even knowing they were doing it. They would return to the present only to find that people who were once a part of their lives were no longer there. Different career paths were chosen. Loves were lost. Children disappeared. It was a dark period in the history of time travel.

Perhaps the most horrendous of the traveling effects involved retribution. Once there were enough travelers that people were changing timelines outside their own, it was inevitable that those affected would eventually realize their lives were changed because of another person's voyage. Some began to go back in time in an attempt to prevent the former traveler from affecting their timeline. Many times, these voyages ended in brutality. Sometimes murder.

NOTES:

* call Dr. Rudlough
@ meeting
Wednesday

Avoid the SNOWBALL effect!

Changes to make:

Prevent Branson from using methotrexate
cream for his rash

Prevent Branson from working at
Cooper's Hardware Store – roof replacement
may = asbestos exposure

Good Snowball = Branson doesn't die

Government Intervention

The United Nations was eventually forced to step in, as generations of people were in danger of having their lives, and more dangerously, other people's lives, irreparably destroyed. The problems of time travel were well-documented, but there seemed to be a part of human nature that assumed bad things only happened to other people.

Legislature

When the government became involved, politicians fought bitterly about the crisis. Split down party lines, there were those who believed our ability to time travel was just another evolution of our species that should be allowed to play out accordingly. Still others believed the practice should be obliterated and never attempted by humankind again. They also argued over trip monitoring, debating whether traveling surveillance amounted to an unconstitutional invasion of privacy. In the end, an agreement was reached to allow for one government-sanctioned trip per individual, per lifetime, with random monitoring.

Established Laws Governing Time Travel

Beginning with the third generation after the discovery, new laws were put into effect limiting access to time travel.

- No citizen, military or civilian, shall travel through time outside of government-sanctioned means. It is unlawful to operate or utilize any time travel facility which is unlicensed by the government.

- The highest regard must be placed on maintaining the sanctity of life during travel. This includes both the destruction and preservation of life.

- Any citizen choosing to travel must be a minimum of eighteen years of age.

- All travelers must undergo a thorough background check and mental health screening to be facilitated by the government. If it is determined that you are mentally incapable of following the time travel laws or that your past behavior is deemed "unworthy for travel" due to illicit, dishonest, or criminal behavior, your time traveling privileges will be revoked.

- At birth, all citizens, along with their identification tagging, are coded with one trip voucher. Once you have redeemed your trip, the only way to travel a second time is to be gifted a trip by another individual who still processes an unused trip voucher.

- The maximum duration of any trip back in time is six consecutive months.

- All travelers, regardless of age, must attend two months of mandatory time travel preparation classes for a minimum of three times per week, pass a final examination with a minimum score of 85%, and willingly sign all release waivers indemnifying the government from any liability in the event that any laws are broken during the course of travel.

- Every effort must be made to retain the integrity of the timeline. No changes of any kind should be made.

Punishable offenses include but are not limited to: saving a life, ending a life, purposely changing the past for monetary, social, personal, or societal gain.

NOTES:

<u>My Time Travel Checklist</u>

✓ 18 years old
✓ using licensed government facility
✓ completed background check
✓ passed mental health screening
✓ using trip voucher
✓ traveling < six months
✓ taking manditory classes
  pass final exam
  maintain timeline integrity
  ~~do not save life~~

* SAVE BRANSON'S LIFE!!!!

Methods for Maintaining Timeline Integrity
Preparing to Maintain Your Timeline Before Your Trip

In order to properly prepare yourself for your journey into your past, it is imperative that you spend a considerable amount of time familiarizing yourself with the specific details of the world into which you are returning. Strategies include:

- Interviewing friends and family members about specific details they remember.

- Reviewing old emails, texts, and other correspondence for specific details.

- Considering current habits and whether these habits were exhibited in the past. If not, it is vital that you divest yourself of these habits prior to and during your trip.

- Brushing up on current world events for your destination time period. Great sources are old news articles and almanacs.

- Reflecting upon old photographs taken during the time of your return.

Best Practices for Maintaining Your Timeline During Your Trip

Every effort must be made to preserve the integrity of your timeline during your trip in order to prevent changes to the present. Please remember that you are responsible for the outcome of your trip and that fellow citizens are depending on you to maintain their present timelines as well. Changes will be randomly monitored and discovered offenders will be prosecuted. Strategies to remain lawful include:

- Staying calm. Practice rhythmic breathing and focus on maintaining the correct series of action and dialogue as it was performed in the original timeline.

- Using context cues, your surroundings, and other people to help you remember what to do and say next in any given situation.

- Not revealing yourself as a traveler under any circumstances. Doing so is grounds for immediate removal from the past and imprisonment. Instead, remain present in the moment, focusing completely on your current situation. If you happen to make a mistake (i.e. – speaking about something you shouldn't have knowledge of or mentioning something about the future) you must immediately convince listeners that you misspoke or that they misunderstood what was being said.

- Speaking about the future is strictly prohibited and is a punishable offense. Be mindful of only speaking about the present and remove yourself from any conversations about upcoming events.

- If you find yourself in a situation where you are unable to remember what happened in the original timeline, it is best to remain quiet or remove yourself from the situation until such time as you remember the precise series of events. Reintroduce yourself into the situation as soon as you are able.

Reestablishing Yourself in the Present Timeline After Your Trip

If you have successfully followed all of the time travel rules your return to the present should be both seamless and uneventful. Regardless of the amount of time you spent traveling to the past, your return to the present will seem virtually instantaneous. Theoretically, you should be able to return directly to your life in the time and place where you left off.

If, however, any changes were made in the past, you may notice small differences in the present timeline. In order to navigate them effectively you should:

- Check personal calendars and logs to refamiliarize yourself with your daily schedule.

- Perform a search of your social media outlets to assess your personal status with regard to local and global affairs.

- Ask questions of others if you can do so without revealing that you have recently traveled.

- Consider maintaining a daily journal from the point of your extraction from the past back to the present as a means of recording events which might be useful to have knowledge of in the future. Decide on a location to hide the journal before traveling as it could be a liability if it is found my someone else.

- Monitoring inquiries can be made at your local time travel facility.

NOTES:

Maintaining my timeline:

1st night back

October (five months before symptoms)

rainy Thursday night —
　Soccer practice canceled
　Branson will be HOME!

HIM: writing English paper on Edgar Allen Poe
ME: studying for biology quiz - cell division

did we eat ice cream that night?

Remember Homecoming dance discussion...

　Branson asks Mandy on this day

Application Process
Application

All applicants must be a minimum of 17½ years of age at the time of the application request and must still be in possession of their initial trip voucher to begin the application process. Applications can be filled out electronically at your nearest Time Travel Facility or can be completed via the official government website at:
 www.timetraveladministration.com/applications. Additionally, before initiating the application process, potential travelers must first submit their completed screening for mental health and compliance forms which must be filled out by a participating physician. A directory of health care providers can be found on the government website.

Mandatory Classes

All travelers, regardless of age, must attend two months of mandatory time travel preparation classes for a minimum of three times per week, pass a final examination with a minimum score of 85%, and willingly sign all release waivers indemnifying the government from any liability in the event that any laws are broken during the course of your travel. Classes must be completed within six months of the initial application.

Familiarizing Yourself with the Equipment

On the final day of class, applicants tour the Time Travel Facility to become familiarized with the equipment. They will have access to the waiting rooms, observation spaces, and travel chambers.

The 8x8 foot square chambers are constructed of stainless steel and are fully encapsulated with hydraulically sealed doors. Each includes one Plexiglas paneled wall which allows travelers to see into the viewing area. Travelers are monitored via video surveillance and verbal communication is transmitted between the chamber and the control room. A timer, predominately displayed on the wall, is used to countdown the seconds leading up to the departure.

Several methods of extraction from the past have been successfully used over the years. In some instances, travelers are returned directly to the chamber at the facility. In other cases, travelers are extracted to a location of their choosing. Returning to the chamber is the preferred method, but depending on availability, you may be asked to choose a different location. Please see your final affidavit for specific instructions.

Final Examination

To be approved for travel, each candidate is required to score no less than an 85% on a final examination. This test will be administered at your local time travel facility on a government-issued computer. Travel candidates must take the exam within one month of completing the time travel course to be eligible for travel; beyond that point, travel candidates must retake the class to reinstate eligibility. Once a candidate has passed the examination, travel must be initiated within three months or eligibility is waived and the course must be retaken.

Acceptance/Rejection/Reapplication

Once a candidate has passed the examination, their test score, mental health and compliance forms, and any other pertinent documentation will be sent to a caseworker for review. Travelers will receive written notification of their scheduled meeting with their personal caseworker to review their file to determine if traveling privileges will be granted. If an applicant is accepted for travel, their voucher will be authorized and the trip will be scheduled immediately. If a candidate is rejected for travel (as determined by the sole discretion of the caseworker) he/she may be permitted to reapply within one to five years, based on the cause of the rejection. Some applicants may receive a lifetime ban. If this occurs, the candidate will be ineligible for reapplication.

Sample Test Questions

1. Circulating light beams can produce which of the following:
    A. Time travel to the future.
    B. Time travel to the past.
    C. Material transport
    D. All of the above
    E. None of the above

2. True or False: Gamma/Magnetic fields can be used to create circulating beams to warp or loop time.

3. Who was the first human to travel back in time?

4. Which institute used the radioactive substance beryllium-14 to prove the possibility of time travel?

5. List three strategies to use BEFORE your trip to help maintain the integrity of your timeline. Be specific.

6. What type of laser produced the world's first artificial gravitational force?

7. True or False: Once a candidate has passed the examination, travel must be initiated within six months or eligibility is waived and the course must be retaken.

8. List three punishable time travel offenses.

9. Which is NOT a best strategy to maintain the integrity of your timeline during your trip?

    A. Stay calm.

    B. Use context clues.

    C. Ask about the future.

    D. Remove yourself from the situation.

How long was Dr. Muhammed Khanna's longest trip into the past?

WANT TO FIND OUT MORE?

Purchase the Marked by Fate boxset and get
The Clay Lion plus 24 other full-length novels

What if you could go back in time to save the person you love the most?
The rules are simple. If you want to travel back in time, you need to be at least eighteen years old. You can only travel within your own lifespan for a maximum of six months. And above all else, you must never, ever, change the past.
But that's exactly what Brooke Wallace plans to do.
As Brooke faces existence without her beloved brother, his life cut short by a rare disease, she can think of only one solution - travel back in time to prevent his death. However, her attempts at fixing the past challenge her to confront everything she believes to be true about herself. And ultimately, she is forced to discover whether or not we can ever truly be in charge of our own destiny.

Connect with Amalie

I hope you've enjoyed Time Travel: History and Legal Procedures
A Manual for Travel Candidates

To find out what happens next, check out the rest of my series available now
The Clay Lion | Tin Men | A Straw Man |
Visit me at AmalieJahn.com to hear my latest news and to get your free copy
of Under the Rainbow

Follow me online
Twitter: @AmalieJahn | Facebook: @AmalieJahn | Pinterest: @AmalieJahn

About the Author

Amalie Jahn is the recipient of the Literary Classics Seal of Approval and the Readers' Favorite Gold Medal for her debut novel, The Clay Lion. She is a contributing blogger to the Huffington Post, Southern Writers Magazine, as well as a finalist in the 2015 Kindle Book Awards. A TED speaker, human rights advocate, and active promoter of kindness, she lives in the United States with her husband, two children, and three extremely overfed cats.

When she's not at the computer coaxing characters into submission, you can find Amalie swimming laps, cycling, or running on the treadmill, probably training for her next triathlon. She hates pairing socks and loves avocados. She is also very happy time travel does not yet exist.

INSTINCT

YA Dark Urban Fantasy

Shifter Chronicles Companion Book Two

Melle Amade

CHAPTER ONE

The plane swoops low over the striking red, yellow and purple rivers of tulips growing on the flat plain below. A windmill stabs up from the horizon. I clench the handles of the leather seat, trying not to show my excitement too much. I mean, Aiden sees this every summer when his private jet lands in Holland, but this is my first time. It's kind of crazy. I've known we'd go through the Bloedhart ceremony now that we're all sixteen, but I had no idea we'd do it in Aiden's ancestral home.

Muiderslot castle, the original seat of the Van Arend family. Unbelievable. The history of Muiderslot blows my mind. This is where the Order was forged, where everybody first came together. And this is where we're going to do our Bloedhart ceremony and become shifters ourselves.

For real.

It feels like my blood is made of champagne. It bubbles inside me at the thought of finally being able to turn into a coyote. Instead of just talking about it. Instead of just sitting on our asses being tutored about all the rules and the regulations and the history of the Order. Instead of all that boring crap, we finally just get to be who we really are.

This is the moment I've been craving my whole life.

"What're you thinking about, Wolfie?" Roman grins across at me, his teeth sparkle brilliant white against his dark skin. He's got his gold 70's glasses pulled down over his eyes, but I know he's looking out the window, too.

I kick him.

"Don't even get me started on cute nicknames to call you. You'll end up a lizard in no time, frog face."

Roman shrugs. "That's a term of adoration."

I roll my eyes as I turn them to the window. "It's a fact."

"You don't have to hide it, Zan, I know you like me." He taps my toe and I chuckle. He's such a dork. Roman moved to our tiny community of Topanga, California when we were in second grade and he's been one of our group ever since.

"Don't act like you're not excited," I say.

"Oh, I'm excited," Roman says. "I'm gonna have awesome superpowers." He holds up his hands like he's shooting some sort of magic out of his fingertips.

Laughter bursts out of me. "I don't know, dude," I say, thinking about his small, bespectacled parents. "I wouldn't get too grandiose about any of that. I mean, your parents are super smart, but their frog genes haven't exactly made them overly badass."

Roman lowers his glasses a bit, his brown eyes blinking at me over the slim golden rim. "Clearly you haven't seen my old man play horseshoes. Total. Bad. Ass."

"That's about all that happens up in Topanga," I mutter.

I wonder what it's like in other parts of our shifter world. Maybe we'll get a taste of it while we're here. They might know more about the Hunters than we hear about.

"It's just the way Lord Van Arend likes it." Roman returns to looking out the window. "But you know, we don't have to stay there. We can forge our own destiny."

"Yeah, that's probably exactly what those two are thinking," I tilt my head toward Aiden and Callum on the other side of the private jet. Aiden is Arend Lord Van Arend's son and the Heir to the Kortsrijk, the high seat of Muiderkring West. Basically, it means his dad is in charge and has all the money. And one day, so will Aiden.

I don't even think Callum's awake yet. He's got his arms folded over in his black leather jacket, sunglasses on, and chin practically against his chest. I frown and look away. I miss Callum. I miss the Callum he was, but after everything he's been through, he might never be that same Callum again.

Aiden is quiet and staring out the window. No doubt thinking about Shae. It sucks we had to leave her behind. But humans don't belong in our world.

The plane banks toward a private airfield near the castle. It'll allow us to be collected quickly and transported behind Ravensgaard lines. It's strange how there's a lot more Ravensgaard here than in Topanga. Especially when the Lord of the Kortsrijk sits in Topanga. Why do they need so much more protection here? Is it the Hunters?

Don't they have a ward like Topanga? Muiderslot has been here so long, the Hunters must have a general idea about it. But for some reason they've never attacked. Maybe they're low on numbers. I bet it takes a lot of convincing for a human to be trained and conscripted into becoming a member of the Alliance of Righteous Humanity. Shifters don't have to worry about that. We're born into our world and trained from our early years to be fighters.

"How many days to the Bloedhart?" Roman asks.

"What am I? Your personal assistant?" I mutter.

He stares at me through the dark shades that protect his sensitive eyes.

"It's tomorrow," I mutter. "They're expecting that we're already well-trained. They want us to shift early so we can spend the next two weeks training with the Ravensgaard and learning to use our animal forms."

"Oh, I think I got a handle on my animal form." The side of Roman's mouth lifts.

"I'm pretty sure you have no idea what to do with it," I retort.

His laughter is so loud, Aiden glances over. Life with my friends is so easy. We can turn everything into fun, even our sexual prowess, or lack thereof. I'm sure we're all virgins. What choice do we have? We're shifters. We're only allowed to mate with our own kind, and up in Topanga, well, I'm the only coyote, Roman is the only frog, Aiden is the only eagle, and Callum is the only Raven. So, no one up there is mating with anyone.

"Are you worried at all about the ceremony?" Roman asks, his voice playful.

"What is there to be worried about?" I was born for this.

Roman takes his glasses off and drops them in his black spiked hair. He leans forward, all serious for once.

"But I've heard," he says conspiratorially, "that when you first go through the Bloedhart, well, I don't know exactly how to say this, but you know, everyone starts to get a little bit turned on."

My laughter bursts out so loudly that Callum starts and Aiden looks over curiously.

"Right." I choke the words out through my giggles. "So you're afraid you're going to jump Callum's bones, is that what you're telling me? Or is Aiden more your type? I've never been able to quite figure that out."

Roman laughs out loud. "I'm either-or, not picky."

"Are you going to buckle in for landing or what?" Aiden asks, no hint at humor on his solemn face.

"What is the point of owning your own jet if you still have to buckle up and follow some silly rules?" I ask.

Roman looks at Aiden. "You do realize that if we crash, seatbelts aren't going to do a dang bit of good, right? Like the plane is going to go up in a fiery ball of hell?"

"Put your seatbelt on," Aiden repeats. And there something in his voice that triggers us, something I still don't quite understand. Without even thinking about it Roman and I reach over and grab our seatbelts, buckling them snuggly around our hips.

"You've got to follow the rules," Aiden says. "That's the deal."

"Aye-aye, captain," Roman mumbles.

I turn to Aiden and give him a salute before blowing him a kiss. This is an exciting time of our life and I won't let Mr. Rules ruin it for us.

We're collected by a black limousine from the small airport where the jet lands. Lord Van Arend has roused himself from the back of the plane, but doesn't do much more once inside the limo. He simply curls up in a corner, eyes closed, head resting against the tinted window.

The limo cruises slowly along the green fields and canals before turning onto the long straight drive that heads up to the main gates of Muiderslot Castle. A team of Ravensgaard, Callum's kin, guard the gate, but waves us through. In minutes we are at the massive red castle, its towers stretching into the overcast Dutch sky, where so much of the Order's core history happened. It's on the edges of Holland, with water from the North Sea lapping at the dykes that surround it. The Castle was built more than six hundred years ago as a fortress by the Van Arends but now it serves as a home to the Lord's sister, Lady Annalise.

We step out of the limo to walk across the draw bridge, though the massive curtain wall and into the inner ward, which serves as the courtyard to the castle. The Ravensgaard, clad in their black sealskin uniform with sharp metal weapons glinting in the low-lying afternoon sun. They stand at attention on the battlements looking deadly and fierce.

My gaze goes over to Callum, wondering how he's going to respond to all the Ravensgaard around him. These are his people. I may not be around many of my people in Topanga, but at least I have my parents. The muscles at the base of my neck tighten as I think about Callum's parents. I hate his mother. You shouldn't hate the dead, I know, but she destroyed him. What kind of mother commits suicide? Just because her husband abandons her? She gave no thought to the two young men she left behind. Callum's jaw is clenched tight. The preparation for the Bloedhart has been worse for him. He doesn't talk about it, but I can see it. The herbs Zaragoza has given us to deal with the rage don't seem to work as well on Callum. When the rage comes, he has to white knuckle it, grab on to something, and hold on tight, trying not to let it explode inside him or perhaps out of him.

People wearing the crimson and gold of the Van Arend family lead us into the courtyard where all the castle staff stand in a long row outside. What the heck. I duck my head behind my short red curls, hoping we don't have to greet every single one of them. But apparently, that is something just for Aiden and his father. The castle and the staff all belong to Lord Van Arend. His sister only lives here because he lets her. I hang back with Roman and Callum until the acknowledgements are done and Lord Van Arend turns with his prim and proper sister and enters the dark interior of the castle.

The Ravensgaard disperse after a quick inspection and we are left standing in the courtyard with Aiden's cousin, Matilde. My parents never seemed too fond of her mother, but have always admired her beautiful blonde daughter. They say she is strong, intelligent, and a killer. Because she lives here without any peers, they always thought she was a bit lonely and spent all her time in training. Aiden greets her warmly and kisses her on each cheek.

"What did you bring with you?" she asks, looking over his shoulder.

Her features are sharp like an Eagle's. It's the first time I've ever met a female eagle.

"Not what, dear cousin," Aiden says with a smile. "Who. These are my friends, Zan and Roman and Callum."

Matilde folds her arms across her chest and tilts her head to the side, looking the three of us up-and-down as if we're available for inspection.

"Ravensgaard," she says with an easy glance at Callum.

No surprise there, his raven sharp features and black hair are a complete give away, not to mention his dark mood and brooding stare.

Then it's my turn. I meet her gaze with a raised eyebrow. It will be interesting to see if this Dutch-born girl can even guess what I could be.

It takes her a little longer. She steps forward, forearms folded in front of her as she circles me, her eyes cruising up and down. I stick my hands in my back pockets. Regardless of her position, now or in the future, I'm not afraid of her. My loyalty lies with the Van Arends, and she is one of them. So she can look and inspect and think all she wants.

"I don't think I've seen this kind here," she says.

"That would be right," Aiden says. "This species doesn't exist here."

"Good. Well, you can't be a dog, because those Passiefs were all exterminated in the war. As for the wolves ..."

Roman glances over at me. "She's got you nailed for four legs and furry."

"And with sharp teeth." She smiles and it lights up her face.

"I'm a coyote," I say. "I'll show you after the Bloedhart."

My skin prickles even as I say it. Tomorrow. One more night and then I'll be able to let loose of this compulsion inside me to run, to howl, to ... well, kill things.

She shrugs as if she never would've guessed it anyhow and then turns to Roman. Her eyes open almost as big as his naturally are. "A poisonous frog. An agalychniscallidryas." Her gaze flies to Aiden. "I didn't know your father had some of those."

"You make him sound like he's a possession," Aiden says, throwing his arm around Roman's shoulder.

"More like your secret weapon," she says. "It's a lot of firepower."

Roman's chest pops out and he stands a little taller. I cover my mouth to stifle a yawn. The time difference is going to get to me, but I've heard that the coffee here is strong.

I also kind of don't like the way Matilde is looking at Roman. It's a little annoying and puts a rock in my stomach.

"But come on," she motions us forward. "I'll take you to the tower and show you the rooms."

My gaze spins around the courtyard at the high brick walls that surround us, then over to the main part of the castle and the towers that jut high into the dismally overcast sky.

A tingling sensation moves across my skin. I can't believe I'm going to stay in Muiderslot, the castle where legends were made.

The next morning, we gather on the lawn outside the castle to watch the Ravensgaard's formal presentation to Lord Van Arend. A bunch more shifters have arrived to make sure the leader of Muiderkring West knows they are sworn to him.

As if there was any doubt.

I stand in the blustery northern winds hoping the big party tomorrow night, after we complete the ceremony, is going to be inside. Even in June it's too cold for me out here.

Everyone else is drinking wine, but I'm sipping a cup of tea, holding it close to my face to keep my nose warm. Roman's in the middle of a bunch of Eagles, regaling them with his American brand of humor, a bit coarse and a bit loud, but everybody seems to like it. It's kind of annoying. Everyone likes Roman no matter what. He is so light. It's like the world could fall down around him and he would still find some way to make everyone laugh about it. I stare at his bright laughing eyes and wonder how on earth he is supposed to be the poison arrow among us.

Callum is standing by a hedge at the far end of the party near the drinks table. It doesn't look like he's drinking, so maybe he's just using it as a barrier between himself and the rest of us. There's no indication he wants to spend time with the Ravensgaard at all.

I walk over to him, trying to tuck my curls behind my ears, but the wind keeps blowing them in my eyes.

"You okay?" I touch his leather jacket lightly, breathing in the musky warm scent.

His movement is nearly imperceptible, but it happens. Without even looking like he's moved at all, he leans away and puts a good three inches between us.

"Do you still have your meds from Zaragoza?" I ask.

He nods, shoving his hands into the pocket of his black jeans. But then he jerks one of them out and starts fidgeting with the silver chain threaded through his belt loops.

"Yes." He's quiet and serious. "I made sure I had enough. I went to Zaragoza and got some more." His shoulders shiver and I recognize it. My body does that, too, when I taste the powder. It's nasty, but it's the only thing that combats the anger.

"It's been really hard," I say, hoping to ease his isolation.

"It's been all right." He shrugs. "There's not much longer now."

"What are you going to do?" I ask.

He looks down at me. "What do you mean what am I going to do? I'm going to learn how to shift."

"Yeah but, well you know … Are you going to stay in Topanga?" I ask.

His body recoils. His shoulders hunch forward and his nose wrinkles. "Whatever made you think I would leave Topanga?" He asks.

"Well …" I don't really know what to say. "I mean, your brother left." I finally mutter.

"My brother was asked to take a hiatus before he takes on his duties as the Ridder," Callum says. "You know why."

"Because of Naomi." I nod.

Callum raises his shoulders and lets them fall. "Hopefully the time in Ireland will let him get her out of his system. Nothing good comes from breaking the laws and being with humans."

"Yeah it's a totally bad idea. But it's hard to let go of people you care for." My mind immediately goes to Shae. It hurts, like my hearts being yanked away from me. My best friend since we were in preschool. Since we were tiny. She knows everything about me. Well, I guess not my whole life. She doesn't know I'm a shifter. And, that … she can never know.

"It's better this way," Callum says.

My head jerks up to look at him. "Don't you miss her?" I ask.

"No," he says quietly. "I just saw her last night at Aiden's party."

"That's not what I mean and you know it," I say. "We can't be friends with her anymore. And don't pretend you don't care for her. I know you do."

"Listen, Zan." Callum turns away from inspecting all the shifters milling around the garden party and turns to me, fully looking down at me. He's a good-looking guy, but there's something dark and fierce about him I don't think I'll ever understand. But I do know I will always want him on my side.

"I've lost a lot of people. I've lost so many people that now there's just me. So, losing one more doesn't really seem to make much of a difference."

There's nothing I can say to that. I don't know what it's like to lose your mother and your father. Both my parents are still alive. They're slightly older, even for shifter standards, but they're going to be around a long time I'm pretty sure.

"Your father only left," I say. "He's not dead."

The words don't come out quite the way they sounded in my mind. I want to slap myself upside the head. But I stand there looking at him, because it's like cement is forming on his face. it's like he is becoming stone.

"He is to me," Callum says. "He is to me."

Without another word, he walks off toward the castle. In moments the dark red bricks envelope him in darkness. I take a deep breath and slowly exhale. I wish I could make it better for him. I wish I could just take his pain away. Callum is one of the best friends I have. And it's hard to see him hurting so much. But over the years, as much as I would do anything for my friends, there's some pain you can't help them with.

Aiden and Shae have home problems, too. The only people who seem to have easy-going lives at home are Roman and me.

Roman is still delighting the crowd of Eagles. I don't even know how to join the conversation. My stomach knots as I watch him handle the crowd. He's grown up so much in the last two years, from being that pranking, young teenager. His chest is filled out and chiseled with muscle and glowing brown skin. Looking at him makes my stomach tingle. But I stick my tongue between my teeth and bite down on it. This isn't a good idea. Whatever it is my body is feeling for this science geek friend of mine, it's just a bad idea. Roman's a frog and I'm a coyote and I have no doubt about that. We all have to stick to our own species.

We didn't know we were shifters until we all turned thirteen. I remember one afternoon Shae and I were sitting on the hammock on her on my front porch making kid jokes about which of our three best friends we would go out with. Roman, Callum, or Aiden. I told her I didn't know. Aiden has a manor home and he's nice and upstanding and righteous and firm. But Roman just makes me laugh. And that's a hard thing to pass up on. It's so hard to choose between bright blue eyes and deep brown eyes, but I'll go with laughter every time.

Shae only ever had one that she would choose. Time and time again it was always Aiden, Aiden, Aiden. But we always laughed it off. We were young and had no idea what our futures would hold. I thought I would be friends with Shae forever, yet our friendship is over. And as I watch Roman charm the crowd, I know that's all we will ever be.

A short while later we are all led back into Muiderslot. I'm surprised we're going inside, I thought we'd go outside; to a cave for something. Zaragoza, the badger warlock of Topanga has taken me to the cave where they've done the Bloedhart there. Such a deep and beautiful cave full of stalactites and stalagmites. I love them. Probably because I'm an animal that burrows. But clearly, we're not going into a cave for this Bloedhart.

We enter the great hall of the castle, where the ceiling soars high above our head and a great fire burns in the massive fireplace. The red brick is unadorned except for three massive tapestries. One is a winter scene of Muiderslot where rain pours down on the castle and its lush green surroundings. Eagles fly above the castle and on a ribbon at the top is written the family crest "Rain is the Birdsong." The second tapestry matches the first except it shows Van Arend Manor, the baroque manor house that was built when they grew tired of living in a castle. It's strange to see the manor house in the low green lands of Holland. Today it sits high on the top of a dry canyon in California, moved brick by brick to its new home when the Order insisted Muiderkring West move its High Seat to the new country. The third tapestry shows Lord Reginald Van Arend sitting in the high seat with a group of shifters swearing fealty to him. And the third tapestry.

There's no sign of the Order or the Berzerken on any of the tapestries. This is the Van Arend home and heritage. It doesn't matter that in this room they created an alliance of all shifters. They bound together Muiderkring East, Muiderkring West and Muiderkring South. Even though the Berzerken came out on top and now they rule us all, they do not get represented in the great hall of the Van Arends.

My gaze falls off the tapestries and onto Roman, who has clearly charmed at least one European girl. She walks with him into the hall, her hand daintily looped through his.

"What is he doing?" I ask Aiden who stands next to me. "She's an eagle."

Aiden shrugs. "They're my cousins. He's not doing anything, just relaxing and having a good time. Why are you so bothered by it?"

"Me?" I straighten myself and smooth my jeans, which didn't really need smoothing. "I'm not bothered by it. It's just, well, we're not supposed to do it."

"Do what?" Aiden says. "He's just talking to her."

My skin heats up, because it's obvious what I was thinking, which is dumb anyway.

"You're jealous," Aiden says, raising his eyebrows.

"I am not," I say "I just don't want anyone to get into trouble."

"No one's going to get into trouble." Aiden looks at me. "My father's here. We're going to do the Bloedhart soon and then we go to training. In two weeks, we'll be gone. I don't know what you're so upset about."

"I'm not upset," I say, but my voice is a little bit shrill and it's obvious something is bugging me. "I guess I'm just nervous." I wave my hand trying to push off the feelings and his inquisition.

"It's going to be okay." His voice is low and reassuring as he puts his hands on my shoulders and squeezes them gently. Roman glances over for a second but then returns to the blonde his attention has been going to all morning. I sigh as Aiden's taut grip presses gently into my muscles.

"Wow that feels good."

"Yeah, don't underestimate jetlag," he says. "Doesn't matter how many times I do it, I can still be a wreck when I get over here. The only reason it's not got us lying flat right now is probably because of the adrenaline rush."

As he finishes his words he takes his hand and rubs it down my spine, pinching the bones between his thumb and index finger. A thrill shoots through my body and down to… well, down. And then a warm feeling rises through everything. I swallow hard. What the heck is wrong with me? Whatever's going on inside is totally screwed up. I'm anxious and excited, I'm nervous, I'm jealous. Now something else, whatever Aiden just did has got me a little hot and uncomfortable in all the wrong places. I want to say something casual and funny to lighten the moment but I don't.

"You look like you're about to faint," Aiden says.

"Okay," I murmur. "I'm okay. Just tired." My throat is tight and suddenly dry, my heart pounding loudly in my chest. Aiden's looking at me funny. But fortunately, I notice something I can distract him with. I point toward the small side door leading out of the hall. It's the kind of door the Lord of the castle would normally sneak in or out of the room through. But Lord Van Arend is already in the room.

Aiden looks over and his eyes grow wide. "How the hell did he get here?" he rumbles.

I never thought I'd be so happy to see anyone in my entire life. But the hunched over, shriveled little man in the brown smock, clicking the moving sticks continually in his hand well, it's like seeing family.

"But I thought he refused to fly," Aiden says.

"Or maybe he just didn't want to fly in your private jet," I say.

"Oh, maybe he has some other way of getting around that we don't know about." Aiden parries. "Because I'm pretty sure his exact words were 'I would sooner cut off my own testicles and eat them than ride a cursed plane.'"

I nod and chuckle.

"That sounds like Zaragoza. But I just saw him two days ago in Topanga," I say. "There's no way he could have taken a boat to get here."

"Never mind that now," Aiden says. "It's time."

He motions me forward as he leaves me to stand next to Lord Van Arend. I glance over at Roman and flick my wrist, letting him know it's time to leave the bevy of beauties and join us. Callum is already falling in step right next to Aiden, as he always does, and if I were to make a bet on it I'd say he always will.

There's no pomp or circumstance in this moment. I've been to enough shifter ceremonies to know we like our pomp and circumstance, but not yet, not for us. Because we're not fully fledged shifters yet. We're all awkward pre-shifter teens. I can't quite figure out exactly what's going to happen next. But everything is about to change. And through this one ceremony we're going to lose our angst and become our true selves.

Zaragoza's beady eyes are trained on me, but I lower my lids and keep my eyes to the ground. I have too many questions about how he got here and right now, he's not going to give me any answers. I'm pretty sure of that. So, it's best if we just get on with it.

The room quiets down until it's silent, except for the Zaragoza twigs.

Lord Van Arend's voice rings out so loud it startles me and I jump.

"I put them in your care," he says stiffly to the warlock and motions us to follow Zaragoza.

Zaragoza doesn't exactly welcome us with open arms. He turns his back and shuffles out of the room. Aiden and Callum follow dutifully right behind, but I come in behind with Roman. He and I exchange a look and raise our eyebrows at each other. He bows low with a slight smile.

"After you, little pooch," he says, and instantly my mood is lighter and a big smile pours over my face. Being with Roman is being at home.

I step in front of him but I know he's close behind, making sure I'm protected. He's going to make a great weapon for Aiden. The Ravensgaard might be the soldiers, but it's shifters like Roman with special skills that really make the difference in the protection of Muiderkring West.

It quickly becomes apparent we're not going to a cave. Zaragoza leads us to a back hallway. I certainly don't know my way around the castle; I only just got here yesterday. As I glance at the profile of Aiden's face just ahead of us, I can tell he's not clear where we're going either. This dark stairwell is clearly one he's never traversed.

I've got pretty good stamina, all shifters do, but by the time we make it up probably more than one thousand stairs, I'm pretty winded and I can tell that we're in the highest point of the castle, right under the eaves. The weather outside hasn't exactly been like California, I would say it's quite cold, but up here under the eaves it's not bad. Zaragoza doesn't leave any time for us to talk.

"I've spent the last three years training you to be ready for this moment. Are you ready to be your shifter self?" His voice grates like gravel against my ear.

He should be talking to Aiden, the Heir, but his eyes are focused on me.

"Yes," I say. I hate the way my voice squeaks when I say it, but it doesn't matter. It's been said.

Zaragoza looks at each of the guys in turn and repeats the question. They all answer in the same simple way I have. "Yes."

We all must agree to do the shifter ceremony. Once that is done, there is no turning back. If we don't do it, we'll end up wytes, shifters who are unable to shift and live a life full of pent up anger. Better to be our true selves. Was it Roman who was saying the world demanded evolution or death. That is how I feel right now, that I must evolve or die.

To my surprise, there is a chimney flue set up in the center of the room. It's a pipe going up to the top for the smoke to escape. It reminds me of the starlight hole in our Topanga cave.

On the floor in the center of the attic room, a pentagram is drawn in chalk. We all take our place around the pentagram and wait while Zaragoza sprinkles herbs in the fire and begins to chant. His words are no surprise. We have heard them, memorized them and practiced them.

"Hud feroaring ontstaan."

The world is not as it seems.

We take our places around the circle and add our voices as Zaragoza stokes the fire. The flames inside me burn as well, rising threw my guts and bones and to the edge of my skin, but they can't escape. I want to cry out and scream as the edges of the world go dark. My gaze stays on the fire as my blood calls out to it.

Zaragoza burns the blade in the fire until the knife glows orange. The scent of burning herbs fills the air. He steps to me, pulls out my hand and slices the knife across my finger. My inhale sounds like a scream, but nobody notices and I don't stop chanting. Zaragoza cuts his own finger and lifts the back of my shirt. He presses his bleeding digit against the Threnton Crest on my lower back, the pressure point for releasing the shifter. I inhale sharply as my shifter blood surges to the edge of my skin, like an undulating wave trapped inside a balloon.

He moves to Roman and I follow him. We all must join in the ritual and release the shifter in each of us. First Roman, then Callum, and finally Aiden. It is Aiden, the Heir, who will apply the final pressure. It is almost an instantaneous transformation. Callum is gone and a black raven flies in circles cawing in the attic. Roman disappears and somewhere in the dark, I'm sure there is a frog.

"You two, at the same time," Zaragoza instructs and Aiden and I are standing face to face by the fire. My heart is racing trying to keep up with the surging blood inside me.

There is only one way for us to press the Threnton Crest at the same time, he steps toward me until our bodies are touching fully. I'm staring up into his bright blue eyes, his golden hair falling forward. My breath is heavy, my chest rising and falling against his. We stretch our arms around each other and in that moment, I'm not sure if he's going to kiss me or finish the spell or both. Nothing would thrill me more than if it were both. My tongue moistens my lips as I lift the back of his shirt.

"Are you ready?" he asks.

I nod silently. Yes. I am ready for anything.

And together we place our bleeding fingers against each other's lower backs.

I scream in joy as my body transforms and shrinks and my senses come alive with scents and sounds and sights I had no idea were locked away inside me. I'm on the ground and on all fours and racing in circles around the room, my energy free. A high-pitched howl fills the attic and sails out the flue with the smoke.

And this is me.

I am a shifter.

Finally.

When we re-enter the great hall we are in our human form. A great cheer goes up from the assembled crowd. Lord Van Arend personally congratulates every one of us and we are surrounded by a sea of well-wishers. Each giving us advice on how to be the best shifter possible.

I nod and I smile and I respond as expected.

But every now and then I catch myself looking across the room. Callum has disappeared, but Roman seems in his element. Aiden is staring straight at me, ignoring the people who are talking to him. They don't seem to mind, being quite happy listening to themselves talk.

Aiden jerks his head to the side. My gaze follows his movement and I see the door he's talking about.

A single short nod of my head is all the answer he needs.

I slip quietly into the dark room not quite sure where I am, but trusting the Heir wouldn't steer me wrong. All I can think of in the dark is his blue eyes piercing me as my chest pressed into his.

This is crazy.

What am I do?

Standing in the dark waiting for the Heir? Waiting for Aiden? What about Roman? It doesn't matter. None of this matters. We are not allowed to choose. We are not allowed to mate. None of these boys can be my chosen ones.

But the door cracks open and Aiden slips in. He smells of forest and fresh rain as he locks the door and reaches for me.

His hand pulls me toward him. But my blood is already racing for him, returning to the place it was as we stood waiting for the final moment of the Bloedhart, waiting to become shifters. Now we are shifters.

We are free.

I follow him down the darkened hallway and he pulls me through a small door at the far end. My eyes have adjusted and there's a pale blue light from the moon slipping in through a high window. Shelves line the walls. It's some sort of a storage room.

Aiden crashes his mouth against mine in the dark. The magic of the Bloedhart still racing through our veins, setting us on fire, pushing us together. I lift his shirt and press my finger against the spot where my blood still rests on his lower back.

He moans against my mouth and I dissolve.

Nothing about this is right, but I am powerless to stop it. We are lost in each other and in the newly awakened animals within us whose only desire is to live by instinct and be free.

WANT TO FIND OUT MORE?

Purchase the Marked by Fate boxset and get
Sanctuary plus 24 other full-length novels

It's survival of the fittest, but first you have to fit in. Shae is sure the icy rage that claws at her is driving away her friends and pulling her closer to the wrong boy. After all, it's Aiden she has always secretly wanted, not Callum, who has barely spoken to her in the last year.

But, as her protected life unravels, she discovers the violent supernatural world that lurks in her quiet hometown and the ancient feuds that threaten to destroy both her friends and her family.

To save those she loves, Shae must succumb to her own fury and take on the Ravensgaard, the renegade warriors of the Order, but as the battle approaches her deepest fears are coming true, she's becoming just like them. Shae's not sure she can afford the price she'll have to pay—her own humanity.

Connect with Melle

I hope you've enjoyed Instinct, Shifter Chronicles Companion

To find out what happens next, check out the rest of my series available now
Sanctuary, Shifter Chronicles | Remnants, Shifter Chronicles |
Iron Cage, Quest for Shifter Magic
Visit me at MelleAmade.com to hear my latest news and to get your free
copy of Heritage, Shifter Chronicles Prelude

Follow me online
Instagram: @melleamade | Twitter: @melleamade |
Facebook: @melleamade.Author | Pinterest: @melleamade |

About the Author

Since I was eight I have been writing stories that capture the adventures in my head and the characters strong enough and flawed enough to have them. When I look at an empty field I see a formidable citadel. When I meet a vulnerable old man, I greet an emeritus warrior. When I walk through city streets I feel dimensions hiding around every turn. It has been my lifelong passion to explore these worlds that reveal the pain of loneliness, the joy or self-actualization, and the hope of magic.

I grew up in a place called Potter Valley where the Milky Way is held aloft by a circle of mountains and the central business district consists of a bait store and a saloon. At 19 I moved alone to London and spent the next ten years exploring the world, even becoming an Australian citizen, before I returned to California and found a new home in Los Angeles. My world revolves around my two wee children, storytelling, and my love of travel.

A Becoming Attribute

A Balance Bringer Chronicles Short Story

Debra Kristi

Chapter One

A Becoming Attribute

"From the moment of inception, I was born into greatness." I scratch at my hairline and tilt my head in consideration. "No. No. No," I chirp. To cliché. I can do better. My English teacher would push me to do better.

I bite my lip and narrow my gaze upon the metallic flecks embedded in the floor tiles, pushing my unconscious mind to solve this hidden riddle and wow me. "In an ordinary world lived an extraordinary girl ... ha ha, yeah right," I rattle off my little rhyme, already knowing it's another fail, and shuffle up behind Chris in the checkout line.

It's Sunday morning, and for a lack of anything better to do, Chris and I are going to kick back and watch a rental movie. In our one-high-school town, there aren't a whole lot of options for entertainment. No mall, no movie theater, and no money for dirt bikes. The town fun was yesterday, on Farmer's Market Saturday. Really it's more like a street fair/flea market mix, but in any case, Saturdays are fun and Sundays not so much.

"What are you doing, Crystia?" Chris asks, exasperated, and sets the chips and soda on the moving belt. One person stands in front of us in line.

"I'm writing my superhero theme song." I smile at the back of his head.

He erupts with a sarcastic laugh and turns to look at me. "If you're a superhero, then this boring, dusty town must be Gotham?"

"No ..." I contemplate my options. Our quiet, rustic home of Faredale is nothing like Batman's Gotham or even Superman's Metropolis. Actually, I can't think of any superhero that came from a small desert town. Maybe that's because superheroes need a larger community of people to save. Metropolis is to Faredale as a book is to a chapter. Yet I can't help but believe that Faredale, as uninteresting and unexciting as it is, has well-hidden secrets. After all, there is something not completely normal about me or my sister, and we live here and are definitely meant for something more. "No," I continue, "we're sitting in the closet cabinet, pushing our way past the cloaks and coats toward the entrance of Narnia."

It's our turn, so the clerk rings up our purchase, and Chris hands over the money.

"I think you're a tad confused. I may not have read the Narnia book—"

"*The Chronicles of Narnia*," I interrupt.

"Whatever." He shakes his head in irritation. "I haven't read the books, but I saw the first movie, and it has nothing to do with superheroes. It's all magic and destiny and that crap."

"So what? I can blend my worlds if I want to. I'm being creative," I beam. "I may not look like a superhero, but I'm still walking my path of discovering. Heck, maybe I'm more than a superhero. Maybe ..." I folded my hands together and pressed them down the front of me, "just maybe, I'm a goddess."

Chris laughs, collects his change, picks up our goods, and leads us toward the front door of the market. "Okay, Miss Superhero wannabe goddess. You can show me just how amazing your powers are when we get back to your place." Clear expectation weighs heavy in his banter.

My happiness drops like the first nose-dive on a roller coaster. This is my fault. I created this situation by allowing him to move our relationship to the next step. Only, I didn't see the event of last week as an advancement or betterment. I saw it as a sign we should stop … completely. So why am I still here, going through the motions? I bite the inside of my lip.

The front doors slide open and exposes a typical Sunday scene: the mid-morning sun glistening off the asphalt, a multitude of parked cars, and the buzz of people moving in and out of the market. But today, something is definitely different. Directly in front of us, in the shade of the store overhang, a collection of tables and cages sits on proud display.

"Where did all this come from?" Chris says, mirroring my thoughts. And then colors and sweet softness register in my brain, and my mood instantly lifts.

An uncontrollable squeal leaps from my throat, and I rush to the nearest table with a cage. A cage filled with kitties.

Stripes and splotches, fuzzy fur all around. I want to eat them all up!

"Kittens? You can't get a kitten. Let's go." Chris tugs my arm while attempting to balance the six-pack of soda and bag of chips in his arms.

He's right, of course. I know he is. My mother has never allowed us to own a single pet. That might be why I'm so drawn to animals. The lack of such an experience makes me desire it even more. And these kittens … they're so freakin' adorable! It was smart to set this pet adoption up in the front of the only true grocery store in town. Given it's among Faredale's top five weekend destinations the pets should get plenty of exposure. Plus the sight of these kittens tugs at the must-have heart string. I can attest that it works. I want to take them all home.

"Can you give me a minute?" I snap.

"Come on, Crystia."

Internally I sigh, but externally, I ignore him and stick my fingers through the cage. The kittens are brawling, a frenzy of color toppling and turning. "Come here. Come see me," I coo, beckoning.

As if the sound of my voice calms them, the play stops and the kittens sit up and stare at me, wide-eyed. A sweet, little black-and-white takes the lead and approaches my fingers, rubs against me. I wiggle and scratch her fur.

"How much are they?" I ask the girl working the pet adoptions.

"Fifteen dollars and a signature," she says with a stunning smile.

"Only fifteen? I can do that!"

"You are not taking one of those fur-shedding creatures in my car," Chris says.

Embarrassed, I avert my eyes from the girl. "It's less than a five-minute drive. How much hair is he going to shed in such a short time?" I pin Chris with a glare.

"You'd be surprised." Chris's face morphs into a scowl.

"You no want a meowsers, *anyhow."*

"What?" I balk.

"I said—"

"Not you," I cut Chris off, quick to look at the pet adoption girl. She's staring down the front of the store, avoiding looking at Chris and me. Maybe she's embarrassed for me, too. Or maybe playing witness to our bickering is overly awkward.

"They too little. Immeowture. *Tear and chew everything."*

Who else is here? I glance back and forth, but there's no one. Only the girl, myself, Chris, and the kitties. No one else lingers around the cages at the moment. My body jerks, and I stare closer at the cats, my gaze moving away from the kittens, until I pause upon an older, wise-looking cat, beautiful with long orange fur.

"Yes, I talk to you, furless one." The cat blinks.

"What?"

"What's wrong with you?" Chris yanks on my arm.

I pull away, wave him off, and stare at the cat. *Holy flipping kitties!* Did I just understand cat speak? "How am I hearing you?" I ask the cat, totally not caring how crazy I appear.

"Supurrb *question*." He lifts his paw and begins to groom, then pauses and looks up at me. "*Don't know*."

I glance to the kittens, then back at the cat. "I haven't gone mental, I am hearing you, aren't I?"

The cat tilts his head as if bored by the question and watches me through slits for eyes.

My gaze snaps to the sign, taking in the information. Normal cats. Nothing special, besides being homeless, adorable, and awesome. I chew on my thumbnail, and gnaw on the need to figure this out. Today only, the sign says. I can't let this cat go without understanding what's happening. My eyes widen, knowing what I must do. He has to come home me.

I wrench open my purse and dig out my wallet, tearing it open. My cheeks flush. Five dollars and change. How can I not have fifteen dollars? My gaze darts to Chris and then back to my bare wallet. I sigh. I could ask Chris for the money but I don't want to owe him.

"Can we go now?" Chris says.

"In a minute." I turn my attention back to the girl. "What's that one's name?" I point to the orange tabby.

"That's Oscar. He's a sweetheart." Again, she smiles, and I feel a tiny pang in my chest.

"Can you save him for me?"

Her smile falters. "I can't make any promises. Of course, the kittens are always the most popular, so there is a good chance he will be here if you come back fairly soon."

"How late will you be here?" I ask, feeling a sense of urgency spread through my body.

"We're here until two o'clock."

I look at my phone. Ten fifty-seven. I have plenty of time. Still, I don't want to push my luck. "Let's go." I grab Chris's arm and make way for the parking lot.

Heat rises through me, and my feet fall heavy against the pavement. I imagine steam rolling off my skin as we make our way to the car. I don't say anything, just walk directly to the passenger door and wait for Chris to let me in. I stand there, fuming and waiting, and then look back at Oscar and the girl. The clench on my heart loosens, if only a little.

Chris unlocks the door with a click of his remote. "What's your deal?" he asks, then pulls open the driver's side door and slips in behind the wheel.

I drop into my seat and sigh. "Just take me home."

He grunts an ugly sound of disgust, then starts the car. We drive away from the store and from Oscar the orange tabby in silence. Less than ten minutes later, we're pulling up to my house. My mom's Ford Explorer sits in the driveway.

"Great," Chris mutters, pulling the car to a stop at the back of the driveway.

Relief washes over me. If the Explorer is here, then my sister is home, which means no alone time for Chris and me and no repeat of last week. "Doesn't matter. It's not like you were going to get some," I say, then turn my body to face him. He looks like I just punched him in the gut.

"Is this about the stupid cat thing?"

I take a deep breath, steel my core, and think about all the emotions that have been swirling within me over the last week. Ever since we took our relationship to the next level.

"That comment makes you sound like an insensitive jerk." He starts to open his mouth, but I throw up my hand, stopping his rebuttal. "Right now, I'm asking myself why I would want to give so much of myself to such a person, and the truth is … I don't. I think it's time we call it."

His nose wrinkles; his brows furrow, and he stares at me in silence.

All week, I felt this brewing, but I didn't think this process out. Didn't plan what I would say or how the breakup would go. Not that something like this would ever stick to a plan. He used to make me laugh and smile—once. We used to be happy. Somewhere along the line, things changed, yet out of habit, our relationship continued. But now it's time for us both to find something better.

"We're done, Chris," I say. "You deserve someone who's more into you."

"What is that supposed to mean?" His voice slams into me like a hammer. "I've invested two years in you! You can't cut me out now."

My mouth drops open. I snap it shut, jump out of the car, and turn to look back at him. "It's over!" I yell, then slam the car door and march to the house, refusing to look back. *Invested two years. What a steaming pile of cat poop!*

I burst through the kitchen side door. Only after I am inside with the door shut do I hear Chris drive away. The tension that has seized my body unfurls, and I lean against the door, close my eyes, and attempt to find serenity.

Chris and I hooked up in the middle of my freshman year. I never even considered anyone else, and yet when I think about him, I don't get the slightest bit excited. Now I'm not sure I ever did, even in the beginning. But I should be excited by my own boyfriend, right? He became a favorite sweater or hoodie. The one you grab for comfort and ease. That was Chris, comfortable and easy and always there. But when did he become such a jerk?

"Bad day?"

I jolt ramrod straight and stare across the kitchen. I didn't hear my sister walk in. Ana carries a dirty glass to the kitchen sink. She pauses, glass still in hand, and looks me over, then meets my gaze.

"What happened?" she asks, a crease forming between her brows.

I relax and step into the room. "I just broke up with Chris."

She sighs sympathetically. "You can do better."

"Probably." I set my bag and phone on the kitchen table and wonder if my lack of emotion toward Chris is a sign of a deeper issue. Maybe I'm incapable of feeling that kind of connection, of finding love at all.

"No probably about it. You will. When the right one comes into your life, you'll know it." Ana turns toward the sink and begins to run water into the dirty glass.

I mull over her words, consider smarting off about her own lack of effort in the area of relationships and dating. The thought lasts all of a second. It's more time than I care to spend on boys, especially my now ex-boyfriend. "Can I have fifteen dollars?" I move beside her and lean against the counter.

"That came out of nowhere." Ana shoves the dish brush into the glass and swooshes it around in circles. "What's the money for?"

"I'm getting a cat."

She spins toward me so fast I think her head might snap off. "Are you crazy? Mom will kill you!" Her voice pitches; the kitchen sink gurgles and thumps, and suddenly water is spraying the ceiling and falling upon us like the overspray of a fire hose.

I squeal screams of delight, holding my hands up. I'm five again and running through the sprinklers, only this time the sprinklers are inside the house.

"Holy Gaia!" Ana yells. "What's happening?"

A devilish smile takes hold of my face. "You're a beautiful freak, just like me."

"I am not a freak!"

"Are!" I get right up in her face. So close I can see the water drops fall from her lashes and the zig-zag of her green-blue-brown irises. "Just accept it. It's why you're so great on the swim team."

"You think I cheat?" Her voice rises and cracks.

I don't answer. I'm captivated by the sight before me. My sister is about to shove me. Her hand is raised, and I recognize the look on her face, but I don't think she realizes her fingers are sparking with blue electricity. *That's new.*

Ana's hand slams into me, the current sending my body into a wave of quakes and twitches.

"Oh no! Oh no!" she says, her voice washing into garble. She sounds so far away.

My body jolts, jolts, jolts. My world hardening and pitching. And now Ana's in my face. Or is she? My body drops, and I fall into feathery softness. Everything becomes mushy and wet and blotchy.

Then darkness consumes until there is only black silence.

And sleep.

A low moan rumbles through my chest. *Did I make that sound?* Something squeezes my hand. Heavy with the weight of sleep, my eyelids fight the desire to open. I'm damp like I threw myself on the bed after walking in the rain. Weird. I take a deep breath and stare, blurry-eyed, at the ceiling. I don't recall what day it is or what I was doing before I lay down. I don't even remember lying down.

"I'm so sorry, Crystia," Ana says and squeezes my hand a tad tighter.

I blink. Everything that led me to this point illuminates. My thoughts reel, and the memories surge. I sit up with a bolt. *What time is it?* My head throbs, but still I need to know. In a frantic motion, I twist toward my nightstand to see the clock. One twenty-three. *Oscar!* In a leap, I tear my hand from Ana's, spring from the bed, and start tossing clothes out of my dresser drawers. I don't care if what I grab matches. All I want are dry clothes. Dry bell-bottom jeans, a dry gossamer top, and dry pink tennis shoes.

Ana is sitting on the bed behind me, her eyes narrowed and face tight. Her head tilts to the side. "Are you alright?"

"You mean after you electrocuted me?" My tone is irritated, but I don't care. Waking up wet, confused, and with a headache, and more importantly, losing all that time, is not my idea of fun.

"I didn't …" Her gaze drops to her lap. "I didn't mean … I don't know what happened."

I can sense the onset of a sisterly moment, and I don't mean to be insensitive, but—ugh, I have to go. I scan my dresser and nightstands but don't see my phone. It must still be in the kitchen.

I'm gonna make it. I'm gonna make it, I chant silently as I turn to leave Ana alone in my room, but then stop short. In the doorway I pause and look back. "One of these days, you're gonna have to admit the truth, and when you do, I hope I'm there to hear it." I leave her, mouth agape, my bedroom door slamming shut between us.

Phone, keys, cash, car. I power down the hallway, through the dining area, and into the kitchen. Remnants of a puddle remain, along with several sodden towels in a bunch. I step around the mess and grab my bag and phone off the table. *Phone and keys, check.*

Now the cash. I retrieve Ana's money jar off the shelf above the sink, not even caring that she'll know what I did. To save Oscar, I need the money. Within the jar, is a mix of coins and folding cash. I snatch a twenty-dollar bill and slide the jar back into place.

Ana calls my name from down the hall. *Kitty crap. She's coming.*

"Please, Crystia! Let me explain." She moves closer, still talking, but I don't know what she's saying. I've stopped listening.

"It's fine, Sis." I fish my car keys from my bag. "I needed a nap anyway," I snap and head out the door.

Walking across our dirt driveway, I shake my head and wonder why Ana feels the need to be normal and fit in so badly. "When is everyone going to accept the fact that there is something off about our family," I mumble.

I get in my car and pull out of the driveway to head for the market, all the while obsessing over Ana and myself. *She's just not ready yet,* I tell myself. But she will be, must be, soon. And when she is, we'll talk. We'll talk about how I can talk to cats, and she can electrocute things and probably manipulate water. We'll talk about how I've seen her hold her breath underwater for like ever! And how she's the strongest and fastest swimmer on the school swim team. Or how I'm the fastest runner on the track team. And I don't even break a sweat! It all has to mean something.

Are her abilities inhuman? Are mine? Or are we both just crazy?

My face flushes, and my fingers tap, drumming nervously. I rock back and forth in my seat and yell at other drivers on the road. *Move, people!* I need to get Oscar before it's too late. I need to figure out what this is, what I'm capable of. My palms sweat, and I have to grip the steering wheel tighter than usual to keep it from slipping through my hands.

I pull into the store parking lot and catch sight of a truck stopped at the front of the market. The girl with the cats now has someone helping her, and they are loading supplies into the back of the truck. Closing shop. My heart pounds like a rabbit on the run. It's not yet two o'clock, and they are already packing up. Quick as I can, I park the car, lock up, and speed-walk toward Oscar.

"Hey," the pretty girl says, seeing me rush toward her. "I didn't think you were going to make it."

"Almost didn't, by the look of things." I survey the cats. Three of the five kittens are now gone. Hopefully off to loving homes. On the other side of the kittens, Oscar sits at attention, watching me. My heart and breath calm.

"You still had fifteen minutes," the girl says. "I would have waited, just in case."

A weight melts off my chest. "Thanks." I stare at her stupidly, then look down to hide the color I feel warming my checks. Shoving my hand into my back pocket, I pull out the twenty-dollar bill I "borrowed" from Ana's money jar. "Let's get the process started."

"Alrighty!" She grabs a form and pen from the table, and before I know it, I'm a new cat owner, with five extra Ana-dollars to spend on pet supplies. Add that to the five dollars I already had and Oscar will want for nothing. I snort. *As if.* What will ten- bucks get me? A food dish and collar?

"That's it?" I ask when we're done.

"That's all there is," she tells me. "It's not about the money or overwhelming paperwork." Her mouth lifts at the edges and her lip gloss shimmers. "It's about finding our furry friends good homes." She hands me my copy of the adoption paperwork, along with a flyer on proper cat care.

I fold everything up, shove it all in my back pocket, and nod, maybe a little too enthusiastically, but I'm excited to start exploring this new talent. *I can talk to cats!*

"You look so nervous," the girl says, her entire face brightening. "Relax. Owning a cat is a great experience. You're going to love it."

"I don't doubt it." I turn and walk toward Oscar, eager to talk to him again. The girl follows.

As I walk past the kittens, they move to the cage siding, meowing, and press their little paws against the grating. "*Mea,*" they whine. "*Mea.*"

Beyond their cage is Oscar. He lifts his lazy gaze to mine and meows. "*Said* meowsers *were trouble.*" He shifts his gaze to the kittens then back to me. "*We go now?*" He licks his paw and presses it to the barrier between us.

"In a minute," I say, leaning down in front of Oscar's cage to get a better look at him.

"You have a way with the cats," the girl says from behind me.

"So it seems." I press my hand to the metal separating Oscar and me. He moves his paw and rubs his nose to my fingertips. "I need to figure out what to do with this newly discovered talent of mine. Maybe get a job like the one you have." I'm about to say more, but I stop myself, clamp my mouth shut. *Why am I telling a stranger my secrets? I need to contain my excitement and—*

"I don't think you'd do well working a position like mine." The girl starts folding together the cardboard cat carry box. "The animals respond too favorably to you. You'd probably want to take them all home." There's a hidden giggle in her voice.

I sigh and turn to face her. "You're probably right." My heart sinks into my stomach, and my gaze drops to my pink tennis shoes. *I must have this Doctor Doolittle ability for a reason.* My mind starts tossing around all the jobs I can think of that involve animals.

"I might have an idea, though," the girl says, "if the size of the cat doesn't matter to you." She sets the completed cardboard carrier on the table next to Oscar's cage. "My name is Natalie, by the way." She shoves her hand toward me.

My gaze pops up to meet hers, and I shake her hand, squeezing a tad too tight. But her touch is warm and comforting. "Crystia," I say. "What kind of idea?"

"Well ..." She hesitates and looks back at her co-worker, who is now packing the kittens into the back of the truck. "My sister works at the Feline Preservation Center, and I'd be happy to introduce you."

"Seriously?" Mini-kittens are doing somersaults inside my ribcage. "You'd do that for me?"

"Sure." She smiles, and it's like the world just opened up a thousand and one possibilities. "I can't guarantee anything will come from the introduction, but it's worth a try."

I stare into her big, brown eyes, and swallow the lump in my throat. My mind whirls, creating daydreams of working with tigers, panthers, cheetahs...

"Big meowsers *pushy. We're purrfect."*

Guilt stabs me in the gut, and I grin at Oscar. "Can I hold him now?"

"Of course. Just be careful. We wouldn't want him running into the parking lot." Natalie opens the cage and pulls Oscar from his confines, hands him to me.

I pet him, bury my face in his fur. "I'm blessed we found each other, Oscar."

He purrs and pushes his paws into my shoulder in an attempt to knead my skin into dough.

"Ready to go home with me?" I ask my new furry friend.

His forehead presses against me.

"I'll take that as a yes," I say and place him in his temporary cat carrier. "I guess you'll need my phone number or something?" I ask Natalie, continuing to pet my new orange friend through the open lid of the cardboard carrier. His fur takes to the air, shedding as if escaping an impending doom. It tickles my nose, my eyelashes, and I can taste it on my lips. Chris was right. His car would have been filled with cat hair.

Natalie gives me a perplexed look and my cheeks immediately warm.

"My number. To call me about the position?" I quickly follow up and close the top of the temporary cat carrier.

"Of course." Her eyes twinkle like she's privy to a joke. "Can I see your phone?"

Now it's my turn to be perplexed, but I take my phone from my back pocket and hand it over.

"Smile," she says, and then leans into me and takes a picture of the two of us. With lightning quick fingers she presses a bunch of buttons, then grins, and hands my phone back to me. "Now I have your info and you have mine. If for some reason you don't hear from me, you can tap me."

"Tap you?" My nose wrinkles pushing tension between my eyes.

"You know, tap," she says and imitates pushing a button on her phone.

I look down at my phone. My contacts page is open. At the top of my-favorites list, our faces smile back at me. Or really, she smiles and I look confused. I don't know what to say to this so I don't say anything. I simply stare at the picture in a stupid stupor.

"I should know something about the job within a week or so."

"Great. This is exciting. Thanks!" I glance up to see her moving away, toward the truck. Then I glance down at Oscar's paw, protruding from one of the holes cut in the box.

I set Oscar's box on the ground and help the Natalie and her co-worker fold and load the last table. Natalie pulls a small bag of cat food from the back of the truck. "To get you started," she says. "Can I help you get this to the car?"

"Thanks. I didn't know carry-out service was provided." I grab Oscar in his box, and Natalie laughs. Together, we walk to my little, old, silver Mustang parked in the middle of the lot. I set Oscar's box in the front passenger seat, open its top, and whisper to him, "This will be quick. Don't worry." If I didn't know better, I'd think he rolled his eyes at me before looking away. After closing the lid of the box, I wrap the seatbelt around his cardboard kitty cage and lock the belt into place.

"Thanks for everything," I say to Natalie.

A moment of awkward silence passes between us, and then she takes a step back. "Okay, well, good luck with Oscar, and I will talk to you soon." She turns and starts walking back to the front of the store.

"Yeah, talk to you soon," I say to her retreating back.

And then she turns and waves, and a silly grin creeps across my face. *What's that about?*

I jump into my car before I can say anything embarrassing.

Minutes later, I'm driving my car with Oscar at my side, heading toward home. My home that has never seen a pet.

Gah! Mom's going to be so irritated that I adopted Oscar.

A meow from within Oscar's box beckons me to look down. His orange paw is pushed through one of the side air holes.

"We'll be there soon," I say, returning my attention to the road. And sure enough, a few minutes later, we're parked, out of the car, and walking toward the house. "I need you to do me a favor."

"*Meows?*"

"I need you to stay hid ..."

The kitchen side door swings open. "Crystia ..." At the sight of my cardboard cat carrier, Ana freezes, blocking the doorway. "You got the cat?" Her eyes widen with disbelief or shock or both.

"I did." I climb the two steps and push past Ana and into the kitchen, set Oscar's box down on the table. "You need to see how amazing he is. Then you'll understand."

Ana doesn't respond. Instead, she stares at me and at the box and at the orange paw jutting through one of the air holes.

I open the lid, retrieve Oscar, and gentle place him on the kitchen floor. "This is your new home," I say. "Our room is all the way down the hall and on right."

Oscar glances between me and Ana and then walks a circle around the room before disappear through the doorway and into the shadows of the dining room and beyond.

Ana coughs and my gaze jumps from Oscar's departure point to her. "You talk to him like he knows what you're saying," she says.

"He does." I shrug. I'm not going to lie, even if I know she won't believe me. Not until she hears it for herself. That's what I'm waiting for, her to hear Oscar and vindicate me.

"Mom is going to be infuriated," she counters, ignoring my admission of cat intelligence.

"Only if she finds him." I grin, mischievously.

"Oh, for the love of Gaia and God!" Her hands rise and then fall at her side. Her lips torque, and her nose wrinkles. "There is no way you can hide that cat from Mom. He's gonna shed and smell and ..."

Oscar yowls from somewhere at the back of the house.

"See?" She points. "And meow." Her hands drop with a solid *cerplump* on the table. "Unless mom suddenly becomes blind, deaf, and loses all sense of smell, she'll be on to you before you can spell that cat's name."

I'm grinning from ear to ear. She can blow hot air at me all night long, and I doubt I'll mind. Mysteries have always been a love of mine, and this—Oscar and the ability to understand him—is the most intriguing mystery I've yet to come across. It's even better than the mystery of the anonymous valentine note left in my locker a year ago. Possibly even greater than our missing Father.

"At least you won't be in the line of fire when she becomes wise." I grin, grab the empty cat carrier and bag of cat food, and then move past her in my search for Oscar. I see no need to drag this conversation out any longer.

"Don't be so sure," she says from behind me. "Mom will likely blame me for remaining silent."

Mom could. Pets have always been one of her trigger buttons. Maybe this is why. Maybe she always knew I'd be able to communicate with them. And maybe, just maybe, she's been trying to keep me from that discovery. A gurgle of lava-hot acid rises in my chest.

"Just put all the blame on me," I yell over my shoulder. "I'll take full responsibility." I walk down the hall toward my bedroom and hear Ana grumbling from the kitchen.

The door to Mom's room is open; so is the door to Ana's, but I see no sign of Oscar in either. When I reach my room, I find the furry feline curled comfortably on my bed.

"Look at you," I say, closing my bedroom door behind me. "Already making yourself comfy." I drop all the cat supplies on the floor and stare at Oscar.

He looks up and his whiskers twitch. *Thought you stank.*" He shakes his head. *"Other very stinky-stinky."*

"Ana?" I don't know if I'm disappointed or happy that my sister smells worse than me. What does the stink mean? I turn my nose toward my arm pit and take a whiff. I don't think I smell bad, but I'm not a cat. "Is that normal? People smelling bad to you?" I take a seat on the bed and start petting him. He purrs and presses his head against my palm.

"Stink ... no. Heard talk."

"What kind of talk?" My insides are exploding with light and effervescence. I can't uncover answers fast enough.

"Talk of mother world. Stinky humans from mother world." Oscar flops onto his side and rubs against my covers.

"Mother world?" My voice pitches and my skin itches. I can hardly remain seated. "What does that all mean?"

"Just mother world." He rolls over. *"Think you stink like mother world."*

Oscar is both informative and not. He creates more questions than he reveals answers. Leaves me to speculate. And yet, what he says fits nicely into the puzzle of me. I never felt right in this world. Now I can say that's because I'm probably not meant to be in this world. Just like Supergirl or Wonder Woman.

"Hiddenkel," he says.

"Holy hot places!" I jump off the bed. Oscar sits up and watches me with his piercing cat eyes. If I had a kitten for every time I've heard that name in my sleep, I'd be so far beyond a crazy cat lady that I'd be institutionalized. I fluff Oscar's fur and then run around my bed to my closet door. A collage of magazine pictures covers the entire surface. It's my dream board, all the places I'd like to visit and all the things I want to do before I die. Along the bottom, I tear free a space, pulling back a paper picture of the canals in Venice. Grabbing a pen from my nightstand, I write the name "Hiddenkel" in the newly exposed place. If this is a real place, then I need to add it to my bucket-list. Possibly move it to the top of my must-do.

"If my family isn't from here," I think out loud while staring at the new addition to my closet door. "Then it's possible all these things we can do are real. Ana and me, we really are different for a traceable reason."

"Ana," Oscar says. *"Stinky-stinky."* He jumps off the bed and sits beside me.

"But she can't understand you," I say.

Oscar sneezes, then wipes at his nose with his paw. When he's done, he sits up straight and looks directly at me. *"She must … if she is to become."*

Superheroes. Goddesses. The words whirl through my head like a sand storm of clean kitty litter. "Become?"

His stare is steady, but his shoulders seem to tighten, heighten. *"Become the needed savior."*

And there it is! Everything I've been searching for and more. Not just superheroes or goddesses, but saviors! Chosen ones.

Adrenaline pumps in a mad rush through my body, and my grin most likely devours my face. I swallow the onslaught of giggles threating to explode from my lungs and clench the bedsheets tight within my grasp. I cannot wait for the becoming to begin. I am ready. Bring it on!

WANT TO FIND OUT MORE?

Purchase the Marked by Fate boxset and get Becoming: The Balance Bringer plus 24 other full-length novels

Ana still blames herself for her boyfriend's death two years prior. Now, what she thought were mere dreams are starting to enter her waking life.

As Eerie shadows hunt Ana, strange new abilities develop. Her dream guy becomes reality, and Ana is becoming something ... other.

Ana feels like she's becoming something beyond human, or maybe she's just going crazy. But theres no one for her to turn to. Her mother and her best friend are keeping a dark secret about who Ana really is—a secret that could restore the balance between worlds or hurtle them deeper into darkness.

Ana is not only discovering the world is far stranger than she ever expected, but that its survival is dependent on her. But for there to even be a glimmer of a chance at salvation, she must make it alive to the home she's never known.

Connect with Debra

I hope you've enjoyed A Becoming Attribute

Haven't read the full story yet? Check out the first book in the series and watch for the second, coming in late 2017.
Becoming: The Balance Bringer | Awakening: The Balance Bringer

Follow me online
Instagram: @debrakristi | Twitter: @debrakristi |
Facebook: @debrakristi.writer | Pinterest: @debrakristi |

About the Author

Born and raised a Southern California girl, Debra Kristi still resides in the sunny state with her husband, two kids, and four schizophrenic cats.
Her love for the fantastical began at a very young age when her imagination magically transformed the backyard swing set into the U.S.S. Enterprise. Since then she's had a lifelong love of science fiction, fantasy, and creative storytelling. Unlike the characters she often writes, Debra is not immortal and her only superpower is letting the dishes and laundry pile up. When not writing, she is usually creating memories with her family, geeking out to sci-fi and fantasy television, and tossing out movie quotes.

Unsweet

A Short Story

Ingrid Seymour

CHAPTER ONE

We sit on the floor of my living room using the low coffee table for all our books, pencils, and studying implements. Nicolas, my best friend, is helping both me and my cousin prepare for a difficult math test. We have been at it for three hours, and my back is starting to hurt from sitting on the floor hunched over the books. I put my pencil down and stretch my arms upward feeling we're due for a breather.

"I don't know about you guys, but I'm ready for a break," I say.

Leonardo, my first cousin on Dad's side, drops his pencil and jumps to his feet without protest while Nicolas frowns and agrees reluctantly.

"I'll go get our stuff," Leonardo says. He stays put, however, stretching his neck from side to side and ruffling his blonde hair.

We bought cupcakes to have something to look forward to during our break. Nicolas thinks we just wanted an excuse to stop studying, rather than barreling through our text problems to get them all done. He's such a slave driver.

After his drawn out, lazy stretch, Leonardo rushes into the kitchen. A few minutes later, he comes back with freshly brewed coffee and our treats. He sets the mugs on the table with individual plates and napkins for the cupcakes. My mouth waters at the sight of the delicious goodie.

It's strawberry, from Kat & Jonna's Bakery, my favorite place in the entire bay area.

I've been daydreaming about eating it the entire three hours we've been studying—add to that an hour since we bought them and call it torture.

Leonardo's brew is good, though not as good as what Dad makes in the French Press. I have to go back for creamer and extra sugar, but I can't complain—not when he actually made it for us.

Once Nicolas tastes his cupcake and sips his coffee, he seems to relax and actually forget about the fact that we're supposed to be studying. Leonardo wolfs down his treat in a couple of bites while Nicolas savors his, looking as if he's trying to suppress sounds of ecstasy. They both finish in record time, while I've barely licked a little icing off mine—all in anticipation of taking a big, decadent bite.

Leonardo licks his thumb and smacks. "I wish we had more."

"Well, we would if you hadn't already eaten three in the car," I put in.

He's going to have to content himself with coffee and whatever he can find in the pantry.

I lifted my mug and, on second thought, set it down. A bottle of water and a half a cup of coffee seem to be more than my poor bladder can handle.

"I'll be right back," I say, hopping to my feet. I rush to the bathroom to relieve myself, then head back into the living room. Just a few steps in, I freeze on the spot.

My cupcake is gone.

Leonardo and Nicolas stare intently into their math books, looking more studious than ever.

I glare at them. "Where is my cupcake?!"

Both keep their eyes on their books, ignoring my question.

"I'll ask one more time. Where. Is. My. Cupcake?" This is not nice. Not cool at all. Who takes other people's treats? It's ... it's ... *unsweet!*

Leonardo looks up. His eyes lock with mine then quickly flick toward Nicolas in clear accusation.

I approach the table and kneel on one of the sofa cushions that lies on the floor.

"Nicolas," I say. I scrutinize his face, trying to decide whether or not to believe Leonardo. If I was going to suspect anyone, it would be my cousin, not Nicolas, but the way my best friend is acting makes me wonder.

"Nicolas, look at me," I say. His gaze lifts to mine very slowly. "Did you eat my cupcake?"

"No, Meadow. I didn't eat your cupcake," he says in an even tone. I purse my lips. The steadiness of his voice is at odds with the expression on his face. It's so unlike Nicolas that I don't know what to think.

I look back and forth between the two of them. One of Leonardo's eyebrows is raised and a small smile twitches his lips.

"Leonardo!" I say accusingly.

"What?!" he says. "Why are you looking at me? I didn't eat your cupcake. I ate three in the car on our way here, remember?"

"Yes, but I also remember you were the one wishing there were more."

"I *did not* eat your cupcake," he says, adamantly.

"I don't believe you," I say.

"Oh, and you believed *him*?" Leonardo thrusts his thumb in Nicolas's direction.

"This is ridiculous!" I say, frustrated.

I don't know who to believe. Either one of them could have eaten my cupcake. I know it's absurd to be so upset about something as inconsequential as a sweet treat, but I feel as if they've betrayed my confidence. When I left to go to the bathroom, it never occurred to me that one of them would so blatantly and carelessly deprive me of what was mine. It's like they've broken something between us and, from now on, I won't be able to leave the room without getting paranoid. Leonardo and

Nicolas are my best friends. We've all lived in the same neighborhood since we were children and always share everything. So it's not out of selfishness that I find it hard to accept the fact that my cupcake is gone.

I scratch my head, wondering why it's bothering me so much. I keep thinking it has to be a trust thing and try to make myself believe it. But something deep inside of me tells me there's a different reason. I make an effort to ignore the nagging feeling, but it doesn't go away.

An incessant itch begins in the tips of my fingers and spreads to the palms of my hands. *"You could find out,"* a voice says in the back of my head. *"You could* see, *right now, who ate your cupcake."*

Anger builds in my chest. I grind my teeth. Not this again. I don't want to use my powers. I don't! I know this niggling sensation well enough, and it's extremely difficult to ignore.

My psychic skills are something I don't like to use.

Nicolas doesn't know about them. Though Leonardo, being my cousin, is much too aware of them. Powers run in the family. Not everyone is "blessed"—Leonardo's term—but he and I definitely are. Although I prefer using the word "cursed", instead. Leonardo heartedly disagrees with my attitude. He never shies away from using his skills— not in the least. Just one of the many ways in which we're different.

I have not used my powers in a very long time. I keep them hidden behind thick walls that I learned to erect from an early age. But for some reason, every so often, I feel challenged to unleash them, as if they have a life of their own and eventually are able to override me. I guess the fact that Leonardo is always trying to get me to use them might have something to do with it. He doesn't think I should hide my powers from anyone, much less from myself. His opinion is that I should embrace my differences, my uniqueness—just the way he embraces his.

And, at the moment, it's his particular brand of powers that has me itching to discover if he's to blame for my cupcake mishap. I try not to let it affect me, but it makes me inordinately mad to think he wants to manipulate me into using my skill to solve this puzzle. It infuriates me even more to realize I'm falling prey to his game.

I should ignore the situation, should go in the kitchen to get a dry Pop Tart to replace my moist cupcake. Instead, I find myself getting angrier and angrier.

Leonardo can manipulate people. That's his power. So he could have told Nicolas to eat the cupcake, and my poor friend would have found it difficult to resist the command. True, Nicolas has lived around us for a while and that has helped him build some immunity to our skills, but he isn't 100% invulnerable—not yet anyway, maybe in another couple of years since every day he's exposed to us he becomes more resilient, subconsciously able to block people like us.

I like that about him, about our relationship. I don't want to touch him and suddenly get a flash of what Nicolas has been doing or saying. I want our friendship to be normal, without the added consequences of what my hands could reveal, even when I'm not trying.

More importantly, I'm glad he's safe from Leonardo, and his suggestive little quips. My cousin can be very juvenile when it comes to asking people to do things he finds amusing. At times, he can even be mean-spirited.

I excuse his behavior. I know I do. His family life with Uncle George and his sick mother isn't the best environment for a growing boy—not that he's a little child anymore; he's now fifteen and knows better than to go around asking his classmates to lick his shoes for his own entertainment. But he has been through a lot. His mother is in a mental facility because, for some reason, her mind cracked, leaving my uncle and Leonardo to fend for themselves.

Maybe that's why I hold him to a lower standard than I hold everyone else—even myself. I know it's illogical because if it's okay for my cousin to go around doing stupid things based on his rough childhood, then I should end up in the principal's office every day. Leonardo's childhood has been rough, but nowhere near as rough as mine. At least he still has his mother.

I shake my head. I don't want to think about that. I hate when my thoughts lead me there. It's far easier to think about my cupcake and who to blame for its disappearance.

I look at the empty plate next to my math textbook. Minutes ago, it had contained a delicious treat, and now, the only proof of its existence is a tiny smear of strawberry icing on the edge.

If I touch the plate and I concentrate, letting my walls down, allowing in the memories that people's essences always leave behind, I'd be able to see who cheated me. But I can't give in, especially when I'm pretty sure I already know what I'd see: Leonardo whispering into Nicolas's ear, instructing him to eat my cupcake, and Nicolas fighting, resisting the urge, but failing. I know he would fight it. He's my friend and he wouldn't dare break our trust, not even in that small way. We already share enough. There has to be a boundary somewhere. We can't go around taking from each other without permission. Trust begins with the small things, even if they appear unimportant. Otherwise, how could we ever trust anyone with the major things, the things that can turn our lives over their heads?

Regardless, I feel bad for distrusting Leonardo. He means well most of the time. He simply wants to have fun and that doesn't necessarily mean he's willing to break my trust just for the sake of it. At least that's what I'm trying to believe.

I fight the insistent pull, but my hand is already on the plate, and I'm taking a deep breath, allowing my mental blocks to fall away. The walls lower slowly, and little by little the images of the pasts that surround us all begin to unfold inside my mind.

Like thousands of old movies playing on top of one another images flood me. They range in color, from black and white to the brightest rainbow hues. The monochrome images seem torn at the edges, old and far away. They show me an empty lot and men in construction clothes. They walk around with tools, building the house I now live in.

Other images are not so frayed, not so dark. They possess a bit of color, like old sepia pictures or the faded images on a magazine battered by the sun. I understand these are more recent. I can tell from the clothing. It's more modern.

The sepia images blend into brighter ones. These show me the people who used to live in this house before us. I've seen their faces in other occasions. They are a family of five, one mom and four kids, no father. They move around the room like ghosts, thousands, millions of them just shuffling about in an endless cycle. They never leave. They're always here, stuck forever in time and space.

If I concentrate, I can also see slightly more colorful images. Traveling through the rainbow, time speeds up right before my eyes. I recognize the kids' faces, though now there are only three of them. They're older, and I assume one of them moved out, went to college.

I fast-forward from there to the images with the liveliest tones. They are the memories that Dad and I have left behind, memories of Nicolas and Leonardo's visits, even memories of my cat. They all live on, with no one the wiser.

With a shutter, I remove my hand from the plate and let my walls rise in a split second. I hate feeling open, vulnerable. I hate my weakness against the temptation that they represent. But, most importantly, I hate what they did to me when I was just a little girl.

I shut the thoughts away. I don't like to think about the past and recall what my skills forced me to *see*. And it's ridiculous and stupid for me to try to use them now just to figure out who ate a stupid cupcake. It doesn't matter—not compared to the possibility of inviting the kind of trouble that almost drove me crazy when my skills took on a life of their own all those years ago. I can't let myself forget that. My powers are not a game. They aren't something to be used carelessly or at all. But I get too relaxed when I'm around Nicolas and Leonardo, and I start pretending my world is normal and nothing awful has ever happened to me and my family.

Leonardo looks at me from across the coffee table, one eyebrow raised. There is a silent question on his face. He looks smug because he knows I've found out the answer to my question. He didn't use his powers to persuade Nicolas to eat my cupcake. Nicolas decided all on his own to snatch it.

But my friend didn't eat it. He hid it, carefully putting it in one of the drawers of the cabinet in the corner. Neither one of them was lying. Neither one of them betrayed my trust. They just played a joke on me.

I heave a heavy sigh. God, I have to lighten up. I should have guessed they wouldn't eat my cupcake. I should have known they'd hidden it to play a joke on me.

And now, after all my outrage and accusations, how do I get it back?

I can't just walk to the cabinet to find it, not after I accused them of wolfing it down with such certainty. So I just sit there pouting and looking sad. Maybe if Nicolas thinks I'm resigned to my *cupcakeless* fate, he will take pity on me and return it.

As sullenly as possible, I grab my notebook and pencil and pull them closer, making sure to stick my bottom lip out as far as it'll go. I put my index finger on one of the problems we've been working on and start copying it on a blank page. After writing it down, I take a sip of coffee, then stand up with a shrug.

"I guess I'll get some cookies to eat with my coffee," I announce.

I walk to the kitchen and find a box of Girl Scout cookies in the pantry. I put them on a napkin, not really planning to eat them; I know Nicolas and Leonardo will snatch them right away once I get to my cupcake back.

As I walk back into the living room, my eyes fly straight to the cupcake. It's back, sitting on its plate, looking as delicious as in the beginning. Nicolas is averting his face, probably hiding a smile that he doesn't want me to see.

Sadness hits me like a wrecking ball, then.

God, I can't even enjoy a simple joke. I've ruined it. If I was normal I would be surprised, relieved, glad, to find my cupcake back in its place. Instead, I feel nothing. No satisfaction at the thought that I will actually get to eat it or at the fact that my friends have played a joke on me.

I hate myself and my powers so much right now. I wish I could push them away and never *see* again. I don't understand why, at times like this, I find myself helpless against the urge to use the hideous skills that destroyed my five-year-old mind after my mother died.

With a heavy heart, I pretend to be surprised. I pretend to be glad to have my cupcake back. I mock-punch Nicolas on the shoulder and ask, "Did you hide it? Or was it you Leonardo?"

My cousin shakes his head in disappointment. He thinks my efforts to conceal what I can do are pathetic. For my part, I think my weakness against the desire to unleash my powers is what should be considered pathetic. Nothing else.

I want to be normal. I want to live life the way average people do. I don't want to know what happened in my house before I was ever here. I don't want to see the hordes of students that have gone through my high school year after year. I don't want to see the awful things that people do to each other, even if that means I get to see the nice things too. I just want to be like every other girl out there. And I will be. I'll never stop trying. I'll never take my walls down again.

I make this promise to myself like many times before. The last time I broke my vow was a few months back, but this relapse took longer. I know I can get there. I know I can win the battle against my curiosity, my weakness, the temptation of my powers.

I know I can live in *unreality*.

WANT TO FIND OUT MORE?

Purchase the Marked by Fate boxset and get Unreality plus 24 other full-length novels

Meadow's psychic powers ruined her life once. Now they're back and just as bent on destroying her as before. Ever since she helped solve her mother's gruesome murder twelve years ago, Meadow Bright has kept her psychic abilities locked away. As a five-year-old, the brutal visions of her mother's death nearly destroyed her. Now, a senior in high school, she still fears her nature and what opening up could do to her. But when a classmate is found viciously tortured and murdered, her powers return with a vengeance, flooding her mind with new visions and opening old wounds. Worst of all, the new victim wears the signature of her mother's killer, a man who's still in jail under a life sentence without parole. It seems that, all those years ago, she made a mistake and helped put the wrong man in jail. Now, she must redeem herself before more people die.

Connect with Ingrid

Want to find our more? Purchase the Marked by Fate boxset.
I hope you've enjoyed Unsweet

If you liked this short story, find out more about Meadow, Nicolas, and Leonardo in my upcoming novel *Unreality*. Make sure to follow me on your favorite social media outlet for release information and dates.

Visit me at ingridseymour.com to hear my latest news and get your free copy of Keeper, Book 1 of The Morphid Chronicles.

Follow me online
Instagram: @ingrid_seymour | Twitter: @ingrid_seymour |
Facebook: @ingridseymourAuthor | Pinterest: @ingridseymour |

About The Author

Ingrid Seymour loves, loves, loves to write. She's a young and new adult author. She writes in a variety of genres including romance, urban fantasy, paranormal and horror. She loves pizza and sushi, Sunkist and gum. She believes in vampires, witches, but not zombies (uh-uh, never!) She writes to loud music, daydreams constantly and spends too much time in twitter!! Find her there?

Ingrid has incredible fun doing what she does, but more than anything she enjoys hearing from her readers. It's a dream come true.

Kingsman

An Edinburgh Seer Prequel

Alisha Klapheke

CHAPTER ONE

Smoke curled into the pines and starlight, blending with the staccato laughs and muted conversations of everyone chumming together in the forest. Thane sucked the last of his stupid cigarette and crushed it beneath his kingsman boot.

"This is going to kill us," Bran said, raising his bushy black eyebrows at his own cigarette.

Thane shrugged. "Who said I wanted to live?" He immediately hated himself. "I'm sorry, pal. I'm just being …"

"You're being the crabbit lad you always are." Bran grinned. "It's only that golden hair of yours that keeps the girls putting up with your moods."

"Shut your gob." Thane shoved him gently with a shoulder and headed toward the loch.

Moonlight gleamed over the lapping water and a good, cool breeze pushed against his black-rimmed glasses. Insects whirred. Spring creatures were out in force. He wished he could stand here forever.

"If that lot would quiet down, it'd be fairly peaceful." Thane closed his eyes and soaked in the scent of the night air—clean water and pine trees.

"It's only peaceful because you can't see the hunters," Bran said. Thane scowled and Bran nodded at a clutch of low bushes. A branch moved. The white petals weighing it down lost a few petals. "There's surely a feral cat in there beheading a wee mousie. Blood everywhere. And there." He looked up into the twisted tree limbs. "I'd bet my britches there's a snake swallowing cute things above."

"Joyful as a funeral, you are," Thane said. "I thought being crabbit was my job."

"I'm simply pointing out the truth. Now, let's crack open this bit of fun I brought." Bran pulled a shining flask from his pocket and unscrewed the lid.

There were benefits to knowing a bar keep. Bran gathered gossip and information, for Thane's family. Clan Campbell used the intel to help the king keep his crown and hunt down rebels. Bran, with no family of his own, kept Thane company too. It was good to have a friend who could keep secrets when he needed it.

Thane took a swig from the flask. Whisky—better than most had sitting in their pockets—slithered down his throat, hot and perfect. Laphroiag? The stuff cost a pretty penny. "Didn't realize I meant that much to you." He fluttered his lashes.

Bran rolled his eyes.

Thane handed the flask back. "You win this stuff in a card game with a sixth sense you're hiding from me?"

Bran cocked his head and pursed his lips. "You've seen my luck," he said wryly.

"Aye. So, you stole it."

"How dare you insult my honor?"

"You can't blame me for mistakes when you're the one filling me with whisky."

Bran laughed, but the sound lacked its usual full-bellied bark. "Let's head to town. I have early work tomorrow."

Thane probably shouldn't have joked about sixth sensers. There'd been too many rough arrests lately. Many of the sensers were tied to those plotting against the king, those lousy Dionadair rebels.

Pushing the worry away, Thane followed Bran to his friend's very red, very fine car—the only thing Bran put his bar keep money into. Bran tossed Thane the keys.

"Really?" Thane asked.

"Och, sure."

Thane's phone buzzed. Cupping the cool keys in his palm, he read the caller's name on the screen. It was a punch in the gut. His father, Nathair Campbell, head of the king's security and the second most feared man in Scotland, didn't call to simply say *Cheers*.

"Thane?" Bran had just opened the other door. He shut it quietly and came back around the car.

"Hold on." Thane pressed the button and turned away from Bran, tucking one arm under the other and feeling sick. "What is it?" he said into the phone.

"You answered on the second ring." Nathair's voice was rough like he'd been yelling. "I'd call that progress. My last lesson must've made an impression."

Thane knew his father was on the right side—the king's side—against the insidious rebels that were creeping their foul way south and claiming the king wasn't the true heir, but the way he went about his business …

"I have a job for you," Nathair said.

Thane swallowed. The weird tremor Nathair's voice always shot into Thane's chest hit hard. "I'm listening."

"You're in the bit of forest near the loch, aye?"

"I am."

"A girl is there. About your age. Red hair. A tattoo of a stupid four-leaf clover on her neck."

"What about her?" Thane forced himself to ask. He looked at the scars that crisscrossed his knuckles.

"Nothing that means you need to have that tone of voice with me, boy."

Thane gritted his teeth, but kept his tongue. Bran shrugged, asking what was going on.

"Her mother has some information she doesn't care to give us," Nathair said. "I'd like you to influence the girl. Show her the Campbells aren't so bad. Maybe she'll go home and mention she spent the evening with one. It doesn't have to get ugly."

Thane understood. It'd be a quiet, subtle threat to the family's safety. The Campbells could reach anyone anytime they wished. It was a better situation than it could be. Some people were taken for questioning and Thane didn't want to think about how that went. It definitely wasn't pleasant. "All right. I know what to do." He ended the call, staring at a finger smear on the shiny car's red surface.

"Thane, pal. What is it?"

"Nathair."

Bran tucked his lips to one side and mumbled something. He was loyal to the Campbells, to the crown, but he had a word or two to say about the way things ran sometimes.

Thane tucked his phone away. The energy cell inside heated his leg through his trousers. A part of him wanted to toss the thing into the loch so all he'd have against him was the cool night and colonial cotton. "There's a girl. I'm supposed to … talk to her."

"I have your back, pal," Bran said, voice dark as a grave.

A smile surprised Thane. He rarely had much to smile about after being assigned to a job. "Thanks. It's good to have a friend even if he is as old as Granny MacAllister."

Bran hit him hard in the kidney and Thane let out a *whoo*. "Three years more than you and I get granny status. Kids today, I tell you." He shook his head.

The pine needles hid their approach as they made their way toward a group of girls and guys by the biggest pine. The red-headed girl in question stood with a hand on her hip and said something that made her friends laugh and elbow one another.

Maybe she was smart. Determined. Proud. Good.

Or maybe she wasn't any of those things. Still. She didn't deserve to be played just because of what her mother may or may not know.

Stopping, Thane yanked his glasses off and rubbed his face roughly. Why was he thinking like this? Nathair was terrible, but he was on the right side. The king's side. The side of peace. Besides, it wasn't like Thane could have any relationship with this girl even if she *was* all the things he'd love to see in a girl. He was about to trick her, fool her, scare her family.

He had to focus on the job and his goals. That was it. He wasn't a good guy today, but in real life, heroes had to be bad sometimes too.

Chapter Two

They made it to the girl and her group and Bran tossed the shortest of the guys his fancy whisky.

"That's not a bad way to start it," the short guy said. "I'm Rog. Cheers." He tipped the flask up, took a drink, then passed it to another guy with a lot of fluff around his middle.

"What did you lot think of that crash on Front Street last night?" Thane asked, trying to break the ice.

"A real mess, that was," the girl said. "Hi." She nodded at him in greeting and ran a finger over her tattoo like she was nervous about it, like she wasn't really the kind of person who had the guts to pay for a needle to the throat even though she obviously was. "I'm Jodie."

"Thane."

"Heard the lorry driver lost an arm," Rog said.

Jodie's eyes widened. "Ah no. I hope not."

Thane touched her forearm with one finger, then let his hand drop away from her freckled skin. Jodie blinked and didn't step away. A good sign. "He'll be all right, hen. His family has money. They'll get him a fine prosthetic."

"A what?"

"A replacement arm. You know. It's a rough life, I'm sure, but maybe with the prosthetic, it'll be a little easier." He wouldn't be plying this girl for information. She wasn't the sharpest. He'd have to give her something to talk about at home, some reason to bring him up. A bit of macking was in order. Trying to get interested in the line of Jodie's neck, Thane leaned close. She could've done with a little more flesh on her bones. He had to remember that despite the disgusting nature of the job—trying to snog a girl because one's father told one to—this was for peace, for his beloved Scotland.

"How do you know about the lorry driver's family?" Rog asked.

Bran asked Thane a silent question. Did he want to reveal his family name? Would it help? Thane gave him a nod.

"Our Thane here is a Campbell," Bran said.

Rog laughed nervously. His friends crossed their arms over their chests and shifted their weight. They were worried. Good. They wouldn't bother too much when he tried to pull Jodie away for a bit.

Jodie studied Thane's mouth, suddenly even more interested in him. "You are a Campbell?" Awe shaded her voice.

"Aye."

Bran took the flask and put it to his mouth, acting like he was still drinking. "His father is Nathair Campbell."

The group was properly wowed and Thane felt his cheeks heat a bit. His stomach twisted. He was glad Bran was staying sober though. That was wise. Good of Bran to do it for Thane. This was a real friend. Not someone simply impressed with who his father was. Thane would have to pay Bran back somehow, but for now he had to focus on the job.

Jodie touched the back of Thane's hand. "Want to take a walk?" she asked. "Just to the loch. To talk."

"Jodie." Rog started forward.

"We're just going over there." She pointed. "Just for a chat."

Bran held out his flask again, then bumped Rog with it. "Three drams left and I bet you can't finish it in one go."

Rog snorted. "Oh you're on, my friend."

Giving Bran a nod over Jodie's head, Thane led the girl toward the silvery water, just a little ways from the group. Thane let his hand trail down the girl's knobby spine. She went on about classes she'd taken down at St. Andrews, where Thane was going soon. The study talk turned into chatter about a club that was supposed to open in town. Thane let her go on for what felt like an eternity. By the time she was done, Thane was nearly dead with boredom and he felt awful about it. This was a serious job, a dangerous situation and he needed to care more about this girl. She could've said something of worth.

"Are you listening?" Tossing a smooth stone into the loch, she smiled over her shoulder. Then she spotted Bran's very nice car in the park. "That yours?" She produced a wee tube of gloss and slicked her lips.

He did still have the car keys. If they drove away, the group wouldn't interfere with his job. "Um. Yeah. Want to go for a ride? We can come right back."

"Aye. I'd like that."

Daft girl, going off with a near stranger. They'd only talked an hour or so. Not nearly enough to know anybody. Thane's phone buzzed from his pocket. A message from Father blinked across the screen.

Take her to the safe house near the fisheries. Now.

He gripped the phone, hoping the message didn't mean anything too nefarious. Knuckles aching as he pressed them into the metal, he prayed, he wished that taking her to the house only meant the kingsmen there wanted to talk to Jodie. Or maybe have a meeting with her and her mother. That Nathair had already worked it all out and Jodie's family was firmly on the right side of things and no one needed bloodied. It was true. Had to be true. He couldn't bring this girl to the safe house if he thought anything different. And he *had* to bring her. There was no other choice that involved him living through the week with his face intact. Yes. He was only worrying. All was fine.

Unless it wasn't.

Jodie climbed into the car. It was all so painfully convenient. He should've been pleased that the job was going to be this easy, that as he drove down the winding road the air tumbled through his hair pleasantly, that the car under his control was a great, powerful beast, and that a red head's hand had slid up his leg. But his heart burned and crumbled along its edges. The muscle beat weakly in his chest. This wasn't a fun, free time like it appeared to be. This was work, what he did every day for his mother's safety, for his Scotland with its towering, green mountains, fierce men and women, gray sea, and peat-brown rivers. Thane's heart healed a bit and thrummed, stronger now remembering the reasons he did what he did. He refused to let Dionadair rebels tear Scotland apart with blood, lies, and death.

Jodie's skirt fluttered and showed her thigh. She noticed him noticing and took his hand off the gearshift. Smoothing his hand up her leg, she gave him the look that said he'd be permitted to do exactly as he pleased if he wanted to stop the car and have a bit of fun.

A jolt of heat traveled the length of him. His mind and the better parts of his heart knew why he was here now with this girl, but his body … it had simpler motivations. He started to say now was a good time to pull off to the side of the road, but he bit the words and swallowed them. Nathair had said take her to the house and that what he would do. He didn't need to canoodle. His lesser needs would just have to wait until he found someone he could maybe actually have a relationship with. Or the next girl Nathair ordered him to get close to.

"You from Inveraray?" Thane asked, moving his thoughts back into focus.

"No. We're from up near Inverness. But my mum took a job here so here we are. I like it though."

"Oh?" The road pulled left and showed them the backside of a tavern and an inn.

A man in a dirty apron sat on a barrel outside the latter's door. He whistled. "Richie! Nice ride. We all know whose side you're on, eh?"

Jodie paled and gripped the edge of her seat.

"It's all right. The glaikit ape is no real traitor. He is just taking the piss out of a man with a better date and a better ride."

Exhaling, Jodie smiled, and her perfume whuffed through the air, all sour fruit and too many flowers. "You're a kind one."

Urban legends flowed around the Campbell name like diseased floodwater. Stuff about assassins and the underground cells in Edinburgh where all sorts of torture supposedly went on. It wasn't that bad. It couldn't be. But Thane knew what she meant: he was more merciful than most Campbells.

"You know, we aren't as horrible as some like to think," he said, his words darker than he'd meant them to be.

Jodie went white again. "I didn't mean that."

He held out a hand and she glanced at the formulas and symbols tattooed along his fingers. "No, it's okay, hen. You've heard things. I mean, my father is … well, he is what he must be in his line of work." He pushed away the thought of Nathair's hand raised against his mother, how Nathair did *not* need to be like *that*. Not ever. "And not all of us Campbells enjoy scaring the shite out of people." Cousin Rodric did, but that was beside the point.

"I didn't think you were evil or anything."

He raised his eyebrows.

"All right. Maybe a little. But a good kind of evil." She pressed her chest against his arm, her sour sweet perfume choking him. "You proved that by taking me on a drive. And you must be smart with all those number tattoos."

Pouting a little, she clicked her safety belt, moved it away, and pushed even closer. She sat nearly on his lap, his left arm under her leg. Her lips landed on his neck, then feathered up to his ear. She wasn't a bad kisser, he had to give her that. If only she didn't smell like a market fruit stall left in the sun for a week, she probably would've been more tempting.

"I enjoy chemistry and mathematics. You always know exactly when you're right and when you're wrong."

Her teeth grazed his earlobe. "Why's that?"

"If you're wrong, you either explode something or end up on the ground not realizing how you ended up there."

"Oh," she said absently. She took his chin in her fingers and turned his mouth to hers.

"I do need to keep us on the road," he said around her lips.

Huffing, she slid back into her seat. "Where are we going anyway?"

"One of my houses." He had to reassure her. Keep her from growing tetchy.

"One?"

"One." He smoothed a circle on her bare knee and watched her grin reappear.

The only sound was the engine's thrum and the wind. Thane's palm began to sweat on the steering wheel as she stared at the side of his head.

"I would've said we could go to my tenth palace, but it's pretty far off," he joked.

Then she broke into laughs and he joined her. It was ridiculous. The Campbells had so many houses, properties everywhere. A weight pressed into Thane's shoulders. This girl, this Jodie, looked like every girl he'd ever met, full of kind fun and if not innocence, then the joy of living. He gritted his teeth, wishing for things he shouldn't again.

Chapter Three

The safe house welcomed them with a curving drive and a red brick face. They slipped out of Bran's car and headed up the front steps. Inside, the hand hewn wood floors and red-painted walls smelled like tart lemons and years of choking cigar smoke. A woman in a crisp, long skirt and a kingsman jacket clicked out of a back room and came forward with a hand outstretched.

"Are you Mrs. Campbell?" Jodie asked, shaking the woman's hand.

She laughed breathily as another kingsman appeared in the hall, his Campbell colors giving Thane that same old feeling—a head-spinning mix, two parts fierce loyalty and one part a cold, cold fear. His mother wore the colors as she talked to him about her latest addition to the garden at their estate. But the Campbell colors also showed on Nathair when he beat Thane with a belt after a particularly difficult lecture session on the ins and outs of being a Campbell.

"They're … my father's employees," Thane said, not caring that both the man and the woman had pinched up their mouths at the disrespect. These two were probably pretty high up in Campbell ranking, but if they were only at this safe house, they weren't as high and mighty as they wanted to think. "We're going to the gardens out back to see what's in bloom."

Jodie wrinkled her nose. "Gardens?"

"It's actually really beautiful this time of year."

"Don't you have a room here? It's late. I could use a rest." She smiled like a fox in the henhouse.

A rest. Right. Sure. "No. We're headed to the flowers, hen." He grabbed her hand to tug her out of there before the two insulted lackeys could do something she'd like a lot less than boring greenery.

The woman's hand flashed out and tore Jodie from Thane's grip.

"What are you doing?" Jodie snapped. Her red hair was mussed. It stuck to her forehead.

The man nodded at the woman and she produced a cloth from her pocket. "We'll take it from here, young Thane."

"No. I haven't heard from my father and I don't think you are supposed to do anything. I'm just here to talk to Jodie and—"

"What is this?" Jodie's voice grew shrill. "What are you doing?"

The woman pushed her way between Thane and Jodie. "It will be fine, Miss Jodie, if you simply come with us. Your mother won't be hurt if you simply come with us."

Red splotches sprang up all over Jodie's cheeks and neck. Thane's stomach churned. His hands wanted to reach out and grab Jodie and take her away from here. Arguments tried to crawl up his throat, but he pushed them down and kept his hands at his sides. Nathair's words, Clan Campbell's motto, rang through his head like bells.

Ne Obliviscaris. Never forget. No matter what, Nathair had said hundreds of times, you are a Campbell and you are loyal to the crown and loyal to your family and none else. You do as you're told by your Campbell elders. The rebels have tried to kill us but we never die. We never forget what it means to be a Campbell.

Thane stared at the scars on his knuckles and that one on his thumb, remembering the day he earned it. He'd only been ten and there had been so much blood. Not his blood, another man's. A traitor's blood he himself spilled.

Never forget.

And so Thane turned away from the now hysterical Jodie whose questions fell to a muffled yelling as he slammed the front door and walked down the steps. His head spun like it always did after a tough job.

Bran ran up the drive. "What is it? What's happened?"

A blue van sat behind Bran's red car. Bran must've borrowed it. "They're taking Jodie and her mother in for questioning, looks like. They took custody of her. My father's people did. Right when we walked inside. He didn't warn me. But it's right. This is the side of peace. Right, Bran?"

Bran's eyes drew down at the sides. "In the darkness, there is no peace, only hunters you can't see."

Heat seared Thane's throat like he wanted to scream or shout. Bran didn't understand. He hadn't lived this life. He was a good friend, but he didn't understand this.

"That's the only peace we can have," Thane spat. "A peace given by hunters in the dark. I am a hunter and I will give Scotland peace."

Pain leeched from Thane's hands. His nails had cut into his palms. Bran put a gentle hand on his shoulder and let Thane be Thane. It would've been better if Bran had yelled. But when did life go as Thane wanted? Despite the prestige, money, brains, and looks he'd been given, his life was a hell crafted by vicious rebels and a devil of a father.

WANT TO FIND OUT MORE?

Purchase the Marked by Fate boxset and get The Edinburgh Seer plus 24 other full-length novels

Magic. History. Romance.

In an alternate, modern-day Scotland, a king runs the country like it's the 17th century rather than the 21st.

Sixth-sensers like Aini MacGregor face the firing squad if they're found out, and when her father is abducted, she fears her time is up. The kingsmen and the Campbells who do his dirty work must know something is off at her father's lab. But why would they take him instead of her?

Alongside her father's mysterious apprentice, Aini sets out to find some answers. A trail of artifacts embedded with visions takes them through passageways, ruins, and age-old cemeteries where they find rebels.

But nothing is more dangerous than the ruthless betrayal she doesn't see coming.

Connect with Alisha

Want to find out more? Purchase the Marked by Fate boxset.
I hope you've enjoyed Kingsman

Visit me at alishaklapheke.com to hear my latest news and to get your free
copy of Claimed, An Uncommon World Prequel

Follow me online
Instagram: @alishaklapheke | Twitter: @alishaklapheke |
Facebook: @authoralishaklapheke |

About the Author

Alisha Klapheke is the author of the Uncommon World series. She began writing as a child and hasn't stopped since. When she isn't crafting new stories, she can be found teaching kids, teens, and adults Muay Thai kickboxing, Krav Maga, Brazilian Jiu Jitsu, and self-defense at a Nashville martial arts school she and her husband own and operate. Traveling inspires much of Alisha's fiction. The varying art, architecture, foods, and rituals worldwide fuel her passion for creating fantastical people and places with heart and soul. This year, she is off to Japan for another adventure.

BEFORE THE MAGIC

Prequel to Unlikely Magic

Lena Mae Hill

CHAPTER ONE

It's around noon on a Monday when I find my father's body.

"Dad?" I call, tapping on his door with my knuckles. No answer. I turn the knob slowly, because you never want to walk in on your dad getting dressed. "Dad?" This time, I whisper, peering into the darkened bedroom. The blinds are drawn, but they let in enough light to illuminate the outline of his body in the bed.

I step into the bedroom, leaving the door open, and cross the room, my bare feet silent on the thick beige carpet. "Dad." I give his shoulder a shake. Instead of the usual sigh and groggy mumble, he doesn't respond. And the way his body moves when I shake him, the slow and heavy feeling of it, sends a shiver running through me. I repeat his name, this time louder, almost shouting. My dad can be a heavy sleeper, but not this heavy.

I keep repeating his name, like he's going to wake up suddenly and say, *"Gotcha!"* Because sometimes, Dad has a weird sense of humor. Just not usually when he first wakes up. I woke hours ago, so used to getting up for school that I woke even when he didn't come in to wake me. When he didn't come in, I remembered that he was out late for a university function the night before, and he would probably sleep in.

Instead of getting up, making myself breakfast, and catching the bus or calling my best friend Emmy for a ride, I rolled over and went back to sleep. I'd been up late, too, talking on the phone to Emmy about modeling agencies that might take a look at fourteen-year-olds. I almost never missed school, so it wasn't like one day was going to hurt. As I fell asleep, I thought I heard Dad moving around, and I thought any minute he'd come get me up and take me in a few minutes late.

But now it's the middle of the day, and I can't wake him up. In a panic, I scream at his body. "Get up, Dad! Get up! I mean it!"

He doesn't move, doesn't so much as twitch. I lay my hand across his forehead, then pull it back, horrified by how cool he feels. A shudder goes through me as I stand over the mountain of his body. My father is a big man—burly would be putting it nicely. He used to be burly, when I was a kid. He'd tower over the other dads at school events like a beardy mountain man. But a botany professor only gets so much time to be active, and aside from some racquetball games with the other professors, he doesn't do much. He definitely put on some pounds as he approached his fortieth birthday. But surely not so many that he's in danger of a heart attack.

"Dad," I whisper one more time, backing away from the bed. Then I run out of his room, down the hall, and out the front door. Still wearing the oversized t-shirt and cotton shorts I wore to bed, I run barefoot along the sidewalk to the small white house next door. I run up onto the porch and bang on the door with both fists.

"Hold your horses," comes a slightly irritated, quavering voice from within. After what seems like ten minutes, the door opens a crack and Mrs. Nguyen peers out at me from under the chain lock. "Stella? Why aren't you in school?"

"My dad," I say, my throat tightening. "He's ... he's not ..."

"Not what?" She unlocks the chain and thrusts her head out the door to survey our tan brick, ranch-style house as if it might have suddenly been converted into a heroine den.

"He's not waking up," I tell her. "I shook him, and ... and ..." It strikes me then how stupid it was to run over here before I checked all the usual signs, like his pulse and breathing. "When I yelled for him to wake up, he just … didn't."

"My poor dear," Mrs. Nguyen says, her whole demeanor changing from suspicion to concern. It's not as if she doesn't know us. She was my babysitter for years, until last summer, when Dad decided I could stay home alone as long as she was next door in case of emergency. But she's suspicious of everyone, so I don't take it too personally that she acts like I'm here to rob her.

"Sorry," I mutter as she steps back and opens the door wider.

"Come in while I get my shoes," she says, turning away from the door to the row of tiny shoes neatly lined up against the wall in the entrance. "I guess you've called for help?"

"No," I admit. I step back to let her pass, then follow her down the steps to the walkway.

"Well, that's a first," she says as we move at a snail's pace toward my house. "I've never seen you without your phone glued to one hand or the other. I'd think you'd need a surgeon to get that thing removed."

"Want me to run ahead and call an ambulance?" I ask, cursing myself silently for not doing that first. These precious minutes could have cost Dad his life.

"For what?" she asks. "You don't know anything's wrong yet. Maybe he had a glass too many last night. I wouldn't put it past Owen. I'm always telling him …" I grind my teeth and fight the urge to push past her as she takes our four front steps one foot at a time, muttering about "this old body."

Finally, we step through the front door. Mrs. Nguyen stops to sniff the air, as if she might smell what's wrong, as if she can smell death from the front door.

"You had microwave popcorn for dinner last night, didn't you?" she asks, turning an accusing glare on me.

"That's not important," I explode. "My dad might be dead right now."

"Then there's no hurry," she says, shuffling down the hall. "I told him I'd keep a watch on you. Popcorn for dinner. Imagine! You know what that kind of junk does to your skin?"

"My skin is fine," I assure her, balling my hands into fists to keep from pushing her aside, running to Dad, begging him to be okay. To wake up. To be alive.

"You think you'll be young and pretty forever," she says, shaking her head.

Finally, after what must be several hours, we reach the door to my room, and I slip inside to grab my phone. When I step back into the hall, Mrs. Nguyen has made it another three steps. But we make it to Dad's room eventually. Mrs. Nguyen approaches the bed and pokes my father in the shoulder with one sharp, yellowed nail. "Owen?" she says. "Wake up or I'm going to climb in bed with you. It's been a while since this old body's held a nice young man like you."

Oh my God. My ears are going to bleed.

I'm about to text Emmy and share the horror, but the realization hits before I can.

Dad might be dead.

My father, the indestructible mountain of a man, the guy who could take a walk in a state park and name every kind of tree in the park by the leaves alone in summer and the bark in winter. A guy who came to every parent teacher conference and father-daughter dance and bring your daughter to work day. The guy who explained puberty and periods to me, red and sweating all the while, but determinedly powering through what was probably the most embarrassing moment of both our lives.

Dad can't be dead. He'll get up, he'll tie on the ruffled Barbie apron I bought him as a gag gift, the one he's worn proudly ever since, and he'll make a batch of carrot muffins, because if you call them carrot muffins instead of carrot cake, it's okay to eat them for breakfast. "That's one serving of vegetables down," he'll say with a wink, as he does every time he makes them. And then he'll ask if I'm sure other girls wear that kind of thing to school, because, ahem, that's an awful lot of skin showing.

"He's okay, right?" I ask from the doorway of his bedroom, not daring to go in. If I stay out here, I don't have to see him and admit that living bodies don't move so very little.

"If that threat didn't get him up, I can't say he is," Mrs. Nguyen says, straightening from where she was bent over him. "Call Dr. Golden."

"Dr. Golden? Why? Is he alive?" I ask, confused what the family doctor is going to do for him if he's not.

"I'm afraid it doesn't look good, honey," she says, hobbling toward me. "But we'll have her take a look."

"Shouldn't we call an ambulance?"

"I don't think he's going to need one of those," Mrs. Nguyen says quietly. She puts a hand on my shoulder, and the lines in her old face look suddenly deeper than before.

"Are you sure?" I whisper.

She nods, her lips tight. "Come sit in the kitchen while we wait," she says. "Have you called your school?"

"My school? For what?"

"I'll let them know you're not going to be in today," she says. "Or the rest of the week, if you need it."

Together, we walk to the kitchen. I sit at the table while she makes her slow way around the kitchen, grumbling about our lack of a tea kettle. I think her head might explode when I tell her we use the coffee maker for hot water.

While she puts on water to heat in a saucepan, I watch dust motes fall through the warm autumn sunlight slanting in from the kitchen window. After a few minutes, Mrs. Nguyen brings a cup of tea and sets it in front of me.

"I guess I should text Emmy," I say. But when I try, I don't know how to say it. There's no good way to tell your best friend that your dad is dead. Finally, I send the simple line, as if saying it bluntly will convince me it's true.

My dad died.

Chapter Two

Dr. Golden arrives, her kind face earnest and concerned as she asks what happened. I tell her what little I know, which is nothing. She looks exactly like the kind of doctor who still makes house calls. She's wearing scrubs today and carrying her doctor's bag, but she still looks like what Dad jokingly calls her—a witch doctor. She has two long, thick blonde braids that hang down her back all the way to her hips, and she never wears a drop of makeup. "I'll go have a look," she says, slipping from the kitchen.

I start to rise, but Mrs. Nguyen puts a hand on mine. "No need to upset yourself," she says. "Let's wait and see what she has to say."

Five minutes later, Dr. Golden comes back and sets her bag down next to the entranceway between the kitchen and living room. "I'm so sorry, Stella," she says.

Numbly, I nod my head. She asks why I'm not in school, then about Dad—when was the last time I saw him, alive presumably, and how he's been lately. If I've noticed any symptoms. If he's been acting strange. Eating anything unusual. Complaining of aches and pains. I answer the best I can.

I saw him yesterday morning, when he told me he had a work function and would be home late. I didn't wake up when he came in, as I'm used to his late nights, and him coming home past midnight is nothing unusual. Honestly, I don't pay much attention to his health, as he never complains about it. As far as eating unusual things and acting strange, I'd have been more concerned if he *wasn't* doing that.

Dr. Golden smiles sadly at that. She's been my doctor since we moved to Oklahoma when I was a kid. In fact, she was part of the reason we moved here—to be near good doctors, because I was a frail and sickly child, prone to everything from allergies to night terrors to migraines. She and Mrs. Nguyen are the closest thing to family friends we have. Now, as they stand there looking at me, I feel like I should say something, but I don't know what to say. There are no words for this situation.

"Why don't you come stay at my house for the rest of the day," Mrs. Nguyen says.

"That's a good idea," Dr. Golden says. "I'll call in an ambulance, and they'll have to confirm the cause and time of—" She breaks off, obviously realizing that I'm sitting right there, still too shell-shocked to absorb this. My dad, my tree-nerd dad with his big laugh and his backyard barbecues, is dead. How can it be true? He was just alive yesterday, just talking about the candy store that doubles as an old-fashioned soda fountain that we've loved since moving here. And I was rolling my eyes at him and telling him I wasn't a baby anymore. But I let him wear me down and convince me to go with him this weekend, because I secretly still love it.

I stand from the table, my tea untouched. Dr. Golden puts a comforting hand on my shoulder and asks if I'm okay being alone.

"I'm fine," I say, and to my surprise, my voice sounds totally normal. "I'll just go change, and then I'll go to Mrs. Nguyen's. Like you said, it's probably best." My legs are stiff, as if I'm maneuvering a doll's body as I walk down the hall to my room. I stand in front of my dresser with the drawers open and clothes spilling out. It's such a mess. How will I ever decide what to wear?

And then it hits me. It doesn't matter what I wear. For the first time in years, I don't plan an outfit, take a picture, and ask for Emmy's opinion. I just pull something on, the first thing on top of the mess. When I reach the kitchen, Dr. Golden and Mrs. Nguyen exchange looks. Apparently cut-off denim shorts and a tight halter top are not appropriate when your father just died. But how am I supposed to know this? How am I to know anything without Dad? If he hadn't been there to poke good-natured fun at my drag-queen-esque first attempt at makeup, I would never have learned how to apply it at all.

"Why don't you grab a sweater to bring with you?" Dr. Golden says with a pained smile. "It's not that warm today."

Right. Because it's October, not summer. I pull one of Dad's hoodies off the hook near the door. It's huge, engulfing me in an ocean of his dad-smell, drowning me and saving me at the same time. They don't say anything. They let me take it. After all, I'm his only family. Everything he has is mine. Which is not saying much, but it does give me the rights to his grubby hoodies.

Chapter Three

There are arrangements to be made and no one to make them. Up until this moment, I never really missed having a family. Dad was enough. We had each other, and we had friends. I didn't know how to miss something I never had. But now, as Mrs. Nguyen asks me what kind of flowers I want at the funeral, where I want it held, I just shake my head. I have no idea how any of this works. I've never even been to a funeral.

I tell her to do what she thinks is best, to do what she thinks Dad would have liked. They were friends, in some weird way I never understood, some grownup way. Sometimes, after I went to bed, she'd come over, and I'd hear them laughing into the night. Dad said old people get insomnia. Although I never knew his mother and therefore never missed having her in our lives, maybe he missed her. Whatever it was, Mrs. Nguyen knew him well enough that she can plan a funeral better than I can. She's planned one before, when she lost her husband.

But I can't stay in my shell forever. Mrs. Nguyen comes into her guest bedroom the second night to tell me the hospital reports came back showing that Dad died of natural and ordinary causes, that there is no reason for autopsies or investigations or anything to delay the funeral.

Then she sits on the edge of the quilted, flower spread next to me. "You'll need to meet with a case worker tomorrow," she says. "They're sending out one to talk to you about a placement."

"A placement?" I ask. "What's that?"

"You can't live at home," she says. "You're fourteen, Stella."

"Oh. I … I hadn't even thought of that."

"I know you haven't," she says, patting my knee. "I'll talk to them, too, see what we can all come up with together."

"I guess you don't want a kid."

"Oh, they wouldn't look at me. I'm too old," she says, reaching out to pat my cheek. "But I'll be watching over you, wherever you go. Your father is, too. Don't ever forget that, Stella." She takes my hand in her gnarled one and squeezes.

For the first time since Dad died, I start worrying about myself again. Dad always took care of me. I was loved, cared for, safe and wanted. I belonged. What's going to happen to me now? I'm an orphan. I have no one.

The next day, I meet with a group of people from the state—a case worker, a lawyer, a social worker, a child advocate … I don't even try to keep them straight. All I can think about is the life I had. It wasn't perfect. We didn't have a lot of money for stuff like cool clothes, Dad was clueless about ninety percent of things relating to teenage girls, my best friend was allowed to date but I wasn't. But now, all those things seem trivial beyond imagining. I had it all, and now it's gone. My family. My friends. My school.

But even knowing that, I can't seem to summon any more tears. I know I should be sad, but I'm not. I'm not anything.

"Do you have anyone we can contact?"

"No," I say. "It's just me and Dad."

"Actually," Mrs. Nguyen says, scratching her head. "There was an ex-wife …"

Tears swim in my eyes again. I barely register what they're saying. Of course there was an ex-wife. One who died in childbirth.

But the next day, they're back.

"We've tried to contact your mother, but so far, we haven't been able to reach her," a sympathetic but tired-looking black lady is saying. "Do you have any idea where your father would have kept her contact information?"

"My—my mother? No," I say, shaking my head. "She died when I was born. And she didn't have any family."

"Actually, your mother is very much alive, according to our records," says a bespectacled man with thinning blonde hair. The lawyer? Social worker? "She lives in Arkansas, just a few hours away."

"That can't be."

"You're one lucky girl," the black woman says. Her subtle lipstick is seeping into the fine lines around her mouth. "You have family to take care of you. We always prefer that to foster care. Don't worry, we'll do everything we can to track her down for you."

"Right," I say. "I'm lucky."

Four days later, I'm standing over my father's coffin, saying goodbye. I want to reach in and touch him, to convince myself this is real. But I don't want it to be real. He looks so ordinary, as if he's only sleeping there, with his big barrel chest sinking almost imperceptibly as he breathes out.

My eyes snap back to his chest. I saw it move. I'm sure of it. But I stare for a full minute without so much as blinking, and it remains as still as death, as still as what he is now—remains. He's not my father anymore. When they talk about him, they don't call him Owen. They call him *the remains*. What do you want done with the remains? Did he leave any instructions for the handling of the remains?

We were never religious, but Mrs. Nguyen says they call him that because this is all that remains. All I have left, for another minute, maybe two, until they close the lid and take him away. I try to keep the words of the social worker in my mind. I'm lucky. I have family who will take care of me. A mother I never knew existed. Maybe more than that. If she's alive, who else is there? Grandparents, aunts and uncles, cousins who could have been like sisters to me?

That's what Emmy has. A big extended family that fills her house with noise and laughter on Christmas, while me and Dad have our dinner-for-two and watch a classic Christmas movie. I curl my hands around the lip of the casket, fighting the urge to grab him and shake him. To ask how he could have lied to me about something so important all this time. There must be a reason.

But it's too late to ask him why.

I look down at him, waiting for him to become a stranger, a corpse, an unconnected body. He doesn't. He's still Dad, lying with his big hands folded across his big chest, his big body clad in a big suit, so unlike the usual khakis and flannel he always wore to work or the huge t-shirts with cheesy tree quotes he wore at home.

"He looks peaceful, doesn't he?" Dr. Golden asks, stepping up beside me. I know what this means. It means I've been standing over the casket for too long. I'm freaking people out. That, or they're ready to haul away the body.

"I think I saw him breathe," I whisper out of the corner of my mouth.

"Oh, honey," she says, resting her hand on my back. "Sometimes, there are … gases trapped …" She stops speaking and draws a long breath, touches her fingers to her red-rimmed eyes.

I haven't cried today. If I cry now, it becomes real. At home, in my room, no one sees it, so it doesn't have to be real. It can be a nightmare. I can still wake up.

"I think it's time," she says after a minute. "I'm so sorry, Stella." Her kind blue eyes shine with tears.

I nod, and turn one more time, trying to memorize Dad's serene face before they close him in the casket. "Bye, Dad," I whisper.

And then it's time to lead the procession. No one comes to the gravesite, like in movies. It's just me and Mrs. Nguyen and a couple guys with a machine to lower him into the ground. Dr. Golden didn't even come. The guys look bored and impatient to do something more lively on this beautiful autumn day. Mrs. Nguyen takes my hand as we watch them lower the casket. It isn't Dad anymore. It's just a box.

We each throw a handful of dirt on it. I wanted it to have meaning, to be symbolic. But it's just dirt, thrown out of tradition and duty. It means nothing.

"Let's go to the reception," Mrs. Nguyen coaxes, steering me back toward the parking lot.

I follow without resistance, but I answer her. "I'm not going."

"But Stella, that's the best part. We're past the sad part. Now people get to say nice things about your father, tell funny stories. Celebrate his life."

I plant my feet on the paved pathway and speak loudly into the bright, cheery afternoon. "I'm not going."

"Are you sure, dear?" she asks. "It's customary for the family to be there. People will expect you to make a short appearance. They want to offer condolences."

"What about my mother?" I ask. "Won't they expect her? I'm fourteen. I'm sure people will understand. What's her excuse?"

Though it's inexcusable to leave a slow old woman to walk through the cemetery on her own, I can't stay any longer. I break away from her and run. I don't need condolences. I need my dad.

But I've already said goodbye to him. Now it's time to go home and pack. Tomorrow, I say hello to my mother.

WANT TO FIND OUT MORE?

Purchase the Marked by Fate boxset and get Unlikely Magic plus 24 other full-length novels

Devastated by her father's sudden death, Stella barely protests being shipped off to live in a secluded forest encampment with the mother she never knew. Upon arrival, things go from bad to downright creepy. Everyone in the cultish community stares at her like she's a mutant, including the two sisters her father failed to mention in her fourteen years, and her mother promptly locks her in the attic. Her only companions are a mouse and fantasies of befriending her own sisters.

Desperately lonely, Stella watches from the window as her family leaves for a night each month to attend mysterious "lunar meetings." While they are gone to one of these meetings, Stella escapes the attic, only to discover why her mother has kept her locked up her since her arrival—the entire community is made up of werewolves. Intensely protective of their privacy, they would do anything to keep their secret from outsiders…outsiders like Stella.

Connect with Lena

I hope you've enjoyed Before the Magic

Visit me at lenamaehill.com to hear my latest news and to join my VIP Reader's Club and get your free copy of The Last Soul free

Follow me online
Instagram: @lenamaehill | Twitter: @lenamaehill |
Facebook: @lenamaehill |

About the Author

Hey, y'all. Thanks for checking out my work! I'm a southerner, born and raised, which means I mostly mind my manners but I also have the cussing streak of my Italian grandpa when the mood hits. I'm a serious chocolate addict, a coffee lover, and a restless homebody. I love writing more than almost anything, and I'm so excited about publishing my first YA fairytale series this year. I hope you'll come along on the adventure!

PRINCE OF HAWKS

Prequel to the Unweaving Chronicles

Sarah K. L. Wilson

CHAPTER ONE

I am honor from my spine to my skin.

Pwaaa Bwaaa Bwowww. Vultures circled in the distance, their cries echoing over the Kosad Plains far further than their dark forms could be seen. I felt the rhythm of their movements, even though I couldn't see them. Why did they feel so significant today? I didn't usually notice my affinity for birds. It was just natural, like blinking.

I blew into my hands to warm them. I chose to stand watch tonight. Why did burdens feel lighter when you chose them yourself? I'd never know the answer to half the questions I asked, but there was no need for answers on a day like today. The purples of dusk cloaked the low, craggy hills of our western border. Even the moons, hanging low to the earth like they were fishing for trite in the Penspray River seemed pleased. There was little to disturb the peace here, a hundred miles from the nearest city and twenty from the nearest town. A sense of rightness settled in my chest, as it always did when I stood on the low border wall. It streamed out on either side of me, tails to my comet. One day, perhaps, I would push the border forward, dragging these walls behind me, and lead my nation to better things. Not on the western front, next to our greatest ally, but perhaps to the north where savages tore jackal-like at civilization.

It wasn't difficult to watch for danger along a peaceful border, the only real difficulty was keeping my mind focused on the task at hand and not on the rolling steps of the sa'lara dance Serenada had danced for me before I left for the field. She was still too young to wed, but not for long. I would have kissed her then, as her flirting steps and perfumed scarves were begging me to, but I am honor from spine to skin. I couldn't deny I was tempted by those full ruby lips and the heated smiles that curved across them.

I cleared my throat. Distraction was the enemy of the watchman. I needed to lead by example and stand watch with my men this night, so I could not allow it.

"Watching vultures circle, War Leader? That's a bad omen," Brand said, climbing the steps behind me onto the walkway on the wall.

"Still awake, old friend?" It would be nice to be as free and unburdened as my best friend, but duty held me tight.

"Who are you calling old? Neither of us has gone past twenty summers."

I smiled slightly, scanning the border. Rays of gold touched the trees, and there were scant minutes left from now until full dawn. At dawn, I could go find my tent and sleep. I could already feel the down-filled pallet and silken blankets. Ahhh, to be there now. Focus, Rusk!

"I came to tell you there are riders spotted from the east."

"East? At dawn?"

"Maybe your kingly father is so anxious to see you that he rode through the night. Maybe he heard that a shapely girl with dark hair is stealing your heart away before he can make a man out of his youngest war leader."

I felt my cheeks heat and cursed myself. Could anything make me appear less of a man than a blush? Had everyone noticed? It would undermine me with the men. I owed them more than boyish distraction. I needed to be strong and sure, a war leader in truth and not just in name.

I cocked my head to the side, feeling for the songbirds that slept on the branches above us. Their sleepy minds were waking with the dawn.

Who comes? I asked them.

Horses. Stomping. Flies. Flicking tails. Banners, like dawn.

Golden banners. That was my father. But what was he doing here when he should be entertaining our guest? Had he considered my request to wed Seranada? No, that wouldn't lead him to ride to the furthest reaches of the Plains. He could have answered in a letter.

A young soldier hurried up to me, bowing with fists crossed over his chest. He smelled of soap and polish. I saluted him in return, and inspected his presentation, holding back my smile. My reputation as a stickler for decorum was preceding me again, but without discipline, there could be no honor.

"Soldier Wesna, are you here to relieve my watch?"

"On my honor, I will watch the plains, War Leader."

I made a show of looking him over and then grunted in approval. He'd done a good job, but with a small mistake.

"Your spatha is buckled into the sheath, Soldier."

His Adam's apple bobbed as he swallowed in fear, but he cracked his boots together instead of reaching for it.

"You may fix your mistake. See it does not happen again. We can't defend our homes if our weapons are not ready."

"Yes, sir!" He snapped the buckle loose so quickly that I almost expected to see it come off in his hand.

"Take the watch, soldier, and do not fail in your oath."

"I will not fail, War Leader. It also is my honor to inform you that the royal entourage has been spotted arriving on the road from Kosad."

As if I couldn't hear the hooves of their horses growing louder as they approached. I saluted him and stepped away from the post, giving up my watch, and Brand and I climbed down the stairs from the wall, turning to the East. Our camp lay beyond us, but beyond that was nothing but sandy plains, tufted grass and the sandstone crenellations that marked this region. Anyone coming from that direction could only be coming here. Their cloud of dust sparkled in the dawn and I took a steadying breath filled with the heady scent of creosote.

"They seem hurried, Brand." My stomach fluttered slightly. Why did I feel so nervous? What was the worst my father could say?

Brand grinned, still more boy than man, despite his rank as one of my lieutenants.

"I think I can see her, Rusk. The diplomat from Canderabai. She must have ridden with the King of Hawks from Kosad. They say you can smell the exotic spices flowing from her scarves even before you see her. Do you smell anything?"

"Only whatever you were drinking all night." I gave him a half-smile. Honor was my master, but it didn't have to be his.

"I wonder if she will really be dressed in those scandalous dresses they wear. My father says they leave nothing to the imagination."

"Then what will fill your dreams all night?"

"And this year, in Al'Karida, they will race for the Teeth of the Gods. My cousin is heading there for the race. I wouldn't mind going myself if I wasn't bound to serve."

"You want to hunt for something that doesn't exist with a bunch of gold-blinded fools? Why not look for happiness like everyone else?"

"You shouldn't be so serious, Rusk. Life will pass you by. What you need is a wild girl. Someone with some flair to push you out of yourself. Give you a bit of an adventure."

I cleared my throat, trying to clear the images from my mind along with it. Seranada's dance had promised more than adventure.

"And I don't mean Seranada," Brand said. "She's pretty, I'll allow, but she's a sweet garden flower. You'll crush her with your heavy principles. You need someone with a spirit like a hunting falcon."

"You really will have to tell me what you've been drinking, Brand. I think I could use some myself," I joked. What was wrong with a garden flower? A falcon sounded less than appealing, although they sliced through the air in a way that made me envious.

The entourage was close now, edging around the permanent encampment with the practiced precision of someone who had been here many times. My father. That was his heavy-chested paint leading the long line of horses. His banner flowed behind the standard bearer at his side, but only he could wear the Crown of Hawks, and I could see it glimmering there, its golden wings fanning out to frame the sides of his head. He was solid muscle and authority. I'd worked hard for my own solid build, but how many years of service would I need before I could radiate authority like he did?

Behind him, leaning toward each other while riding their husky ponies, my mother and another woman were deep in conversation. No one but the diplomat from Canderabai could look so foreign beside my mother. Where Mother was tall, she was tiny. Where Mother's skin was dark as night, her companion's skin was the color of the sandy Kosad plains – and there was so much of it to see. Mother wore a high-necked, lace-lined dress that showed her status and maturity, but her companion's filmy garments left her middle bare, and the shining jewelry only drew the eye to her perfectly shaped belly that should have been hidden in swaths of cloth. What there was of her dress, trailed and flowed like the surf against a beach, and it matched the surf in color. I swallowed hard when her eyes found me, their irises so dark they were almost black, so different from my mother's honey-light eyes. The only thing they shared was their age. I could see that if I concentrated my attention past the stranger's captivating beauty. She was of an age with my mother, too old for the thoughts that swirled unbidden in my mind.

"And this must be the son," she said in a tinkling voice like a silver bell. She was a songbird made human, a soaring heron on the wing. I swallowed again. "Like his father, but green as a new stick."

Ouch. That stung. I straightened, clenching my jaw at the smile that flickered over my father's expression as he reined in his horse. A new stick? Really? I'd served five years already in the Kosad Cavalry. My title of War Leader wasn't all inherited. What armies had she led?

"She's one of the consorts of the High Tazmin," Brand whispered beside me. As if I didn't already know. She was as attainable as a rainbow, as touchable as a star. "They say she has a daughter."

Could her daughter have even a fraction of the fascination of her mother? It seemed impossible…and treacherous. After all, I had asked my father for Seranada's hand, had I not? It was dishonorable to think of another, no matter how unlikely it was that anything would come of it.

"My son, War Leader Rusk Hawkwing," my father said. "Prince of Hawks."

I felt warm at the approval in his voice and the hawk-like look in his own eyes. Is there anything more powerful for a son than the approval of his father?

A nightendahl sang, strange in the light of dawn. I cocked my head at the sound, my parents doing likewise. It was a bad omen, a nightendahl singing in the day. My mother sent a soothing smile in my direction. I stiffened. She needed to start treating me like a man. The thought of being called a 'new stick' still stung.

The tiny ambassador dismounted, and my mother followed suit. My father joined them, gesturing to our visitor.

"Allow me to present the High Tazminera, visiting us from Canderabai. Your mother and I are delighted to show her every corner of the Kosad Plains."

I crossed my fists across my chest and bowed quickly.

"My welcome be upon you, High Tazminera."

Emotion flickered behind her eyes. Was that pity? Did she see me as so far beneath her that I deserved pity? I clenched my jaw in irritation. How many more summers must I wait before people saw past my youth?

"Let us show you our western wall, High Tazminera," my father said, assisting her to the steps that led up to the winding lattice of the western wall. She looked like a nightendahl between the two hawks of my father and mother. "Isn't it as we promised? Wrought by the magic of our ancestors, it extends many leagues in either direction, but what artistry!

Even the wonders of Al'Karida's lace bridges can't fully eclipse the beauty of the boundary here. Don't you think?"

The High Tazminera touched the winding curves of the gleaming white wall with her tattooed fingers. The rings on that hand alone could have set one of my soldiers up for an early release from service.

"It's truly beautiful, as you promised, King of Hawks. As if it were wrought by the hands of the Gods," she said as she ascended behind him. My mother was close on her heels, patting me on the shoulder as she went by. She really needed to stop doing that. I was a grown man, not a child tied in the saddle. "But it hardly looks strong. Is it only for decoration?"

My father laughed. "Its beauty certainly improves the landscape, but you are correct. It is not crafted to withstand an assault. It has never had to. Our peace with Canderabai goes back a thousand years."

"Of course," she said with a smile like the sunrise.

We stood on the walkway at the top of the lattice wall. There were no rails and no need for them. The wall stood only as high as I did, more of a reminder of the border than any kind of defense.

A hawk keened in the sky and I sought his mind, far more interesting than a history lesson on a peace that would never be broken. I found it hard to concentrate on the ground when the allure of watching everything from above constantly called to me.

How beautiful the dawn, brother?

Bright. Beautiful.

I could see him high in the azure sky, wheeling in great circles. If I could have one wish it would be to fly, not just in the mind of the bird, but in my own body. For a fleeting moment, I saw through his eyes to the spinning world below. Everything looked different from the sky. The mountains to the south appeared larger, and the city to the east smaller. As I fell from his mind I thought I saw something glimmer to the west.

I strained my human eyes to the horizon. The tree line was ragged and if there was someone on the road from Canderabai it would be hard to pick out his form. Was that a gleam there?

Brother, do travelers come from the west? From down that road?

The High Tazminera was watching me, though it was my mother she spoke with now. Something glittered in her eyes that seemed more hawk than songbird after all. She smiled at my mother, sweeter than summer wine.

There! On the horizon there was a gleam again, and another. There was nothing there that should be shining …

Elephants come. Many. Many. Men and sharp steel.

I gasped, turning to my father, but fast as lightning the tiny ambassador turned to my mother, her smile still sweet, and then she pulled a slender knife from the folds of her barely-there dress and plunged it into my mother's belly. My shout mingled with her scream, but the small demon was not done. She twisted the dagger. My mother wailed, crumpling to the ground in agony. I fumbled with my sword.

Her eyes were fiery as she pulled a second dagger from her dress, spinning to fling it into my father's throat as he drew his sword. He stumbled, dropping the sword and pawing at his throat as blood bubbled up, spilling down his snowy white coat.

I pulled my sword free, shouting to alert my men. "Attack! We are betrayed!"

I lunged forward, discipline and endless hours of training rising up and commanding my actions for me. I thrust my spatha into her belly, twisting, just as she had done to my mother, and then yanking it free. I didn't watch her fall. Instead, I dropped to my mother's side, lifting her head and cradling her to me.

"Mother." My voice was hoarse.

"Rusk. Your brother Ajur." Her eyes were already glassing over. I clutched her hand, tears flooding my eyes. I was a man, but too much of a boy not to feel lost without my mother. It wasn't her who was supposed to die for our country. That was my duty.

"Don't go. Please, Mother."

Her fingers lost their strength and her head lolled to the side. I drew in a long breath, laying her gently to the side and crossing her arms reverently over her chest. One glance told me my father hadn't lived to reach the ground, but I still went to him next, closing his eyes and crossing his arms.

I stared for long moments at his golden hawk-wing crown. I was not ready. I glanced up at the hawk sailing in the sky. He was so free. He had nothing that tied him to this land but the currents of wind that he floated in. This crown was nothing like the bird it depicted—nothing like the weightless soaring of that predator.

I was honor, though, from spine to skin.

I lifted it with care from my father's head, pulled off my helmet and placed the crown on my own brow. It was too heavy. Heavy with duty and expectation. Heavy with unmet promises.

Brand stood to one side, his mouth hanging open, frozen in fear and horror.

I cleared the lump from my throat, running a gloved hand over my face to dispense with my tears. No one wanted to see a prince cry. No time for mourning, time only to preserve what might still be kept safe.

"Gather the lieutenants and sound the alarm," I ordered. "They come from the West. Send messengers - as many as we have - to the near settlements and to Kosad. Tell our people to flee. We are betrayed."

Brand ran to obey. There was one more thing to do before I prepared for my last battle – for I had no doubt I would die this day. We were smaller than Canderabai and our army, though brave and true, was nothing before the ranks of the High Tazmin.

I stepped over my father and crouched above the heaving, coughing body of the High Tazminera. She was broken, like a snake with a snapped spine, but I could see now that she was just as deadly. I took care to remain outside her reach.

"You have betrayed us and killed us all. For what purpose did the High Tazmin send you? What good does it do for him to destroy his allies?" The voice that spoke sounded cold – too cold to be mine.

She smiled, that same charming smile, and said, "He saw this in a dream, and what the High Tazmin dreams I deliver to him."

"You have delivered our corpses."

"Maybe not yours. I could still save you, Prince of Hawks. You could live, and they would only make you san'lelion to one of our Tazmineras. It is not a bad life. I have asked the High Tazmin to give you to our daughter if you live. You'll like her—" she cut off, coughing too hard to speak. "—she has an adventurous streak. She'll let you fly to places you'd never reach, even with golden wings on your head."

My mouth twisted with disgust. She wanted to negotiate with me after she'd slain my family? She wanted to make me choose slavery willingly? I knew all about their foreign customs. I had read their Canderabaian Chronicles of History. I would not be tied to a preening princess. I'd rather die.

"Just promise you'll protect her and I'll spare your life. When they come over the walls, minutes from now I'll still be alive and I'll give the order. Promise."

"Your hubris knows no bounds, Tazminera. If I ever meet your daughter, I'll tell her that her mother had no honor."

"Please—"

I stood, shook the blood off my spatha, and then cleanly split her head from her shoulders. I was not her plaything. I didn't ask for her to 'save' me.

The horizon was black with our approaching doom and above them, clouds of vultures swirled, headed toward us.

Feast to come, feast, they said when I reached to them. I swallowed my bile and straightened my shoulders. I had an army to lead. I would die with honor today.

I put on duty like a cloak: for my family, my nation, and my own soul. I was wrong about the hawk. He only flew because the wind was under his wings. I would fly on the strength of the duty that held me up.

I was honor from spine to skin.

WANT TO FIND OUT MORE?

Purchase the Marked by Fate boxset and get
Teeth of the Gods plus 24 other full-length novels

Chained to an enemy general. Determined to be free.

After years in seclusion and training, eighteen-year-old Tylira Nyota is summoned by the High Tazmin to be chained to a fallen enemy general. She is a terrible choice to receive this honor – her magic is useless and she finds it impossible to fit in the world she was born to.

Determined to keep her freedom, Tylira instead joins the legendary race for the fabled Teeth of the Gods. With an angry step-mother chasing her and the handsome general chained to her wrist, Tylira must learn to control her magic - which is turning out to be deadly – before it destroys everything she's fought to gain.

Connect with Sarah

I hope you've enjoyed Prince of Hawks

To find out what happens next, check out the rest of my series available now
Teeth of the Gods | Lightning Strikes Twice

Follow me online
Instagram: @sarahklwilson | Twitter: @sarahklwilson |
Facebook: @sarahklwilson |

About the Author

I believe fiction can help us connect with something greater than ourselves. It's my mission to provide you with those kind of stories. My books have wide-sweeping storylines and absolutely epic endings. I try my best to weave transcendent themes throughout that will get your mind spinning and fuel your creativity and philosophy. Happy reading!

Hag's Hut on the Hill

A Short Story

D. L. Armillei

CHAPTER ONE

Deleted Scene

With no money, only enough food and supplies to last a week, and one cool holographic map, Vanessa Cross and her five teammates headed north, into the savage land of Yesod.

Has it only been ten days since I traveled through the portal to the Living World? wondered Van, as she trudged over the rocky terrain. Her hiking boots tightly squeezed her swollen feet, which ached with each step. Her stomach growled with hunger, and her muscles felt warm from exhaustion. Experiencing this physical discomfort intensified her already irritable mood.

Barely two weeks ago, her sole focus had consisted of the three items on her summer break to-do list: boyfriend, bikini, and beach. The loss of her plans—lazing around Buzzard's Bay beach with her best friend, Paley Ash; shopping on the Boardwalk; and deepening her relationship with her boyfriend, Ken—filled her with indignation.

At least one good thing came from this miserable journey, thought Van. She would never take her cozy bedroom for granted *ever* again.

Yet her bedroom resided far away on Providence Island, off the coast of Massachusetts—in the Earth World. The world where she was raised.

Not born, but raised. Van felt compelled to add this last bit about living in the Earth World to remind herself how far she had traveled.

Her shoulders heaved with an exaggerated sigh.

Van could pinpoint the exact second when her simple, carefree life had careened off track. It happened the morning one of the Island's Elders, Uxa Huxatec, who was also her father's boss—*of all people*—barged into her house to inform Van she had been one of the students awarded to participate in a summer project, starting immediately.

Awarded. A term loosely used by the Elders. Being bound by the Island's Rules of Testing, Van didn't have a choice. The Native Island tribe owned and partly occupied Providence Island, so the U.S. government considered the whole island a sovereign nation with the ability to govern itself. The Elders were the ruling body of the Native Islanders, and if any resident didn't bend to the will of the Elders, that person was banished from the island. Van considered this a fate worse than death. She loved her quaint island home.

With a warm, snuggly feeling, she visualized wrapping her comforter around her body and hugging her pillows and stuffed animals, safe at home in her soft queen-size bed. Uxa's project required her to leave all of that behind for thirty days.

Van didn't like leaving the island. She had been off-island as required for school field trips and had found the mainland crowded with angry, violent people. Ignorant too. They often referred to Providence Island as "that cult," because the Elders restricted residents' use of the Internet and TV and because the island had too much interference for smartphone reception. Now, she was trapped in an alternate world that she didn't know existed two weeks ago.

During Van's encounter with Uxa, everything she knew about herself and her life had begun to crumble.

First, Van learned that her summer project involved being part of a team that would help Island Security, the secretive department where her father worked. She grimaced. Her father's job remained a sore spot for her, because it often took him away from home, away from her—leaving her alone with her ever-watchful stepmother, Iphigenia, or Genie.

Whenever Van felt good about how she looked or proud of a hard-earned achievement, Genie always managed to make "helpful" suggestions for improvement. Like the time when Van came home from the Naked Ape, her favorite hair salon, with a new hairstyle.

"It would look better without all those fly-aways," offered Genie.

And the night Van headed to a party, feeling great in her newest outfit, Genie commented, "Not sure that's the best outfit for your figure."

Or when Van won her first trophy at school, Genie asked, "Did everyone get one?"

No matter what Van did, she could never please Genie.

Yet Van's initial thrill over spending the summer away from her nagging stepmother and finally learning about her father's mysterious occupation soon dissipated.

More details had come out during her briefing with Uxa, knocking the last shred of Van's secure life to the ground. Most shocking—her parents and Genie were from the Living World. The world where Van's mother had died giving birth to her. Providence Island, an outpost to that world and Van's *home*, needed tight security to guard the transportation device between the worlds, the portal.

Then, to make matters even more upsetting, once Van started her project she learned the real reason she'd been selected for the team, and it had nothing to do with skill. Her father had disappeared on a mission in the Living World, while trying to retrieve a magical relic called the Coin of Creation. According to the Elders, Van's ancestral duty required her to complete her father's mission. Fearing she would be banished from her island home and desiring to learn more about her father's fate, Van grudgingly agreed to the task.

So here I am, thought Van, *trudging across this strange land, along with a team of teens, all hand-selected for this mission by Uxa.* Except for Paley. Paley had begged Van to tailgate her on this mission. Van happily obliged, having zero desire to go on some crazy mission in an unfamiliar world by herself. So she snuck Paley through the portal, and due to complications with getting Paley back to the Earth World, Uxa allowed Paley to stay.

Van glanced down at her used khaki pants and worn jersey, grimy and wrinkled from lack of proper laundering. And her hair—*ugh*—a total frizzed mess. Though distressed by her appearance, Van felt exhausted and ruled out trying to pull herself together. Instead, she daydreamed about getting a blowout and a mani-pedi at the Naked Ape. She grinned, thinking about Genie's reaction if she ever caught sight of Van's shabby appearance. Her stepmother would faint! Then Genie would lecture Van on failing to live up to the perfection required of those who carry the Cross family name.

Yet even with a hypercritical stepmother waiting for her, Van wanted to get home. For that to happen, she had to retrieve the Coin of Creation. She initially figured that would take a few days, but it had stretched to almost two weeks—and they weren't even close to finding the Coin.

Van flashed on a memory of Zane, a jovial bartender around her own age. She had met him at the Troll's Foot Tavern, which reminded her of the Earth World's Roaring Twenties speakeasies. The tavern provided an underground meeting place for people who secretly undermined the current monarchy that harshly ruled the Living World.

"I have it on good authority the Coin is hidden in a place called Yesod," said Zane. "There, it lies deep in the Caves of Wolfenden." He had taken a fancy to Van, and for a quick kiss, he gave her this valuable information—along with a mug of mead, a type of lager more plentiful than water in the Living World.

Yet Brux, a boy warrior from the Living World and part of their team, and Paley stole Van's thunder by announcing they had already found out about the Caves of Wolfenden. They added that they also knew how to *get* there, and it had nothing to do with following a map— to which Elmot, the team's guide and map specialist, took offense.

"We have to pass through troll territory," said Paley, as if she were an expert.

"We need to bring gnome guides with us to navigate around the roaming troll tribes," Brux explained. "Otherwise, we'll never make it through Yesod alive."

"Let's grab us some gnomes!" Trey announced.

Trey's swarthy complexion, bole brown hair, and hazel eyes contrasted with the rest of his teammates' appearance—all of whom were blondes with blue eyes, with the exception of Paley and her electric-green contact lens colored eyes. Paley had packed her essentials for the trip—enough wildly colored contacts for each day of the summer.

Jorie, the team's leader who was built like a refrigerator, shook her head. "We'll have to coax the gnomes into helping us. They have to come of their own free will. They're not guide animals."

"How do we do that?" Van asked gloomily. It sounded like more work.

"We have to gain the gnomes' trust," said Jorie, with her habitual gesture of running her hand over her Mohawk. Each hair sprang back to place. "We'll need to bring their leader a gift. Did you find out what that should be?"

"I could give them a pair of my contact lenses," Paley said brightly, shifting her body closer to Brux.

Van didn't like Brux and Paley's growing closeness. Despite having a boyfriend back home, Van believed that she and Brux "had a thing." Paley, as her friend, should step aside. Yet Paley stuck to Brux like dirt to overdone hair gel. Now Van regretted even bringing Paley with her on the mission.

"I could give them my gold ring," Van offered. Considering how much she loved her jewelry, she felt this showed tremendous growth on her part.

Brux frowned. "Gnomes are earth creatures. They don't value material possessions."

"What do they want, then?" Van exclaimed. She couldn't fathom these heathen creatures that wouldn't value her precious—and expensive—ring. Her cheeks reddened, and she glanced at the floor, stung at being shot down, rather than getting credit for her generous offer.

"They want the body of a vegetable lamb," said Brux.

Trey groaned. "What in the worlds is that?"

"We weren't able to find out," Paley said cheerily, as if participating in a playful scavenger hunt. "Does anyone know?"

"A lamb that eats veggies, maybe?" said Van, lamely.

No one else had any clue.

Jorie clapped her hands. "Okay, guys, back to working the crowd."

"I'll talk to Zane again," said Van. "He probably knows." She weaved through the crowd back to the bar.

Yet as Zane busily slugged drinks to the thirsty patrons, Van had little time to question him.

Finally, she burst out as he whooshed past: "Zane!"

He stopped short. "Ho-ho! You need another mead? I could use another kiss!"

Van shook her head. "Someone mentioned a vegetable lamb. Ever heard of it?"

Zane twisted his lips in thought. "Hmm. I can tell you it's not a drink!" He shrugged and then zipped away, back to work.

Midnight neared when the team gave up and headed back to the musty barn housing them for the night. Van welcomed the feel of her silky, soft sleeping bag and snuggled in next to the small, contained fire Brux had lit in a rusty metal barrel.

No one had found out any information about a vegetable lamb, but Jorie had learned about an old woman with knowledge of such things. Van didn't think this angle sounded promising, because the patrons in the Troll's Foot didn't even know the old woman's name or her exact address. They referred to her only as the "old hag on the hill."

The rest of the group tucked into their sleeping bags, forming a circle around the fire, and settled in for a good night's sleep.

When morning came, the team headed out, continuing their journey north. Jorie informed them that they would pass by the hag's hut on their way, so they decided to stop and ask about the vegetable lamb. If the old woman didn't know, they would continue on their mission, prepared to give the gnomes some other kind of offering.

"Any shiny trinket will do," Trey suggested. "After all, the gnomes are basically one step above domesticated animals." Arrogance oozed with every word he spoke.

"If it is a lamb, the gnomes will probably want to eat it," said Brux. "We could offer them some of our food instead."

Van glanced at Brux but heard nothing he said. Instead, she wondered whether he had inherited his cute button nose from his mother's side or his father's.

"I doubt either of those ideas will work," stated Jorie. "But in the interest of gaining ground, let's go with it." She nervously ran a hand over her Mohawk again.

They easily spotted the hag's hut on the hill, which could be seen from the main road. They followed a winding, uphill dirt path toward the hut until it ended, forcing the team to hike over rocks and brush the rest of the way.

"Careful," warned Trey. "The hag planted bladerush on the grounds."

"Ouch!" said Van, cutting her hand on the razor-sharp shrubbery.

Trey stopped and dropped his backpack. "Let me get some salve. Don't want you to get an infection."

"Are you okay?" Paley asked Van, her electric-green eyes open wide.

"No wonder they call her the Old Hag," said Van, scowling. She used her thumb in an attempt to calm the throbbing pain and stop the oozing blood. It didn't work.

Trey pulled out salve and a bandage from his medic kit. Brux grabbed the items and tended to Van.

Trey stepped back, palms up, and said, "All yours."

Jorie yelled from ahead, "Quit dragging your feet and get moving!"

"Take it easy," snapped Elmot. "They're coming as fast as they can."

At the beginning of their journey, Van hadn't liked Elmot. His lanky, awkward body and long face made him look like an oversized elf, and his persnickety fondness for pressed, spotless clothes annoyed her. But he seemed to enjoy hanging around Van and Paley, and now that Elmot had stood up to Jorie in Van's defense, she grew even more fond of him.

They reached the top of the hill and stood before a stone hut with a thatched roof. Gray smoke curled out of a crumbling chimney, and tangles of vines climbed the walls, making the hut blend into the natural landscape.

Before Jorie had a chance to knock, the door swung open.

"Don't get many visitors up this way," said the hag. "Been expecting you, though." She wore a black robe that contrasted with her sallow skin. Her crooked nose hung hook-like over a mouth resembling a black slit. Flaming orange hair shot crazily from her head every which way.

Van recalled learning about the myth of Medusa in school and breathed a sigh of relief when none of them turned to stone.

Brux leaned toward Van and whispered, "She could definitely use a vacation in Antares."

Van fought back a smile. She found Brux's comment funny—figuring Antares to be a sunny vacation spot in the Living World—but didn't want to lead Brux on. She decided it wouldn't be fair to Paley, Brux, or her boyfriend, Ken, who waited for her back on the island.

"You were expecting us?" asked Jorie.

The hag tapped a finger to her temple. "*Saw* you coming."

Van shivered. The hag's protruding cloudy eyes hadn't actually *seen* anything in years.

"She's a mountain witch!" accused Jorie, backing away from the hag. "We need to leave. Now."

Van had never glimpsed fear in Jorie before, which scared her. She hastily turned and hurried away from the hut, along with the rest of her teammates.

"I have what you came for," the hag called after them. "And you need it to get where you're going!"

Trey stopped and turned toward the hag. "The body of a vegetable lamb? You can tell us what that is?" he asked, raising an eyebrow.

The rest of them stopped, too.

Jorie growled. "But at what cost?"

The hag cackled. "Many have sought the Coin of Creation," she said. "All have failed, paying with their lives." Her words went up and down in tone, adding a sinister element to the hag's demeanor.

"The cost?" Jorie demanded.

"Balish forbade the gnomes to possess the body of a vegetable lamb," said the hag. "Very risky business for me to help you."

"Tell us what it is already!" screeched Paley.

"It's a plant," the hag said in a rush.

"Paley, no!" Jorie shouted. "We needed to hear the cost first, now it's too late! You entered into a contract with the witch! Now we're magically bound to give her whatever she wants!"

Paley moped. "Sorry."

"What is it you want?" Brux asked with trepidation.

"Blood!" hooted the hag.

In a flash, Jorie unsheathed Zachery, her terrifying war axe. Brux and Trey did the same with their dagger and crossbow, respectively.

The hag grinned, displaying rotted teeth. "I gave you something, you give me something. Your weapons are of no use now." Unaffected by the drawn weapons, the hag danced a twirling jig in the doorway and sang, "Blood! Blood! Blood! Blood!"

Jorie reluctantly put Zachery away, looking stern. "It's true."

Brux and Trey did the same with their weapons.

"If we attack, the magic binding the contract will protect her and harm us," said Jorie.

Brux stepped forward. "Take my blood."

The hag stopped dancing and singing and turned serious. "One of you cut your hand on the bladerush. That's whose blood I want."

"Not a chance!" Brux roared. He stood protectively in front of Van.

Van hid behind Brux, hugging her wounded hand to her chest.

Elmot and Trey flanked Van, poised for a fight.

Jorie put her hand on Brux's arm and gently said, "Brux. We have to."

"It-it's okay," Van said with more bravado than she felt, as she stepped from behind Brux.

Elmot and Trey hung their heads and moved aside.

Paley stared, wide-eyed, brushing an imaginary stray hair off her face. Van noticed that she had bitten her gel fingernails down to the nub.

Standing face-to-face with the hag, Van trembled.

"You'll take mine instead," demanded Brux. He stepped between Van and the deranged woman.

"No, thank you," said the hag, as if declining a second cup of tea. Then she changed to a determined tone and said, "It'll be hers!" She reached out and snatched Van's arm. "Stay put, the rest of you." The hag pulled Van away from the doorway and into the yard.

"If you harm her, I'll slit your throat," cried Brux.

"No harm, no harm," muttered the hag. "Just a little blood, only a little."

Van's heart beat madly, as the hag dragged her around the side of the hut, out of her team's view. She gulped as the hag led her into the middle of a circle marked by stones—a place of worship, a place of sacrifice. Van shivered deep enough to reach her bones.

The hag slipped a dagger out of her cloak and, in a single swoop, cut Van's bandage. It tumbled to the ground. Surprised, Van saw that the salve had already begun to heal her cut.

Without hesitation, the hag dug the tip of the blade into Van's hand, reopening her wound. Blood gushed.

Van screeched from the pain. She heard Brux struggling to come to her aid, and Jorie, Trey, and Elmot grunting as they held him back.

The hag picked up a hollowed-out stone tube from the ground and held it to the bleed, collecting Van's blood.

"There we go. That's it, right there," said the hag in hot ecstasy.

Van felt woozy, wondering when this horror would end.

Finally, the hag released her hand and turned away, clutching the stone container.

"The vegetable lamb, give it to us!" Jorie demanded from the front yard, as the hag and Van returned.

Van wobbled, as Brux and Elmot ran to her. They held her steady, while Trey salved her wound and then re-bandaged her hand.

"You." The hag pointed a mangled finger at Van. "You may pick from the bush of the vegetable lamb. Bring a branch with you and give it to the gnomes. It is treasured among their tribe." The hag clutched her blood-filled tube, scurried back into her hut, and slammed the door.

Van walked to the edge of the woods, to the flourishing bush with boughs of tiny blood-red flowers. As she got closer, she heard a persistent humming. No matter, she reached for one of the branches.

"*Ouch!* Damn it!" yelped Van, pulling her cut hand away from the branch. She eyed her finger. "I got stung!"

Brux rushed over. "Are you okay?"

Van snapped off one of the branches, despite her pain, and extended her injured finger to Brux, hoping for sympathy.

"Boy, you really can't win today," said Brux, forcing a smirk.

Trey appeared next to them and applied salve to Van's finger.

The pain instantly subsided.

Jorie stuck her face close to the bush for inspection, careful not to touch the branches. "You were stung by a bee. The bush is swarming with them."

Paley wrapped Van in a big hug and rested her head on Van's shoulder. "I hope you're okay."

"I'll hold on to this." Trey took the branch from Van. "For safe keeping." He inspected it for bees, gave it a shake just in case, and then tucked it into his backpack.

"How can we be sure the hag told us the truth?" asked Van.

"We can't be sure," said Jorie, throwing a glare at Paley. "We never asked the hag to *give* us the body of vegetable lamb. We only asked her to tell us what it is."

Paley stared at the ground. "I said I was sorry."

"At the very least," added Elmot, "we know it's a plant!"

Jorie nodded. "Van's okay. We have what we have." She started back down the hillside. "Let's keep moving."

WANT TO FIND OUT MORE?

Purchase the Marked by Fate boxset and get
Shock of Fate plus 24 other full-length novels

Vanessa Cross has never traveled anywhere by magical tree trunk. She's never used a wish-fulfilling bowl to create lunch, befriended gnomes, or confronted a troll. Her plans for summer break include lazing on the beach, shopping, and hitting the beauty salon—her usual way of coping with a hypercritical stepmother and an aloof father

Yet fifteen-year-old Van's hopes for summer fun drastically change when she is coerced through a portal to an alternate reality called the Living World. Once there, she discovers the only way to get home is by retrieving a relic called the Coin of Creation.

Along the way, Van not only meets new friends, experiences her first love, and learns about the magic in life, but finds that a great destiny awaits her . . . if she can survive the treacherous journey.

Conntect with DL Armillei

I hope you've enjoyed Hag's Hut on the Hill

To find out what happens next, visit me
at DLArmillei.com

Follow me online
Instagram: @author_dla | Twitter: @DLArmillei |
Facebook: @DLArmillei | Pinterest: @DLArmillei |

About the Author

When Donna was four years old she wrote a "story" in "cursive" and gave it to her mother to read out loud. Her mother tucked the pages into a desk drawer, telling Donna that she should read the amazing story she had created in a few years—after she had learned how to read and write.

Now—able to read and write—Donna continues to create amazing stories. As an Ultrasound Technologist, she draws on the excitement and drama of working in the Emergency Department of a major city hospital to grip readers with her tales, taking them on a journey into an imaginative alternate world—one full of twists and turns and fast-paced action.

A Massachusetts native, Donna now splits her time between living in her home state and FL. She can often be found sweating in a Zumba class, playing in the Universal and Disney parks, or hanging around tiki huts as long as they're on white sand beaches. Being under the impression she's a treasure hunter, she sometimes scuba dives but usually chickens out and ends up snorkeling.

She earned a bachelor's degree in Business Administration from Northeastern University and later an associate degree in Diagnostic Medical Sonography from Community College of Rhode Island, where she graduated Phi Theta Kappa.

DOORMAKER
DEVIL'S HARVEST

A Short Story Prequel

Jamie Thornton

Chapter One

Esson had two hours to prove himself.

Two hours to change his family's future.

Two hours to get the *licatherin* to Barth's father in the first interstellar drug deal of his thirteen-year-old life.

He pressed a hand to his pocket and hurried into the woods—away from the meeting that had changed his family's fortune. Dead, knee-high grasses scratched at his bare legs. Everything smelled dry and brittle. The folded cash in his pocket felt like a good luck charm.

It had been a risk, standing his ground, making Dustin—Barth's father—pay half upfront for the drugs. But it had paid off, literally, and Dustin had looked at Esson with a grudging respect.

But it would all fall violently apart if Esson didn't deliver.

A worried knot of pressure made him want to piss more badly than he could ever remember in his life. He broke out in a cold sweat in spite of the summer's morning heat. Out of the corner of his eye, he saw Dustin stare after him and Barth as the two boys rushed into the shade of the trees.

"How much more of the Devil's Harvest can you even get?" Barth said.

"What?" Esson said, glancing back. The pressure from his bladder made him feel like a balloon about to burst. He needed to find a place to piss, but Dustin was still in sight.

Barth sported a swollen jaw from the punch his father had dished out before giving them the two-hour deadline. If Esson failed to meet Dustin's deadline, his chance for making the money his family needed would vanish. Fury lodged in his stomach, two hours wasn't enough. There was no reason for the deadline except Dustin wanted to be cruel and, Esson suspected, test Esson's commitment to their deal. Dustin said if Esson could make the deadline, there would be more business opportunities ahead.

But if Esson failed—Dustin had smiled coldly.

It had taken everything inside Esson not to shiver in spite of the heat.

Dustin had a reputation. A violent, cruel reputation, especially with those who failed him.

Esson gritted his teeth. He would not fail.

Barth's camo t-shirt was dark at the armpits from sweat, the matching hat stained with dirt and smashed down over his greasy hair. "My dad's expecting a lot of the Devil's Harvest. How much is there?"

Dustin had dismissed Esson's name for the drug—*licatherin*—and changed it to Devil's Harvest, saying it would sell like crazy with the new name.

Esson took a deep breath but immediately regretted the pressure on his bladder. He shouldn't have drunk so much water before the meeting. The drug sometimes took time to work, and he had wanted to dilute it— both to make his last few drops of the oil go further and to slow down the side effects.

Esson had already taken Dustin's money. He should have waited until he had all the drugs in hand, but he hadn't expected the two-hour ultimatum, and it was too late now to undo his mistake. "I'm stealing it. I don't know. A lot."

Esson had stolen two bottles of *licatherin* oil last week, given part of one to Barth's father to try, and kept the rest for himself. The *licatherin* smelled like licorice and made his skin tingle, helping him feel the potential doors around him. It also gave him energy on an empty stomach, clearing his mind, and making him feel a little reckless.

Well, more than a little.

The money Esson had gotten for just that one partial bottle made his head spin. When he handed it over to Grandmother, smiling, proud of himself, she had looked at him funny. He thought for an awful second she wasn't going to take the money. But she did, stuffing it into her bra when she thought he wasn't looking. Then she commented in a tone like she noticed he was wearing a different shirt than normal that he looked a little bruised and was he feeling okay?

Esson ignored her comment. He had also caught the tint of purple to his skin these days. It was a side effect of the drug. For the last several days his mother had looked at him with a grim set to her lips.

And his father?

He hadn't noticed a thing.

Dustin didn't know about the skin color side effect yet. Esson planned to have the rest of the money in his hands first.

Barth opened his mouth. "We should—"

Esson held up a hand, looking behind them. Finally, they were out of sight. He ran behind an oak tree and took a long piss. He chose not to notice the lavender tint to his urine. When he finished, he collapsed against the trunk in relief.

"Come on, Eddy," Barth said. "Stop fooling around."

Esson rubbed his face with his hands. Eddy was his name here because Esson sounded too strange—like it was the kind of name for someone from another world.

Which was exactly the case.

He didn't know much more than that—his family came to this world, Earth, through a door his father opened when Esson had been six. His sister, Maella, had been four, his brother, Josa, one.

Barth loomed into view, a sneer on his face. "Worried about pissing your pants? My dad's not that scary."

Esson put himself back together. Barth only had the guts to say that now that his father was gone. The next task loomed like a mountain. But the cash in his pocket comforted him. He needed to ditch Barth and steal the *licatherin* without Barth discovering his family's secret.

Since before he could remember—this secret rule had controlled every part of his life.

Never open a door.

People in his family who broke the rule tended to unleash otherworldly violence upon themselves and everyone around when they opened something as simple as a drawer.

People in his family who broke the rule—they had all died.

That's what he had been taught, at least.

He came from a family of doormakers. He had been trained from birth to never open a door.

Except.

He had broken the rule.

He had opened a door. Multiple doors, over the past few months, and he was still alive.

Esson hiked through the trees, ignoring the weeds scratching his legs. He took a random path while thinking about how to ditch Barth. What would Dustin use Esson for if he found out Esson could open doors to other worlds? Nothing good.

Suddenly Esson felt a push. He landed chin first on the ground, pain shooting up. He flipped onto his back and blocked Barth's punch, then landed his own punch in Barth's gut.

"What the hell?" Esson said.

"I know this isn't the right way," Barth said, gasping for air.

Esson pushed himself up and rubbed his chin. His stomach flipped. "What are you talking about?"

"I followed you before." Barth's face flushed. "I know your secret."

Esson followed the creek to the back field of some old farmer's property. The field butted up against the woods and was used as a junkyard for rusting tools, broken down cars, an abandoned refrigerator, and a shed that leaned so far over, one more good storm would knock it down.

Esson stalled for a moment, keeping his focus away from the secret door he had left open. *What did Barth know?*

Barth scanned the field, taking in the machinery, the shed, the fridge, then looked expectantly at Esson.

"You don't actually know anything," Esson said, feeling both relief and anger. If Barth didn't know, that meant Dustin still didn't know either. It also meant Esson had fallen for Barth's stupid lie.

"Whatever." Barth grimaced. "I lost you after you got here. Where is it—where are the drugs—on the other side of the field? Don't lie to me."

"It's here," Esson said. "The place is right here."

Barth brought a fist to within inches of Esson's face. "I said don't lie to me. I followed you here, but when I got here, you'd gone somewhere else."

Esson laughed. "Yeah, you could say that."

Barth's expression turned ugly.

"Wait here," Esson said.

"No way!" Barth said.

"Where I'm going ... where the drugs are—it's dangerous."

"Letting my father down—that's dangerous. That's the kind of thing people do when they want to get hurt."

There was a long silence between them. Birds fluttered in the air, bees buzzed from flower to flower, the creek gurgled somewhere behind the trees.

Two hours.

Esson had two hours and he was wasting precious minutes arguing with a jerk like Barth.

He should have gotten all the drugs before making the final deal with Dustin. But the deadline—the made up, just-for-kicks, two-hour deadline had been a surprise. He should have known, but he was never thinking things through—that's what his sister, Maella, would say. His father liked to say that Esson acted first and thought better about it later, when it was too late to take anything back.

He patted the cash in his pocket.

There was at least three months' worth of rent, with more to come.

His way of doing things had paid off big time.

"Fine," Esson said, confidence renewed. "Let's go."

He led them to the refrigerator, feeling its hum as if plugged in, even though it was rusting in a dirt field.

Barth didn't feel a thing of course. That was the Devil's Harvest inside Esson. He had never felt vibrations from doors until he had tried the oil.

The refrigerator was old, dingy white, and sat unevenly on the dirt. Weeds curled around it, yellow, sharp, sticky, brittle. The handle had fallen off, and orange, rusted holes from the bolts remained. Little trails of rust ran down the front of the fridge from the holes like tear tracks down a face. It sat a few feet away from the rundown shed, like someone had intended to lug the fridge inside but gave up on the last few steps.

Esson ignored the stickers that caught in his shoes. Barth cursed behind him but otherwise stayed silent.

If he showed Barth that fridge, there was no going back.

Esson took a deep breath and blocked out the blue sky, the yellow field, the broken down machinery, Barth's anxious breathing, the smell of soil and grease. Because of what he had found on the other side of this door, he had gone behind his father's back and made a deal with Dustin.

He couldn't take back that deal now.

Anyway, he was tired of hiding and running and pretending there was nothing wrong with his family. Esson removed the stone set keep the door from closing on the fridge. He pushed the fridge door open, but stood so that Barth could not see inside. If the fridge door ever closed, he would lose everything.

Doors never opened to the same place twice. At least, not the half dozen doors he had opened and closed over these past few months, daring death each time, searching for a solution to his family's money problems.

The vibrations from the door made his teeth chatter. The inside of the fridge—wasn't. Instead, the door opened to a sort of broom closet lined with shelves, space enough for several people. In front of him were carefully positioned boxes to cover his side of the door if anyone bothered to look. The inside was dark, musty, and filled with equipment—straw brooms, wooden buckets, glass containers, cleaning brushes, a half-broken chair.

Esson ignored all that while he pushed the boxes aside on the shelves, his eyes searching for the *other* door on the far side of the closet. Sometimes it was open, sometimes it was closed.

A faint line of light marked the bottom edge of the doorframe. If he was lucky—

Damn.

The door was closed today.

Esson stepped back and released his breath. He bumped into Barth.

Barth hissed. "Where's the stuff?"

"We have a problem." The door's vibrations made his head swim. Being this close never felt good.

Barth tried to push Esson aside. "Where is it?"

"I need you to do something." Esson didn't know how to explain so he just said it. "I need you to go into the fridge and open the door on the other side."

"You must think I'm an idiot. You want me to climb into that fridge so you can lock me inside of it? Are you trying to kill me? Where are the drugs, Eddy?"

"We're running out of time."

"You're running out of time. I vouched for you with my father." Barth's voice rose, a note of panic in it now. He rubbed his swollen jaw. "He's going to make us both pay."

If Esson tried to open the closet door himself, like this, without any preparation, not only would it not go where he needed it to go, whatever or wherever he opened the door to would likely kill them.

Esson thought quickly. "You don't have to go all the way in. Just lean through. It's a small enough room you can, I don't know, step one foot inside, and just pop it open."

"So why can't you do that?"

"Because it's locked against me!"

"You're not making sense."

What would Barth believe? Every argument he tried in his mind felt more unbelievable than the last. Especially the truth.

I can't just open a door. Every time someone in my family opens a door—cabinet door, front door, refrigerator door—it opens to another place, and someone usually dies because of it.

Yeah.

There was no way Barth would believe any of it in a million years.

They had less than two hours.

"Just do it," Esson said, thinking fast. He noticed Barth's swollen chin again. "If you don't, then we might as well go back now to your father empty handed. This is a test for you as much as it is for me. What do you think he's going to do to *you* if you come back with nothing again?"

Barth's face paled.

Esson backed up until he was at the edge of the field near an abandoned lawn mower. "Look, I'll stand way back over here. I'm not trying to trick you. But I can't take all the risk. You have to prove we're going to be partners in this. That we have each other's back. Just open the door and I'll do the rest."

The tires on the lawn mower were both flat and looked almost like they were melting into the ground. A fraying rope looked like it had once tied the seat to the mower, but the seat had gotten knocked loose and now the rope drooped across the machine like the longest worm in the entire world.

Barth was at the fridge door, watching Esson.

Esson nodded. *Come on.*

He couldn't let Barth know his family's secret, but he couldn't get the *licatherin* unless someone else opened that closet door.

Finally, Barth peered into the fridge. His body froze, probably while his brain tried to make sense of what he saw.

A fridge that wasn't a fridge. A closet to nowhere.

Not nowhere.

A closet to all the Devil's Harvest that Esson needed.

Esson jiggled from foot to foot, nervous, like he had to piss again.

The shed door near the fridge was open, a padlock hung from the latch. Esson stopped moving. All Barth knew right now was something was strange about that fridge. If he took Barth through with him, there would be too many things that would require an explanation. If Barth knew everything, it was only a matter of time before Dustin found out. Esson shivered. He didn't want to imagine what Dustin would do with that kind of information.

If he pushed Barth into the shed and locked him inside, he could keep everyone safe, including his family's secret, for a little longer. That sounded worth it right now. He could think about how to explain it all to Barth later, when he had the drugs in his hands and had returned safely back to this side of the worlds.

He ignored the little voice in his head that sounded an awful lot like Maella's voice. It warned him he was about to act first and think later and it wasn't going to end well. He reminded himself about all of the money currently in his pocket. Her tune would change once she saw what he brought home.

Barth leaned into the fridge, propping himself up with one hand on the door, then stepped through.

Esson fingered the rope coiled on the mower. In an instant, he made his decision. Soil and rust flecks flew into the air. He dashed across the field.

Barth came back through, setting both feet onto the ground and began to turn. "I opened your damn door. Now tell me what the hell is going on? How is that place possible?"

Esson slammed into Barth and sent them both tumbling. The weed stickers shot little needles of pain into Esson as he caught Barth in the rope. First hands, then legs. Barth kicked and punched. The old, decaying rope wouldn't last long, but Esson only needed Barth out of the way for a little bit of time. Which was good, since that was all the time they had left.

Barth shouted, struggled, kicked, and spit out curses.

Esson slapped Barth across the face. "Shut up or they'll hear you."

Barth went blotchy red and his eyes watered. "Who are you talking about?" Barth screamed. "What happened to that fridge? Who are you?"

"I don't know," Esson said, speaking the truth. Anger bubbled inside his chest. He didn't know because his family had kept everything secret. "But I do know there are people on the other side of that door, and if you don't want to get trapped there, you'll quiet down before they hear you."

Before Barth could respond, another problem appeared, standing in Esson's way, literally.

Claritsa.

Esson sucked in a breath.

She had walked up without him seeing her somehow.

She had shining black braids and bangs that made her seem younger than her eleven years. She was thin like a stick and her clothes were well worn like they'd been washed a million times.

She was his sister's best friend, as much as anyone in his family could have a best friend when you couldn't tell that friend about the most fundamental, secret part of you.

"Stop!" Esson yelled.

Claritsa flinched away from the fridge door, but then stood up straight, strong, rebellious.

She had no idea what trouble she had walked into.

"I heard his shouting," Claritsa said, glancing first at Barth, then the open fridge, and then at Esson. "Why do you have him tied up?" She said with a waver in her voice.

"You shouldn't be here." Esson felt the clock ticking. There wasn't time to explain. He had played with her and Maella in the creek often enough, exploring, racing, acting out imaginary battles in the woods. Her parents had ditched her but her grandmother was cool. Claritsa was a nice kid, she didn't deserve to get dragged into his mess. He kicked at the ground in frustration. A dirt clod flew into the air and hit the side of the shed wall.

The shed.

The roof looked partially caved in. A few narrow gaps from missing boards let light enter. The rusty padlock hung from the latch, open, like a gift.

"I'm sorry," Esson said. "Just know ... just know that I'm probably saving your life. You don't want to get mixed up in this. You really don't."

"What—"

Before she could say anything else, Esson dragged her into the shed.

She was like a wild cat, scratching, biting, punching. He wasn't a big thirteen-year-old, but she was a small eleven-year-old. He got her to the shed door, but then she twisted and lashed out, hitting her head on the door frame.

She slumped to the ground, dazed.

This couldn't be happening. "I'm sorry. I'm sorry." He was a monster. He felt the panic rising in him, ready to burst. "Ask Maella. Make her explain what she knows about the doors."

Claritsa looked up at him, horrified, her brown eyes huge and glassy through her bangs. He had put that look on her face.

"Claritsa." He shook her, trying to get her to focus. Instead, it made everything worse. She shrunk into herself.

He scrambled away as if burned, and backed up to the shed door. "Claritsa, ask her. Tell Maella you saw me open a door. I promise I didn't mean to hurt you."

He turned away, sick to his stomach, not sure if she had heard him. He closed the shed door. As soon as the door touched the frame, he cursed himself. Barth was still tied up outside, but now that the door had closed Esson could never open it again. If he hadn't acted so quickly, he could have put Barth inside too. Now, someone else, someone not doomed with this doormaker crap would have to let Claritsa out.

Fine. Maybe he was impulsive, but he was also creative. He'd make Barth open the door when all this was over, but since the point was to keep Clartisa safe inside, he forced the padlock to click closed.

He figured he had less than an hour now.

He left Barth in the weeds and stepped into the fridge, through the open space he'd made between the boxes, into the cool darkness. The closet smelled like cleaning fluids, harsh and acidic. Esson glanced back once through the fridge door. It was like an ugly picture framed on the wall—blue sky, a scraggly line of trees, rusted out machinery disappearing in weeds that had baked too long in the sun. The shed stood at the edge of the picture frame. He could hear Claritsa shouting.

Esson turned. The closet door Barth had opened emptied into a hallway.

He walked through.

The hallway was grey, like concrete, but not quite the same material. Natural light filtered from the ceiling. Each of the half dozen times he had explored this place, he had never noticed electricity. No outlets or light fixtures or switches. The place felt old and different from any place he had experienced on Earth. Probably, he figured, because it wasn't Earth.

He took careful, silent steps down the hallway until it opened up to a larger, factory floor area and headed for what he thought of as the packing station—the wooden crates, the straw used for cushioning, and the *licatherin* bottles ready, he guessed, for shipment. Though he had no idea where the bottles were supposed to go.

He would take what he needed and get the hell out of there and—he decided in that instant—close the fridge door on this place. With as many bottles gone missing as he planned to take, they would tear apart the factory and find his door.

He couldn't let any of what he was about to do lead back to his family.

What he took today would help his family pay the rent and fix the doors and put food on the table for months.

After that? He'd figure out something else.

He listened for footsteps, talking, machinery, security guards. But all was silent. If time on both sides of the door matched up, then it was early morning here—before the factory started its work day.

Several crates were already packed. He couldn't open those, not without risking a door. When he found a half-packed crate, still open, he realized he hadn't brought a bag.

Stupid—his sister would say.

Impulsive—his mother would say while holding his little brother in her arms. His grandmother would shake her head and his father would look at him with disappointment in his eyes.

Creative—that's what Esson would say about himself. It was his job to protect Maella and Josa. He was going to keep a roof over their heads and food on the table. He might not have thought ahead enough to bring a bag, but that wouldn't stop him.

He set to work filling his shirt with dozens of bottles, each no bigger than a hummingbird.

He stopped to uncork one, and took three drops of *licatherin* onto his tongue. Sweet licorice filled his senses.

He didn't need the drug, he told himself. Not to do this next part, but it helped clear his head.

The *licatherin* sizzled through him like an electric shock. His dizziness faded. He could do this. He was so close. He would save his family and his father would have to notice him. The glass bottles clinked together in his shirt. His heart soared. They represented a solution. Money. Answers.

A shout interrupted his thoughts.

He looked around wildly, searching for the source of the noise, zeroing in on a man running toward him with a stick—no, a sword.

The guy was carrying a sword.

Esson raced away, zigzagging through the crates. The man shouted in a language Esson could not understand. He understood the sword well enough. He had forgotten about the security guard.

"Idiot!" Esson said to himself. But no matter. He had what he needed and would make it back through the door in time to close it on this guard's face. He raced down the hallway, slipped into the closet, closing that door behind him. He used the half-broken chair against the handle as a makeshift lock.

He turned, careful of the bottles in his shirt, and saw Barth blocked the way out. Barth held a rusting crowbar in his hands.

In his panic, Esson gripped his shirt too tightly. There was a crunch and he felt wetness seep through to his skin. Licorice smells mixed with the cleaning smells. Energy poured through him, bringing back the dizziness and his headache. No, wait, that was the door. The fridge door was open and he was so close to it, the vibrations pulled at him.

Barth sneered and glanced down. "Finally pissed yourself, did you?"

Esson looked down, the broken bottle of Devil's Harvest had soaked his shorts. It didn't matter, he told himself. There were plenty of bottles left.

"Let me through," Esson shouted.

Something big slammed into the closet door behind him.

The guard.

"Hand over the drugs," Barth said.

Esson bit his lip. He didn't have time for this. He considered barreling through Barth. They could fight it out on the other side. But what about the bottles? How many would break in the process?

"Don't even think about it." Barth swung the crowbar around. "If you make a move, I'll close this door and won't let you out until I feel like it."

"You close that door and you'll never see me again." Esson's stomach sank. Barth didn't know how any of this worked. "You'll kill me."

"Don't be stupid. I won't kill you. I'll just teach you a lesson you and my father don't seem to have learned yet—to never underestimate me."

Esson heard Claritsa's shouts from the shed. Guilt seared him as he pictured the way her head had knocked against the door frame and taken all the fight out of her. He had done that and he couldn't ever take that back. Maella would kill him once she found out.

Esson clutched the bottles in his shirt. The door behind him sounded like it was splintering under the security guard's assault.

He grabbed a few bottles out of his shirt and passed them over to Barth, then rushed Barth like he was a football player. Barth stood, feet planted, ready for him. Esson shouldn't have been surprised. Sometimes Barth seemed stupid, but he was more cunning than anyone gave him credit for.

Barth swung the crowbar, hitting Esson on the collarbone. Something cracked inside Esson and all the bottles tumbled out of his shirt, breaking on the hard floor, scattering glass shards and Devil's Harvest until the entire room filled with the suffocating scent of licorice.

Esson fell to the floor. Each panicked breath shot pain through him.

"Stay there," Barth said, pointing the crow bar at him, and stepping back. His other hand was on the fridge door.

"No!" Esson said, holding out his hand to stop Barth.

"I'm getting my father. You'll wish you hadn't done any of this—"

Barth was a black hole blocking the sun, trees, home.

The door moved. Creaking.

Esson scrambled to his feet in spite of the pain. He wanted to puke.

No, no, no, no.

The sunlight and blue sky became a thin sliver, then it was gone.

Esson forced himself between the shelves and slapped his hands against the wall, searching.

The door closed with a suctioning sound. The rectangular outline of golden light stuck around for a few seconds, then vanished, leaving behind a blank wall.

Nothing.

No door, no handle.

His head spun.

Doors didn't open to the same place twice. Doors didn't always open to any place at all. And now Barth knew something was deeply wrong with his family. Maybe not all of it, maybe not most of it, but enough to somehow use it against them.

He had failed his family.

He might never get back home.

The pounding on the door behind him brought him back. The inside of the closet, all those bottles of Devil's Harvest, looked like how he felt.

Destroyed. Shattered.

He would never be able to fix this.

The chair bowed and slipped an inch under the pounding the guard gave the door.

He waited for his fate.

No.

That's what his parents had done. They had fled some terrible fate and were just waiting now. He didn't know for what, but it was killing them, this waiting. They had stopped living. They were grieving for a life-long dead, waiting for this one to catch up.

No.

He would not live like that.

There *was* something more he could do. It might bring out something worse than the guard breaking down the door. It might kill him. But in that moment, he didn't care.

Let them all go to hell, and if that meant he went too, so be it.

Esson wrestled with the chair, splinters digging into his fingers, pain shooting through his collarbone. He threw the chair aside and pulled the closet door open before the guard could open it himself.

The pounding stopped. There was no guard.

His heartbeat increased.

The door opened to—

Nothing.

Desert.

Miles and miles of sand for as far as the eye could see until the horizon disappeared into heat waves.

The bottles were crushed on the floor at his feet, staining the floor a dark inky purple. He noticed, as if from a distance, that his legs bled, cut up from the glass, adding red to the puddles of *licatherin* oil. He didn't know how long he stared, lost in the insanity of trying to make sense of what he had just done.

When he finally came back, he let out a deep breath, as if waking from a long sleep.

He stepped across the door's threshold and into the heat. A sharp edge dug into his leg. He looked down. The money. It peeked from his jean shorts pocket. He pulled out the cash and felt its smooth paper between his fingers. His family would never see this money now. The air in this new place was dry, the ground grainy. A brief breeze picked at his clothes before settling.

Esson gulped back a sob as he took in the harsh, empty landscape that surrounded him. The cash slipped out of his hand, the green pile of bills landing with a soft thud onto the golden ground. The breeze picked up the paper, throwing the bills lazily into the sky, taunting him.

Dustin would be angry. Barth would guess his secret.

Esson had failed completely.

He was lost.

He had destroyed his family's future.

In two hours he had failed more completely than he could have ever imagined.

WANT TO FIND OUT MORE?

Purchase the Marked by Fate boxset and get Doormaker plus 24 other full-length novels

THREE WORLDS. ONE RULE. SHE MUST NEVER OPEN A DOOR. Since before Maella can remember, one family rule has shaped her life: never open a door. Maella comes from a family of doormakers—people who unleash otherworldly violence when they open something even as simple as a cabinet door. Maella didn't mean to open a door. Maella tried NOT to open a door. She just wanted to save her friend. Pushed through a portal of her own making, Maella discovers worlds of nightmarish flying monsters, magical drug deals, political prisoners, religious cults, and a terrifying prediction: Maella will die upon opening her seventh door. In order to survive, Maella must uncover her family's secrets, all while hiding her identity and outrunning the prediction of her death. But what do you do when the truth you need could destroy the universe? In this thrilling first book in the Doormaker series from New York Times and USA Today bestselling author Jamie Thornton, discover the magic of the doormakers and begin an epic journey of secrets, betrayal, and power.

Connect with Jamie

Want to find out more? Purchase the Marked by Fate boxset.
I hope you've enjoyed Doormaker: Devil's Harvest (A Short Story Prequel)

To find out what happens next, check out
Doormaker: Rock Heaven (Book 1)

Visit me at JamieThornton.com to hear my latest news
and sign up to get your free books!

About the Author

Jamie Thornton is the *New York Times* and *USA Today* bestselling author of the Feast of Weeds series—a post-apocalyptic thrill-ride that follows a group of runaways who search for a lost friend in a world gone mad. Feast of Weeds has recently been optioned for TV. The Doormaker series is her first work of Young Adult fantasy.

Jamie lives in Northern California with her husband, two dogs, a garden, lots of chickens, a viola, and a bicycle. She writes thrilling dark adventures with a hint of romance. Follow her at JamieThornton.com

WRATH OF WITCHES

Shift of Shadow and Soul: A Prequel Story

Hilary Thompson

CHAPTER ONE

Reshra had been watching the girl pick pockets for an hour, so he knew he was likely to lose something.

He crossed the crowded tavern anyway, trusting his true valuables were safe from this dark and beautiful girl's reach.

"Would you like a dance?" he asked when a soldier released her.

She shrugged. "Must it be with you?"

He took her hand and spun her. "I dance well. You'll enjoy yourself."

"I always do."

Her face was less perfect up close, but her eyes were spectacular. So light blue they were nearly silver and rimmed in heavy kohl, like stars on a cloudless night or coins scattered beneath a streetlamp.

"I'm Resh," he said, and she drew closer.

"Shanta." She scanned his face and examined the carefully-arranged waves of dark hair, smiling as she ran her fingers over the expensive leather of his coat.

The tavern grew too loud for conversation as a favored singer took the stage. Resh concentrated on the hum of her body against his as he slyly searched the folds of her dress for hidden pockets. Her hands roamed his figure as well, and a lesser man might have forgotten the mission altogether.

But Resh was a trained Paladin, and an accomplished hunter of women. He appreciated a challenge: although this girl acted easy, she was anything but.

The song ended, and she stepped away from him, draining a mug he knew wasn't hers.

He patted the secret pocket inside his jacket. Empty. He smiled, and she took his outstretched hand for another dance.

"You can keep the coin purse," he said, his lips against her ear. "It's empty."

"Not quite." She tilted her face up, and her delicate hand pushed between them, brandishing the gilded key to his room upstairs.

"And what would you do with such an opportunity?" he asked, dipping her until one of her feet lifted from the stained floor.

She rose gracefully, bringing him close and whispering, "Steal you senseless."

"Is that what you Riatans call it?"

"I'm not Riatan, and neither are you." She reached into her bodice and pulled out a string of Weshen prayer beads.

His prayer beads, Resh realized with a laugh. The very ones he would have sworn still rested around his neck. But there they were, an unbroken strand dangling from her fingers.

He grinned. "You're very talented."

"That's nothing. You should see me when I really want something."

The song ended, and a young EvenFall nobleman approached her. "May I?" he asked, teetering on his feet.

"Absolutely," she answered, bowing low enough to display the tops of her breasts.

Resh smirked. Talk about easy.

"Thank you." She nodded to Resh as she placed her hand in the nobleman's.

Resh stepped into the shadows again. He slipped his hands in his pockets, feeling for the trinket he'd nicked from its stitches along her skirt hem.

And there, in his opposite pocket, rested the beads. He slipped them around his neck, saying a hopeful prayer to the Mirror Magi that this girl might lead him to the talisman he'd come to EvenFall to find: a half-moon blade inlaid with the teeth of a Kitsuun.

Chapter Two

The night sky had nearly faded to morning when Shanta exited a side door of the tavern. She hurried through the sleeping city, and Resh followed.

He nearly lost her several times before she slowed.

A faded wooden building with smashed windows loomed like a toothless grin between two locked shops. Shanta darted through a broken wooden door. Resh waited, but no lights shone into the street.

He stepped across the splintered entrance and listened to the blackness. The faintest echo of voices reached him from above, so he felt his way a few feet at a time until he found a decrepit staircase.

The voices were clearer at the top, and candlelight bled from the edge of a door.

Resh readied his dagger, but as he wrapped his fingers around the knob, the door swung inward, revealing a completely empty room. Not a person or stick of furniture.

"I'm here to trade," he called, and something shifted beyond the room. "I'm a friend of Shanta's," he added, excitement filtering into his voice despite his effort to sound neutral.

A bark of laughter turned Resh to the door as it slammed shut. A boy as tall as the ceiling flicked the bolt. He displayed a disturbing lack of teeth. "Shanta doesn't have friends."

"She has a crew."

Resh swiveled to see a slight blonde girl, much younger than he'd expected.

"And she would have told us to expect a Weshen warrior," a stocky boy continued, entering from a door hidden beneath the tattered wallpaper. He stepped close to Resh, studying his prayer beads, fine black cloak, and crystal-inlaid dagger. "Or are you just playing one for the night?"

Resh didn't resist when the boy spun him and slipped a rope around his wrists. Someone produced a chair and knocked his legs from under him, looping more rope around his waist and ankles. He wasn't worried. This was all part of hunting talismans in EvenFall.

"What do you want?" the young girl asked, twirling his dagger through her fingers.

"I'm searching for a talisman. I have one I'm willing to trade."

"Why trade one talisman for another?" the tall boy asked, pacing.

Resh kept silent.

"Where is the one you've brought to trade?"

"Shanta stole it from me," Resh said, a sly grin forming on his lips.

"And what makes you think I have the one you seek?" a familiar voice asked. Resh's grin stretched even wider. Shanta stood behind him, the heat of her body close enough to warm him from the icy stares of her crew.

"I never said you had it. But I bet you know all the secrets of this city."

She stepped around the chair and sat on his knee, laying her silver eyes on him. She leaned in and whispered against his cheek, "I do. But I don't work for kisses."

"Do you know a girl who does?" he asked. She smiled and flicked her eyes to the tall boy. Without another word, the ropes vanished.

Shanta stood and produced his stolen talisman. "This is beautiful," she admitted.

The narrow fur collar was finely sewn, with velvet ribbons to tie it closed around a woman's slim throat. "It's from a Cheetana. Made before the Shift," Resh added, his eyes darkening at the mention of the war that had brought the Weshen people to their knees before the Restless King.

Shanta slipped it around her neck, running her fingers through the silken fur. "And does it possess magic?"

"Of course not," Resh laughed. "But it did once. When the Sacrifice is reversed, it will again." He was lying, but she hadn't called him on it yet. Maybe his ruse would work after all.

"You could spell it," the stocky boy offered. "The Sulit witches have brought talismans back to life before."

"I'll have nothing to do with witches," Resh answered, curling his lip. "They've never helped the Weshen before."

Shanta raised her eyebrows. "I'll need to test it. What talisman are you hunting?"

"A half-moon blade, inlaid with the teeth of a Kitsuun," he said, enjoying the shock on each face as they grew silent. "You may have heard of it."

"Not the same blade that slit the throat of the Restless King's mistress?" the young girl gasped.

Resh nodded. "The same. It's been missing for decades, but I have new information that places it here in EvenFall."

Shanta considered him for a long moment. "I haven't heard this, but I may know who to ask. If your talisman is worth the price, of course."

She beckoned to her crew, and the four of them slipped like shadows from the room, leaving Resh to find his own way out.

Chapter Three

Striding the streets in the growing light of day, Resh twisted his prayer beads, asking the Magi to lead him to the Kitsuun blade before Shanta learned the truth about the collar around her neck.

He bought a thick roll stuffed with meat and cheese before clumping up the tavern steps to his room. He cursed mildly, realizing he'd have to pick the lock.

But the door swung open before he began, in eerie repetition of the night before. Shanta lounged on his bed, her gaze anything but inviting.

"Liar," she said, somehow making it seem both curse and compliment. She held up the fur collar, and before he could lunge for it, it was smoking on the fire.

"By the Magi, that was expensive!" he cried.

She shrugged. "Not for a thief."

"Not everyone has your lack of morals," Resh grumbled, sitting in the lone chair and biting into his roll. Even though it had never been a talisman, he'd paid good Riatan coin for it.

"I have information on your talisman. The blade, not that cheap piece of ratten fur."

He raised his brow. "Liar," he replied. She either had the information a few hours ago and lied, or she didn't have it now.

She grinned. "Would you care to reconsider your statement about witches?"

"The Sulit have the blade?" He sat up, brushing away crumbs.

"No, but a witch I get herbs from told me where it might be hidden. Coincidentally, it's the same place I lost a man two days ago."

"Were you hunting the talisman?" Resh asked. He'd hoped no one else knew of it.

She shook her head. "We were hunting a Giant Arach."

Resh felt his eyes strain, and a curse slipped out in a groan. He'd trained to fight and kill any sort of MagiCreature. He was one of Weshen City's best Paladins.

Yet he'd hoped to never come across this particular creature. He hated arachs, even the smallest that lived harmlessly in dark corners and under leaves. Giant Arachs were the stuff of childhood nightmares.

"The great Paladin is afraid," Shanta teased.

"The great Paladin is mortal," Resh answered. "And of all the ways I might die, that's the one I dread most. Think of it. Slow paralysis, your blood drained a drop at a time, until there is nothing left to do but die."

"It is the same as any other death. Just slower." Shanta shrugged. But something in her eyes spoke of fear as well.

"The man you lost. Do you think he was caught by one?"

She stared into the fire, silent.

Resh swallowed against his dry mouth. He wanted that talisman. If there were a chance it was here, even in an arach's lair ...

"Do you think the witch is lying?" he asked, feeling childish. Of course the witch was lying.

"I don't know. But I'm going in there to find my friend. I could use a Paladin to help. I'd even say you owe me, after that collar." Shanta locked her silvery eyes on him, and Resh sighed.

"Give me some time to clean up," he said. He didn't want to die dirty and unshaven.

Chapter Four

Barely an hour later, Shanta met Resh at EvenFall's edges, just where the woods began.

"No crew?" he asked.

"I can't risk them, too."

Resh laughed. "You'll risk me, though."

She shrugged. "You're a Weshen Paladin. Isn't this what you live for?" She strode into the trees, not waiting for an answer because they both knew she was right. Resh hurried to follow. She scurried through the undergrowth nearly as nimbly as the creature they were hunting.

In the deepest section of the forest, nearly all daylight was gone. Steam rose from the chilled ground toward an invisible sky. Not a single animal or bird broke the silence, only the crunch of dead leaves beneath their boots.

"The cave is here, somewhere in the heart of the forest," Shanta said.

Resh scanned the shades of darkness around them, trying to separate the brown-black of trees from the blue-black of a cave. "There." He pointed, drawing his sword. He felt a pull in that direction, and adrenaline shot through his limbs.

Today, he would find the talisman and conquer a Giant Arach.

He stepped forward, ignoring the quiver in the pit of his stomach. He was a Paladin. One of the best. He could do this.

The mouth of the cave narrowed immediately, forcing them to step high over shards of rock, like entering a true mouth, with teeth, a throat, and a gullet.

Resh tried not to visualize a stomach ahead, but as the wisps of webbing thickened into ropes and nets of sticky white, the image was harder to contain. Finally, the tunnel widened, opening to a hollowed burrow.

"I can't tell what's behind all this web," he whispered to Shanta. "This could be a giant trap."

She ignored him, rushing to a mass of webbing.

"Lushin," she moaned, hacking at the strands holding a person-sized bundle to the wall and ceiling. "Help me!"

Resh scanned the walls for any sign of movement. The arach could attack any second, if it were here. But he saw no mirrored eyes waiting behind the white curtains of web, and no shine of a half-moon blade, either.

There was no Giant Arach here to conquer, and no talisman to find. And, he knew, no friend to save, despite what Shanta hoped.

"Shanta, I'm sorry, but we're too late. Your friend is dead," he whispered, trying to grasp Shanta's arms to calm her frenzied motion.

"No! He breathes!"

"He may breathe, but he is dead," Resh said, and she choked back a curse and a sob. If the boy was bound, he was bitten, and Great Arach poison was untreatable.

As Shanta sawed away at the bindings, Resh searched the perimeter for any place to hide the half-moon blade. But behind the webbing, the walls were solid, packed dirt. He found nothing but dust and bones.

Finally, the bundle sagged to the floor, and Shanta hoisted one end over her shoulder. Resh couldn't tell if she held the head or feet of the unfortunate boy.

Still brandishing his sword, he bent to grasp the other end, and together they stumbled through the passage and into the forest air.

Compared to the arach's den, the steamy darkness smelled fresh, and Resh breathed deeply, trying to let go of his disappointment.

"Where did it go?" he wondered. The forest was still and quiet, as it had been.

Shanta didn't answer. She adjusted her grip on her dying friend and jerked Resh forward.

They made it to the edge of the forest before Resh confronted Shanta.

"There was no talisman in that burrow."

They rested their burden against a tree. Blinking in the sunlight, she knelt to peel back more of the tangled web. The boy breathed, but his eyes were milky and fixed on nothing.

"Thank you for helping me anyway," Shanta whispered, cupping the boy's bloodless cheek. "I'm sorry you got nothing in exchange. Maybe the witch lied to me, or maybe the Giant Arach took the talisman to a new burrow."

"Creatures care nothing for talismans," Resh argued. "Tell me where to find the witch, and I'll ask her myself." Of course the witch had lied. They always did.

"She has a stall in the market. Help me carry him home, and I'll go with you. I need some wild lotum petals."

Resh doubted pain medicine could help the boy now, but he kept quiet. Shanta finished cutting away the web, and Resh gathered the boy in his arms. He was young, and much slighter without the creature's wrappings.

None of Shanta's crew spoke when they saw their friend. The stocky boy took Lushin from Resh's arms and they disappeared behind the hidden door.

"Come on." Shanta's voice was weary.

At the market, she wove swiftly between the crowds, eventually reaching a lonely alley, black with grime and puddled with foul-smelling water. One stall waited at the end. A figure hunched beneath a cloak, hidden by a deep hood.

"You lied to me," Shanta said, earning a cackle.

"No, you lied to yourself. I tell the truth, but you hear what you want, daughter of Weshen." The witch moved forward enough for Resh to see a crooked slash across her full mouth.

"Witch, I want the half-moon blade," he said, pushing around Shanta. "Was it with the Giant Arach or not?"

"It was."

"The creature was gone, and my friend was already infected," Shanta growled. "You lied."

"I said the creature had not bitten the boy. I said it would bite him soon. Neither was a lie. You were simply too late."

Shanta banged her fist on the table, and the witch slunk into the stall's shadows. She grasped a cup and swirled its contents, staring into the bottom. After a few seconds, she raised her head and grinned.

"The creature now lives in a nearby burrow, and the talisman you seek is with it. Pay me double, and I'll show you myself."

Shanta made a rude noise and a ruder gesture, but Resh bent low enough to see into the stall.

"Name your price, witch."

"My price is what you have already paid, multiplied by what you will pay, and divided by the interest I have in your people," she said, and her chuckle filled him with nausea.

"No riddles. Name your price."

"You will pay me in hatred for my kind and all who befriend them. You will pay me in mistrust and prejudice and ignorance. Your payments will be drawn from the blood of the innocent borne on the dark magic of the glittering sea. Yes, Second Son of General Ashemon of Weshen City. You will pay me so, so handsomely."

Resh startled backward several steps. How did this witch know so precisely who he was, and what did her ramblings mean?

"Meet me in the forest at dusk, and I'll show you where the talisman waits for a strong young Weshen to claim it."

The witch handed Shanta a sack and promptly dropped an oiled canvas curtain, closing her stall. Resh reached to yank it open, but Shanta caught his arm, pulling him from the alley.

"I wouldn't even deal with her if she didn't have the best herbs," she muttered. "She never makes sense, and she lies more than she breathes."

"I'm going to meet her," Resh said.

"You're crazy! Shanta cried. "She'll kill you for certain, or she'll have the Giant Arach waiting to do it! It's just a trap!"

"Of course it's a trap," Resh bit out. "But if there is a grain of truth in this witch, I must wring it from her."

"Why do you want that blade so much?"

But Resh couldn't answer that. Ever since he'd read of its existence in a children's storybook, he'd wanted to see it. Year after year, as he trained and learned to complete missions on his own, he'd listened for rumors of the mythical blade.

He barely believed in magic, but something in this talisman called to him every time he studied the stars on a moonlit night.

Never had it felt real, until this year.

Never had it felt within his grasp, until this week.

He felt that somehow, the blade intersected with his future, one he was eager to begin.

Chapter Five

Resh waited in the forest for the witch until well past dusk. The moon was high over the clearing where he sat when she finally slipped between the trees.

"Do you have your weapon ready?" she asked, her voice floating from beneath her deep hood. "The Giant Arach is hungry from losing its last meal."

Resh glared at her and drew his bow sword and notched a bolted arrow. A long sword was strapped to his back, plus three daggers at his belt, but he had no desire to fight a Giant Arach in close combat.

The witch chuckled and darted away, moving faster than any human could. Resh ran, dodging tree limbs and roots in his pursuit. If he hadn't been going so fast after her fluid form, he might have better processed the cooling of the air, or the strange sponginess of the ground.

But it was a few feet too late when his Paladin instincts yanked him to a stop, toes teetering on the edge of a leafy hollow. Crumbs of dirt fell away beneath his boots. He scrambled for safer ground, but he felt the tingling whoosh of magic in the air and then the snap of a vine as it lashed his back.

Balance lost its battle, and Resh tumbled down the hill, sliding to the unmistakable entrance of an Arach burrow. Wisps of dirty gray webbing cloaked its mouth, and the scritching of claws on stone echoed from the entrance.

His bow sword had been lost in the fall, and as a single, leathery leg tapped its way from the darkness, Resh cursed and pulled his long sword.

His hands were shaking more than he'd ever tell if he lived to share this story.

"Do you see your destiny?" the witch howled from above, her laughter beating the air like the slap of branches in a storm.

A second leg pushed from behind the webbing, and a third and fourth, and then the bulbous, scaled body swayed before Resh. Four pairs of eyes blinked at him, silvery scrying pools full of ancient knowledge.

Resh yelled at the creature and hurled a dagger at its eyes. His aim was poor, though, and it deflected from the creature's scales, only drawing the eyes more intently on his position.

Resh stepped backward as slowly as he could force himself, creeping up the hill a bit at a time. The creature seemed to be tolerating his attempt, as Resh knew the speed it was capable of.

"Do you see it? The blade is waiting for a strong young Weshen!" the witch screeched, dancing around the edge of the hollow above him.

Resh yelled a curse at her as he took a few more steps up the incline and threw a second dagger. It stuck briefly in the meaty body before the Arach shook it away. Resh groaned. He was a dead man.

But then he did see what the witch was on about.

There it was. Shining and mythic and strapped to the back of possibly the largest Giant Arach that ever lived.

The half-moon blade.

It shone in the moonlight, glinting with mockery as the creature examined Resh, taking its time.

A sacred creature, if he'd ever seen one. Eight twinned eyes. Eight legs. And oddly, bearing the blade that carried the blood of his enemy's mistress.

Resh wasn't sure if he believed in destiny, but he recognized a hum and pull between this weapon and his Weshen blood.

Grasping his last dagger in one hand and his sword in the other, Resh struggled a few feet higher on the bank, then lunged and leaped across the open air. The shorter blade plunged to the hilt in the creature's back. It screamed, twisting and writhing to knock Resh from its back, but he used the dagger like a handle.

The witch cackled and sent another vine snaking down the hill to wrap around Resh's arm, pulling the sword from his fingers. He felt his grip slipping on the dagger, too, and yelling a curse, he slid to the leafy floor of the burrow. The creature's legs stomped around him, and Resh rolled frantically to escape the slicing claws.

"The blade is here, but perhaps it isn't waiting for you!" the witch called. "Perhaps it's waiting for the First Son of Weshen!" She was nearly breathless with laughter. Resh vowed to skin her alive, as soon as he figured out how to survive the creature above him.

He jumped to his feet, keeping low beneath the creature's body as it struggled to scrape the blade from its back. In the scuffle of leaves and dirt, he glimpsed his bow sword.

Resh wasn't entirely sure he could make it to the weapon and aim in time, but there were only so many ways to live through this. Clasping the beads at his neck one more time, he breathed a prayer to the Magi.

Then he lunged and skidded across the forest floor. Shouldering the bow sword and flipping to his back, he aimed with trained instinct and loosed a bolted arrow into the creature's screaming mouth, hooking it between the fangs.

The Arach bore down on him, and Resh felt the iron of the bolt press into his own neck as the weight of the creature crushed his chest. All he could see were the black scales of its belly, and the leathery legs scraping him into a shallow grave.

"Hold on, Resh!" a scream filled the hollow, and Resh prayed he wasn't hallucinating. The creature spasmed above him and swerved away, giving him a chance to haul himself to his feet.

"I think I love you!" he called up to Shanta, who was somehow now astride the creature's back, hacking at its tough hide with a pair of longknives.

Resh took aim again and fired, a second bolt spearing through one of the Arach's legs. It bucked and Shanta fell to the ground. A sad sort of hissing noise came from the creature's ruined mouth as it skittered away from them, up the side of the hollow and into the surrounding darkness.

Resh huffed out a half-laugh as he realized he wasn't going to die, but it was cut short by the realization that he wasn't going to get the half-moon blade, either.

"Where's the witch?" Shanta asked, surveying the rim of the hollow above them. But the witch had vanished as quickly as the Giant Arach. The forest was silent.

Resh gathered his daggers from the dirt and followed Shanta up the steep hill, hauling himself to the top with vines and tree roots.

"I can't believe you're here." He leaned against a tree at the top to catch his breath.

"Me neither," she answered, pulling out a cloth and wiping down her blades. "Lushin is dead."

"I'm so sorry," Resh said, and he was almost surprised to realize he meant it. She fixed her full-moon eyes on his, and he reached for her, drawing her slight body against his.

Her hands didn't search his pockets this time, and his fingers sought no trinkets for bargaining.

Instead, he bent his face to hers and kissed her temple. "Thank you," he whispered, suddenly incredibly grateful to be alive and holding a beautiful girl. She tilted her head, giving him access to kiss along her neck. Her hands tightened around his waist.

"I'm sorry we didn't get your blade," Shanta murmured.

"I will," Resh said, pressing the words against her lips. "It's out there, we know that much. I'll find it."

She tasted him, allowed him to open her mouth with his.

Resh knew it was the lust of a battle well-fought and the sorrow of loss that pulled them together, but he didn't care. He took and took of her gifts, feeling stronger with every touch.

A branch fell nearby, breaking them apart, but the forest was empty and still.

"Let's get back to the city," she said, her voice breathless.

"Do you still have my room key?" Resh asked, following her. She slid a glance to him but didn't answer.

As the forest gave way to meadow, then the gravel of the Evenfall streets, Shanta turned back to Resh once more.

She pulled something from her pocket, but it wasn't his key. "I know it's not the blade, but perhaps one of these is good for something."

In her hand rested a slick scale that looked like a slice of moonless night. It held no shine, even in the light of midday.

"A Giant Arach scale," Resh murmured, testing its weight. It was smooth and thick as bark, nearly the size of his palm.

"Maybe I'll make my own talisman," Shanta said.

"Thank you," he said again. "I owe you my life."

"I'll collect on it someday," she grinned. "Be ready with gold, because I don't work for kisses."

His smile didn't fade until she'd vanished into the crowded streets. Resh knew where to find her now, and next time, he hoped to have something more valuable than Riatan gold with him.

Even here in the hot sunlight, the half-moon blade spoke to him, a siren call carried by the rushing force of his Weshen blood.

WANT TO FIND OUT MORE?

Purchase the Marked by Fate boxset and get
Shif of Shadow and Soul plus 24 other full-length novels

There are three kinds of magic in the world, and Corentine has the wrong one.

Long ago, the Restless King forced Corentine's people into hiding as he scoured their blood for the SoulShifter. When Corentine learns she possesses some of the forbidden Shifter magic, she must hide her power or risk the same death her twin suffered.

Raised to trust no one, she rejects the General's son Sy, until she realizes his family secrets might be the key to unlocking hers. When his brother turns against them, they are forced to fight family to save what's left of their home, or accept banishment to find a new future.

If Coren and Sy can't convince their people to accept the light of Shifter magic, the growing Shadow will ruin everyone's chance of freedom.

Connect with Hillary

I hope you've enjoyed Wraths and Witches: A SoulShifter Prequel

To find out what happens next, check out the rest of my series available now
Shift of Shadow and Soul | Twist of Truth and Tomorrow

Visit me at HilaryThompsonAuthor.com to get your free copy of
Rise of Restless and Ruined: A SoulShifter Prequel

Follow me online
Instagram: @hilarylthompson | Twitter: @HilaryLThompson |
Facebook: @hilarythompsonAuthor | Pinterest: @hilarythompson |

About the Author

Hilary used to be such a practical girl. Then she let the stories out, and claimed the titles of stargazer, daydreamer, and believer in all things magical.

Fairy tales, myths from all cultures, and the wonderful "what if" are the foundation of her stories. Villains, heroes, and sidekicks clamor for equal attention. Happily-ever-afters, too (of course), but be warned that the road will twist and turn and seem to dead-end before the magic of a sweet romance leads back into the sunlight.

When she's not writing, Hilary teaches Creative Writing, Literature, and College Writing, drinks too much coffee, and reads as much as her eyes can handle. She plays superheroes and dress up games and reads books in bed with her independent, willful children, and plays at homesteading and world traveling with her soulmate of a husband. She tends to ignore laundry and dirty dishes.

I Want to Be a Pirate

A Short Story

Erin Hayes

CHAPTER ONE

"Ugh."

My voice sounded raspy and hoarse, even to myself. Like I had swallowed bucketfuls of sand and sea water. And as I rolled onto my side in pain and coughed up a lung, I realized that I *had* actually swallowed bucketfuls of *something*, and I needed to get rid of it.

So, I hacked up everything that was inside my stomach and lungs. And when I coughed too much, I retched and let it all out. My left leg ached, and I really, really didn't want to see what was wrong with it.

How did I get here? The last thing I remembered was being on the deck of the *Amphitrite*—a fishing boat where I worked as deck hand. Our fish of choice was tuna, which swam throughout the waters of the Atlantic Ocean.

It was the only job I knew, and as a twenty-six-year-old man, I'd spent as much time at sea as I did on the land.

It was as close to my dreams as I could get.

Growing up at a small seaside town in Maryland, I didn't have many options, except I knew one thing for certain: I've wanted to be a pirate ever since I was a little boy.

Stupid, right?

My pa said that I should stop reading books like *Treasure Island* and get a damn job. Ma had tried to be a little more patient with my wild dreams, thinking that I'd grow out of it. Except I did grow up. And when I turned sixteen, I left home to become a pirate.

I found out, though, that pirate jobs didn't exist, not anymore and not unless I wanted to dress up in some fancy getup for Disneyland for their *Pirates of the Caribbean* ride.

Not my kind of place. I needed to be out on the high seas, feeling the wind through my hair, and hearing the groan of the wood of the ship as we sailed through turbulent waters. Being a deck hand was nowhere near what being a pirate would have been like.

But it was the closest thing I had in 1979.

Except now, I regretted my choice. There was a bad storm. Something bad. And I remembered being on the deck, trying to secure our cargo when a wave came up and …

A chill ran down my spine at the memory of being caught in the powerful wave, being swept off the ship and into the dark waters below.

How did I survive? No one would have been able to fight the current like that.

I pushed myself up on my hands and knees, coughing weakly as I took stock of my surroundings. My left leg splayed out from underneath me, unable to take any weight.

Don't think about it, Neptune, I told myself, concentrating on the beach around me. *Just figure out where you are.*

I was on some sort of beach with inviting, white sand. Which was good. Hopefully this beach connected with civilization and I could find out what happened to the rest of the crew on the *Amphitrite*.

Flotsam and kelp had been pushed up on the beach along with me, and I saw a crab scuttle by. He watched me as suspiciously as I watched him.

"Yeah, better get away before I want dinner," I muttered toward him.

Either he understood English and obeyed. Or he just kept going on his merry, crabby way.

The fight left me and I didn't pursue him, even though my stomach growled hungrily. That wasn't the only thing wrong with me, though.

I rolled onto my back again, wincing in pain. In addition to my leg, it felt like every bone in my body ached, and my headache pounded at my temples. My clothes, which were your average seafaring attire, were soaked and torn at the knees.

And below that, I had a mangled leg.

Perfect. Just perfect.

I blinked up at the sun, covering my eyes with my hand. The sun was so bright and blinding. How could there have been such a bad mother of a storm one night and then have a glorious day like this? Seems like the weather's being a two-faced …

A cough to my left brought my thoughts to a halt. I froze, hearing my own heart shudder to a stop inside my chest.

What could have coughed? Fear was a very real sensation at the moment, and I would have traded it for the seawater and sand in my lungs at that very moment.

I turned my head.

And … *she* … was looking down at me.

I frowned, blinking at her, seeing this *vision* of beauty. She had wild red hair that was bound up with seashells and seaweed. Her eyes, which were watching me tentatively, shone a vibrant violet color. She wasn't naked—but she wore a tattered cloth around her midsection, and her tail …

TAIL?

I blinked furiously looking down at her aquamarine tail, which curled and uncurled around itself, the seawater sliding off her scales and into the sand.

I'd heard about these creatures before. Sailors had told tales of them, how they'd lure a man out to sea and then drag them to their death deep below the surface of the water. Every culture had a myth on them, from the books I'd read as a kid, to the ravings of the crew I worked with. We'd joke about it sometimes whenever a deckhand would get a faraway look in his eyes.

"Looks like ol' Sammy's bewitched again."

There were many names for them. Nymphs. Sirens. Spirits.

Mermaids …

And I was looking at a mermaid on this shore. Not dragged to my death—unless this were some form of Heaven, in which case, I'd have thought my leg would be in better condition—but saved.

By her.

"Who …" I muttered, trying to form coherent thoughts. "Who are you?"

She didn't say anything, she just kept smiling sweetly at me. I must have hit my head harder than I thought because the world swirled around me as our eyes met. She reached out and put a strand of my own sandy hair behind her ear. Her touch was as soft as flower petals, and I wondered how such a soft gentle creature could have been in the ocean.

And then I passed out.

It was dark when I woke up. It could have either been a few hours later or I lost over a day—I didn't know, because time was different when you were stranded on a beach.

At first, I saw the stars. Amazing how whether you're on land or sea, the stars look the same. Two different worlds, the same sky. I closed my eyes, smiling, appreciating it.

And then I heard the rustle of sand to my left.

I twisted at the noise and immediately yelped in pain, clutching at my leg. Something really wrong had happened to it. Something that I didn't want to see, but would have to face soon. An infection would spread or something worse.

I stopped fretting when I saw her again, the pain melting away as I looked into her violet eyes, glowing even in the dark. The mermaid was still here.

And she was holding up a leaf, angling it toward my parched lips.

"Wh—what?" I stammered, trying to push myself back, but she made an irritated little noise and tipped the leaf up into my mouth.

Fresh water.

After that realization, I slurped at it thirstily, and it all too quickly disappeared.

The mermaid giggled, surprised at me, and I couldn't help but grin at her.

"Thank you."

She didn't say anything or even blink.

"Thank you," I said louder and gestured to the leaf. "Thank you for the water."

She nodded, but I wasn't quite sure if it was in understanding. No, she didn't speak English. Or know that nodding was yes. And why would she? She was a mermaid. She swam in the ocean and danced with dolphins in the waves.

But still, talking to her was enough for my own sanity. And it grounded me in a way that I hadn't realized I needed before now. Talking made it feel like I was interacting with a real human, someone who could understand my pain and anguish. Not a creature of the imagination.

Not a mermaid.

Yet, there was something very human in the way she smiled down at me, how she kept brushing the hair out of my eyes. Personal space definitely wasn't a problem for her, and I found that I didn't mind her being so close to me. The wind swept her hair around her face, making her look like something ethereal and not of this world.

Which, I guessed she was.

"Thank you," I said softly. "For saving my life."

She only stroked the side of my face. Like she couldn't get enough of me.

And if I were being completely honest with myself, I didn't think I'd ever get enough of her.

"So, you're a mermaid?" I asked the next morning. "As in a real mermaid?"

She cocked her head at me and chuckled lightly. I wondered if it was because she found my language strange or weird to her ears. But I was relieved to find that laughter was the same, no matter what language we spoke.

Because I knew now that she found me amusing. And I'd take that.

When I had gotten drowsy the night before, she had pushed herself off the beach and into the ocean. Maybe mermaids couldn't spend much time outside of the water. I had watched her frolic among the waves with dolphins squeaking alongside her. In my decade on the high seas, I had never seen anything like it. Nor anything as beautiful.

When I woke up this morning, she was back on land, bringing with her some sort of sea fruit. I had gingerly eaten them. Not the best choice, but my stomach was growling so much, I hungrily devoured them.

She had thought that was amusing, too.

"Do you live under the ocean?" I asked her. "Like in a house? Or do you go somewhere else? Do you have legs on land?"

With that last question, I felt my throat close up. Because if she did have legs, then that could mean that she could spend more time on land. With me. I didn't know if it was gratitude toward her for saving me or what ... but I kept having visions of, well, *life* with her.

Showing her the wonders of my world. And she'd show me the wonders of hers. I'd introduce her to my parents, who'd ask where she got her accent from, and I'd meet her parents—who may have been fish for all I knew. As a sailor, I'd never really ever considered taking a wife.

At least not until now.

And who would be a better match for a man who loved the sea than a mermaid?

Neptune, I thought, *get a hold of yourself.*

Because, for all I knew, this could be some sort of hallucination brought on by my leg, which was still hurting and aching. I had to look at it sometime or other. And I don't think that she would be able to bring medical help or attention.

I groaned, sitting up. She let out a small *eep* at me and cowered away from me, hiding her face in her long, slender hands.

"Oh, no, no," I told her. "I'm all right. I can sit up and everything. And I just need to look at my leg."

She peered at me through her fingers as I glanced down at my left leg. It was still covered up in my pant leg, and the fabric had gotten stiff and crunchy from the sea water.

I pulled up my pant leg, gingerly, afraid at what I was going to see.

And it was as bad as I thought it was. Even the mermaid let out a surprised little whimper at it. Because my leg was broken, and through it, I could see that my fracture had broken through the skin and gleaming white bone peered up at me. It was no wonder that I hadn't bled out or that I wasn't attacked by sharks in the water.

How the hell did that happen?

I dimly remembered that, when the wave had swept me off the deck, that I had smacked into a railing on my way down. I remembered pain in my leg, but I hadn't thought it would be … *this* …

"Guess I have to set it," I told the mermaid, who had lost all color in her face at the scene before her. "This is probably something you won't want to watch."

I didn't even want to watch it. I wasn't a doctor or anything, and I didn't want to put my hands around my calf, because surely that was someone else's calf. I had never set a bone before.

First time for everything.

I snapped it into place, putting my bone back underneath my skin, which was accompanied by a loud, sickening pop. I think my scream of pain outdid it. Stars danced across my vision, and I had to fight to not pass out again.

Panting, I stripped off what remained of my shirt, and I looked around for something to use as a splint.

"Can you hand me that?" I asked the mermaid, pointing to a stick next to her. It was perfect for my leg. "The, uh, stick?"

Please understand English enough to understand that. I didn't know how I'd get a better branch otherwise.

Miraculously, she did. She looked down at the stick, grabbed it, and then handed it to me. I wanted to sob in relief as I took it from her.

"Thank you."

I bent over, wrapping my broken leg to the piece of wood. Securing it hurt almost as much as setting it.

When I sat back up, I saw tears in the mermaid's eyes. First of all, I marveled seeing a mermaid cry. And then I reached over and stroked her face.

"Hey," I said. "I'm all right now."

Although I didn't know where civilization was or where I could go from here. But I was all right for the moment.

Pain and exhaustion overtook me. The night was cold without my shirt, so I huddled up and shivered. Until I felt a warm body press up against my back, and the smell of seaweed and the ocean breeze hit me.

I sighed contentedly for the first time since I wound up on this beach. And the mermaid stayed with me the entire night.

The mermaid was gone the next morning.

I woke up sunburned and overheated with the sun overhead. My leg had its splint as I remembered it, and I felt even hungrier than before.

But no sign of my mermaid.

Was it all just some sort of weird dream then?

I groaned and lay on my back, rubbing at my eyes with my hand. She had to have been real. I needed her more than I needed food or to get off this beach. Even though we had only spent a few days together, I could feel my destiny inexorably linked with hers.

I had to know she was real. I had to know that what we had wasn't the ravings of a madman.

But that's what it seemed like it was.

A splash off in the distance turned my attention away from my anguish, and I watched as a sea creature breached the surface and fell back onto the waves. Tinkling laughter met my ears and I wanted to sob in relief.

My mermaid was here. My mermaid was back.

"I thought I lost you!" I called out to her, waving at her. Whether she was saying hi back or just imitating my movements, she waved joyously back at me. "Where'd you go?"

She didn't answer as she came to the shore. She didn't come empty-handed though. Or, empty-finned. She had a satchel with her, and I couldn't see what was inside.

"What is that?" I asked, looking around her.

She glanced at me shyly and then reached into the bag and brought out a little parcel wrapped up in seaweed. Perplexed, I took it from her, unsure of what to do with it. She poked me once and then pantomimed eating the parcel.

"Oh, this is lunch?" I asked, holding it up. To be honest, I would have preferred the sea fruit from yesterday, but as I nearly balked at the offering, I decided that any food was better than none.

I downed it, grimacing at the horrible flavor. "Oh, this is great. This is just what humans do when they really, really like something."

She giggled again.

And then …

I felt a tingling down in my left leg, right where the bone had broken through the skin. It spread, not uncomfortable, but something that I had never felt before.

"Wha—?"

I could *feel* my leg knitting itself back together. Healing. Becoming whole again.

"What was that?" I asked in amazement, looking back at her violet eyes. She grinned proudly at me in answer, and I would have given all the riches in the world for her to be able to speak to me. "Did you just give me like a … like a spell or something?"

She only pantomimed eating the parcel again.

I nodded. "Yeah, I know," I say. "Thank you."

"So how do I get off this island?"

Since the mermaid had healed my leg, I had been able to walk around the tiny island, seeing that there was no civilization near me. And that there was no way for me to build a raft and get off this island. While I liked my time with the mermaid … well, I knew that I wouldn't be able to live on sea fruit and rainwater for the rest of my life.

Even if I wanted to.

She watched me as I trudged back to her. "You know," I said, even though she couldn't understand a word I was saying, "get back to the mainland?"

At her blank look, I sighed. "Yeah, you wouldn't know, would you?" I put my hands on my hips and looked down at the sand. An idea struck me.

I crouched and drew a circle in the sand. Her violet eyes soaked in everything I was doing as I was doing it.

"Okay, this is the island. And this," I drew a figure within the circle, giving it a swiggly fish tail before pointing it at her, "is you."

She clapped delightedly, following exactly what I was saying. She drew her own figure in the middle of the circle, only instead of a fin, she gave it two legs. One was bent at a weird angle.

I chuckled. "Yes, that's me. And this is the ocean." I drew wavy lines outside of the water. "And this is land. Where I live." I roughly depicted a shoreline for her. "I," I said, making a line from the stick figure with a broken leg, "need to get here," and I ended the line on the shore.

The mermaid gasped so roughly that I looked up at her in alarm. Tears were back in her eyes.

She knew. She knew that I had to go.

"Hey now," I said softly. "It'll all be all right." I wanted to put my arm around her and comfort her somehow. Telling her that everything would have a happy ending.

I didn't know how though. But I knew I couldn't stay here.

She pushed herself away from me and jumped.

"Hey!" I shouted after her as she dove back into the water. "Hey!"

But she was gone. I cursed under my breath and wiped at my pants. I wished more than ever that I could have spoken with her. Told her that I was sorry.

Maybe if we could speak the same language, we would have been able to figure something out. As it was … well, I was just on a beach on a deserted island.

Alone.

She came back later with her satchel, only this time, I could tell that it weighed her down as she swam through the waters.

I ran out to her in the shallows, giving her a hug, which surprised both of us. She dropped the satchel in the water, and I dimly heard the loud splash and thunk as the satchel hit the sandy floor.

All I cared about was that she was back. "I'm so sorry! I can stay, I'll stay with you."

It didn't make a lick of damn sense, but I'd decided it while she was gone. I didn't care what it took, if I had to build a house here with my bare hands, my dream of a pirate's life be damned. I just knew that I didn't want to see her cry like that ever again.

She pulled back and gave me a hard look before shaking her head. Definitely a "no" from her.

"What?" I asked, confused.

She reached up and touched my temples. And *took* my consciousness to somewhere else.

With her, I could see the beauty of her underwater world. So beautiful. So pure. Fish flitted in and out while merpeople—just like her—swam as they smiled at each other and went on with their daily lives. There were sea turtles and whales and fish I couldn't even begin to imagine.

All living in this city that glittered at the bottom of the ocean.

It was the most beautiful thing I'd ever seen. Other than her.

She showed me more. Of seawitches and kings and deeper sea creatures, the kind that made it into *20,000 Leagues Under the Sea*. I shuddered, even though I was in awe that Mother Nature could create something so deadly and wonderful.

And then, she showed me mankind's impact on that world.

How her friends fled when they saw the shadows of a ship above. How there were fewer and fewer fish that visited her underwater city. She showed me how they had gotten caught up in fisherman's nets—*my nets*, the nets that I had spent my life reeling in.

And at the end of it all, there was me. With a decision to make.

I understood what she meant. Understood it without her saying a word. She was entrusting me to take care of this world, that she believed I could make a difference and change our fates.

I didn't know how.

Her fingers left my temples, and I was suddenly back in my body with a shuddering cry as my lungs filled with air once more. Her face was grim as she floated away from me, giving me space. Waiting to see my reaction.

I nodded at her slowly. "I understand," I rasped to her. "I understand what you need. But … I don't know how to do it. I'm just a fisherman. All I wanted was to be a pirate."

Without another look at me, she dove under the waters for a brief second, resurfacing with her satchel. She handed it to me, and I took it, nearly dropping it again.

The thing was *heavy*. And, looking down, I could see why.

The satchel was filled with gold. And not just any gold, but gold coins and diamonds and rubies. Treasure. The kind of treasure that a pirate spends his entire life looking for.

It must have been worth millions of dollars.

She must have found it in a wrecked ship, gathered it, and gave it to me. She must have known this treasure was precious and worth something to my people.

She was giving me the means to make that difference.

I smiled at her. "Okay," I whispered. "Okay."

We spent one more night together, curled up on the sand to watch the night sky. She didn't leave and I didn't try to join her in the water.

In the morning, I hooked the satchel around my shoulders, securing it. I didn't know how she planned to take me from here to the mainland—wherever that was—but I wasn't about to drop this precious loot on my way in. Not when it gave me the means to make a difference.

In the shallows again, I reached out and took her hand, giving it a tight squeeze. She looked down at our clasped hands, a small smile on her face.

And then she dove into the waters, bringing me along with her.

I didn't know how long or how far we traveled, only that I simply needed to open my mouth and she knew to bring me to the surface. Dolphins joined us, skipping along the waves, curious by the mermaid's stowaway.

It was one of the most magical things in my life.

All too quickly, though, it ended.

I noticed when I saw the seagulls overhead and the water changed from blue to a more grayish color, the color of pollution. I could hear different sounds, other than that of the ocean. People laughing and talking to each other. And … *cars* …

She had brought me back to civilization. I saw the cliffs of the shore, and above that, a city. But there was a beach that we could easily access.

It was there where she pulled me up on the shore. Even though I hadn't been doing much of the swimming, I was still tired when I pulled myself up. She was there with me, pulling me up on the beach.

I didn't drop my satchel though.

"Thank you," I whispered. "I—" I swallowed, as emotion overtook me. "I'll never forget you."

Good-byes must not be easy for mermaids as well because she turned away from me, falling back into the ocean where the dolphins greeted her.

And just like that, she was gone, leaving what felt like a huge, gaping hole in my heart.

I swallowed again, unsteady, as I pulled myself onto my feet. What did one do with millions of dollars and a task to save the ocean for a mermaid that had stolen his heart?

It was an impossible task, that's what it was.

With heavy feet, I made my way up the cliffs and found myself on a main road. And next to it, right on the water, was some sort of old touristy attraction that had been boarded up. A "For Sale" sign was placed out front, although judging by the dilapidated structure, I'd have to tear the whole thing down and start again.

But still, I frowned at it as a crazy idea struck me.

I shielded my eyes as I looked out over the ocean, at the spot where the mermaid had brought me back to life. One man couldn't save all of the ocean's creatures, not by himself. Not without changing perceptions.

But maybe I could start with helping out the animals. Maybe by bringing them closer to humans so that we could see that we aren't so different. I glanced back at the old building, and saw the sign saying "The Jacksonville Mystery Spot."

"Mystery Spot, eh?" I murmured, amused. Not a mystery spot anymore.

I was going to buy this place with the money the mermaid gave me. And I was going to build an aquarium and take care of the world that she loved so much. Maybe we couldn't be together, but maybe …

Maybe it would bring our souls closer together.

And, an even crazier thought, although I'd have to figure it out, I could have mermaids there. Not like her of course, but have underwater ballerinas that brought that magic and grace to the world. Like she did for me.

And I'd called it Neptune's World.

It wasn't a pirate's life for me. It was something better.

WANT TO FIND OUT MORE?

Purchase the Marked by Fate boxset and get
How to talk to Ghosts plus 24 other full-length novels

Lita didn't expect to inherit trouble when her uncle died. As someone who can talk to ghosts, Lita's always been more comfortable around the dead than the living. That's especially true with her estranged father, who cares more about building his business empire than her. Then her eccentric Uncle Neptune died, leaving behind an aquarium that Lita's dad wants for himself. The only problem: Neptune left it to someone else. Now Lita's dad wants her to help him to get it back. But her uncle's friends are so…strange. It seems like everyone has their secrets, including her father. And he will stop at nothing to fulfill an ancient conspiracy to take over the world. And Lita may be the only one who can stop it

Connect with Erin

I hope you've enjoyed I Want to be a Pirate

To find out what happens next, check out the rest of my series available now
How to Talk to Ghosts | How to be a Mermaid | I'd Rather be a Witch | I
Do Believe in Faeries | I'm Not Afraid of Wolves |

Visit me at ErinHayesBooks.com to hear my latest news.

Follow me online
Instagram: @erinhayes5399 | Twitter: @erinhayes5399 |
Facebook: @erinhayesbooks |

About the Author

Sci-fi junkie, video game nerd, and wannabe manga artist Erin Hayes writes a lot of things. Sometimes she writes books.

She works as an advertising copywriter by day, and she's an award-winning New York Times Bestselling Author by night. She has lived in New Zealand, Hawaii, Texas, Alabama, and now San Francisco with her husband, cat, and a growing collection of geek paraphernalia.

You can reach her at erinhayesbooks@gmail.com and she'll be happy to chat. Especially if you want to debate Star Wars.

www.ingramcontent.com/pod-product-compliance
Lightning Source LLC
Chambersburg PA
CBHW032101180726
48284CB00002B/388